Three Strand Cord

by

Tracy Krauss

Fictitious Ink Publishing
Tumbler Ridge, BC

Dedication & Acknowledgments

I thank the Lord for the many wonderful friends that have walked across my life's pages – especially the one friend who sticks closer than a brother. I am so blessed to call the Creator of the universe 'friend' and I hope that this story, in some small way, points to that awesome relationship which has no equal and which never fails.

Many thanks must go out to the discerning group of beta readers who helped me refocus this book into a story about spiritual growth, not just a tale of three friends. Also, I am grateful for the dedication of my prayer team, and the love and support of my family. To my husband Gerald – my one true love on this earth - I am ever grateful for your willingness to put up with my writing obsession! Love you forever.

Tracy Krauss

A three strand cord is not easily broken

Ecclesiastes 4:12

PROLOGUE

Stately red brick, manicured lawns, and well kept flower beds – the perfect backdrop for Parkview Private Girls' Academy. Nature itself crowned all with a cobalt sky and warmth from the golden sun. All was exactly as it should be for an institution that prided itself on turning out well bred young ladies of means.

"Quick! This way!" A dark haired girl of about twelve gestured to her companions, her voice barely above a whisper. All three girls ducked around the sculpted hedge and squatted, peeping through the foliage.

The blonde one giggled. "This is sooo exciting!"

"What if we get in trouble?" The third girl pushed her glasses up on her nose with her forefinger. Her chestnut hair bobbed as she shook her head. "I'm not sure this is such a good idea."

"Sh!" The dark haired ringleader held a finger to her lips. "Here comes Casey Brinks."

The three waited, holding a collective breath as their arch nemesis, another twelve-year-old girl, neared the appointed spot under a tree. Suddenly, an explosion of water soaked her as a water balloon hit her dead on. "Ah!" The girl stood frozen while she tried to catch her breath.

"Come on," hissed the leader - and the one with the accurate aim. The threesome crept from the shadows as stealthily as twelve-year-old girls wearing uniforms were able, and made a break for it, letting their excited giggles burst from their lungs unfettered.

"I see you, Stella Crayton!" The enraged mini-diva called after them, hands on hips. "You and your little cronies! The head-mistress is going to hear about this!"

The girls kept running. They'd been caught outright and all that was left now was to wait for the punishment. Stella reached the maintenance shed first, her black hair flying out behind her. She yanked the door open and all three slipped inside.

"What do you think they'll do?" Tempest's eyes looked even bigger and wider behind her spectacles.

Stella shrugged. "Call our parents."

"Do you think they'll send us home? I don't want to live with Aunt Rose." Tempest frowned, her eyebrows disappearing behind the rims of her glasses.

Cherise flipped her blonde tresses back off her shoulders. "Don't worry. Daddy's on the board of directors."

"Oh. Are you sure they won't send us home?" Tempest's eyes were wide, her voice hopeful.

"Nothing is ever for sure," Stella stated. "But our folks are paying way too much for them to get rid of us. Besides, I'm the one who threw the balloon, not you."

"But what if your folks make you go home?" Tempest began twisting her hands together.

Stella snorted. "The last thing my stepmother wants is to have me back home."

"You wouldn't want to go and leave us anyway, would you?" Cherise teased. "Your two best friends in the whole world?"

Stella shrugged. "Not that I don't love you two, but..."

"You miss Texas," Tempest supplied. "Like I miss California. And... and..." She clamped her mouth, blinking her eyelashes rapidly.

"Hey, it's okay." Cherise put a comforting arm around Tempest's shoulders. "I know you miss your folks. I don't know what I'd do if I lost mine like you did. Even if they are a pain sometimes."

Tempest shook her head. "I don't want to live with Aunt Rose," she stated again.

"We won't let that happen. Will we, Stella?" Cherise looked to the other girl for confirmation.

"We'll try our best."

"Why doesn't your stepmother like you?" Tempest swiped at a tear that had strayed down her cheek.

Stella shrugged. "Guess she wants my dad all to herself."

Tempest leaned her head back against the rough wall and sighed. "What do you miss most about Texas?"

Stella furrowed her brow. "Besides the ranch? Zane and Blue."

"Are those your pets?" Cherise asked.

"No, silly. Zane and Blue are my best friends – well, besides you guys," Stella explained.

"You have boys for friends?" Tempest's eyes had become almost as round as her glasses.

"You're so funny!" Cherise giggled. "I'd love to have boys for friends - especially with names like Zane and Blue. Are they cute?"

Stella frowned. "They're just friends. You are so boy crazy, Cherise Hillyer."

Cherise just shrugged. "So?"

"Anyway, there's no chance of me going home now. My step-mother has seen to that. She couldn't wait to get me out of the house just as soon as she married my dad."

"Just like a fairytale." Cherise sighed dreamily.

"Believe me, there's nothing fun about it." Stella sat up and crossed her arms over her chest.

"At least you have parents." Tempest's voice was quiet. She fixed her gaze on her lap, blinking rapidly.

"We're your family now, Temp, right Stella?" Cherise gave Tempest's shoulder a quick squeeze before she shifted, straightening. "Enough gloom! Let's talk about Casey Brinks. We got her good! She is such a snob. I can't believe I used to be friends with her."

"Yeah, until you started hanging around with us," Stella stated. "We weren't cool enough for the Casey Brinks fan club." She shifted her position so she could peek out a small knothole in the wall of the shed. "Coast is still clear."

"You're way more fun, anyway," Cherise declared. "This is so exciting. And kind of scary, too."

"Just wait till Ole Miss Crankypants gets a hold of us," Stella said, her eyes twinkling. "Now, *that* will be scary."

"So what do we do now? Just wait to get caught?" Cherise asked.

"Pretty much," Stella said with a shrug.

"Hey, I have an idea." Tempest dug in her pocket. She pulled out several bright strands of colored embroidery floss. "I read a book on making friendship bracelets and I just got some new colors. We could make some. If you want to, that is."

Stella nodded. "Why not?"

"Okay," Cherise agreed. "So what do we do?"

"It's kind of like weaving," Tempest explained, beginning to work with the threads. "I read that once you tie it on, you can never take it off. It means you'll be friends forever."

"Neat! I want some of this color," Cherise exclaimed, reaching for a few hot pink strands.

"We should make them for each other." Stella took the pink strands from Cherise.

4

"Or, how about if we each work on all three?" Tempest suggested. "That way, we'll be connected forever."

"Good idea," Stella agreed. "Friends forever."

"Friends forever," the other two echoed.

Tempest

CHAPTER 1

*T*he cab wound its way along the tree-lined drive and slowed to a crawl on the circular driveway, finally coming to a halt in front of the mansion tucked well within the depths of Boston's old moneyed district. The grand facade, with its pillars and over-sized windows, spoke of wealth. It was a nervous few minutes as Tempest surveyed the posh brick two story structure. It had been a few years since she'd been here to visit. Cherise's parents weren't much for entertaining strays from boarding school. At least, not strays without a pedigree.

"You plan on getting out?" The cab driver raised his brows questioningly as he made eye contact via the rearview mirror.

Tempest blinked back to reality. "Oh, yes." She rummaged in her purse for the correct amount owing. Her own car was in the repair shop, so taking a cab was a necessity. "Um, here." She shoved the bills into the cabby's waiting palm. She couldn't really afford such a generous tip, but it was just too embarrassing to have to wait while he made change. He was probably wondering what a person like her was doing in this neighborhood in the first place.

She stepped out of the cab, hauling her small suitcase behind her, and shut the car door with a decisive click. She waited until he had driven away before venturing up the wide steps to the menacing double doors, her small black case thumping up the steps behind her.

The bell barely had time to quit resonating when the door swung open.

"Tempest! You made it!" Cherise squealed, enveloping her long time friend in a warm embrace.

A rush of relief swept over Tempest's body. What had she been so nervous about? This was Cherise, after all – the same blonde bombshell she'd grown up with at boarding school. "Sure," Tempest replied, disentangling herself. "The cabby knew exactly where to go."

"Sorry someone didn't pick you up at your aunt's," Cherise apologized as she led her further into the spacious foyer. The ceiling in the entrance rose overhead the full two stories. A large gilded mirror hung over an equally elaborate side table a few feet inside the doors. Polished white marble floors led off in several directions, including toward the grand staircase that curved upward. "The chauffeur had to take Mother to the country club and I just got back from my masseuse."

"The cab was no problem," Tempest assured.

"You look nice." Cherise scanned Tempest from top to toes. "New haircut?"

"Um, yeah." Tempest touched her reddish brown hair with tentative fingers. It was stylishly short, with just a hint of subtle highlights, and still salon fresh from that morning. It would never look this good again. She just wasn't that good when it came to doing hair.

"Well, I like it," Cherise stated with a nod. "Now you just need to get rid of the glasses and update your wardrobe and you'll be a knockout."

Tempest looked down at her outfit. Nondescript slacks and a button up blouse. She was tall and rather willowy and knew she

could probably wear clothes that had a little more pizzazz, but...
"I just like to be comfortable, that's all."

"Comfortable? With that body?" Cherise scoffed. She shook
her head and expelled a dramatic sigh. "One of these days."

"You've been warning me." Tempest smiled.

"And I mean it," Cherise affirmed. "One of these days you're
getting a makeover, lady, and there's nothing you can do about it.
I can't believe we've been friends all these years and you're still
dressing like a librarian."

"My bad."

"In fact, just wait until you see what I've got planned for
tonight!" Cherise exclaimed.

"Oh, oh. Now you've got me worried," Tempest said, still smiling, but in truth feeling a bit uneasy. She wasn't sure she was up
for it.

"Don't worry!" Cherise took Tempest's arm and started
walking toward the stairs. "It's just some good old fashioned girl
fun. It'll be just like old times -" Cherise cut herself short as she
stopped abruptly in her tracks. "Is that all you brought?" She
gestured to the small rolling overnight bag that was following
Tempest like a stray mutt. "You are staying, aren't you?"

Tempest stared at the shabby suitcase for a moment and
blinked before looking back up at Cherise. "It's just one night."

"I thought you were staying in Boston for a few days."

"I am," Tempest replied. "But I have to stay with Aunt Rose for
the rest of the weekend. I don't visit her nearly as often as I
should, and well, you know how it is. She is getting on and she'd
be miffed if I came to town and didn't stay with her." There was a
moment of silence as Cherise pouted. "But I'm here for tonight,"
Tempest offered.

"It's going to be so much fun!" Cherise reverted to her former
animated excitement. "I've got all kinds of things planned, just
like when we were girls at school. We'll do facials and pedicures.
Listen to loud music..."

"Your folks won't mind?" Tempest asked. From what she remembered, they were rather preoccupied with themselves, anyway.

"Silly!" Cherise laughed. "This is an old fashioned sleepover, not some kind of orgy! What were you expecting?"

Tempest blinked and pushed her glasses up with her finger. Sometimes it was hard to gauge whether Cherise was serious or not. "I, um… nothing."

Cherise giggled even more. "That's what I love about you, Tempest. You're so droll!"

Tempest smiled weakly, wondering what was funny. She never had been good at catching on to jokes and things. Oh well. At least Cherise hadn't changed any either.

It was strange the way life worked. They had been so close while growing up – Cherise, Stella and herself – and had remained fast friends even into college. But now, over the last two or three years, they had begun to drift apart. Go their separate ways. Build their own lives apart from one another. Life was like that. People got busy. Stella had sought further education, Cherise was busy as a Boston socialite, and Tempest herself had finally launched into a career as a writer.

Well, "career" was stretching it just a bit. She was writing for a small newspaper about an hour's drive from Boston. It was satisfactory. She was doing what she enjoyed – writing. But sometimes it was difficult. There was only so much that could be said about the local chapter of the dog society.

Tempest started up the steps behind Cherise, the suitcase bumping behind her. Cherise stopped and turned around, frowning. "Goodness! I was so excited about seeing you I forgot to call Crosbie. Just leave your case there and he'll bring it up later."

"It's not that heavy." Tempest retracted the pull handle, and picked it up by the regular one. "I can do it."

Cherise considered this for a moment, as if the thought had

never occurred to her. Then she shrugged. "At least let me take it for you." She snatched the small bag and started up the stairs again. "I can hardly wait to tell you everything that's been happening."

Tempest watched as Cherise skipped up the steps in front of her, her mini-skirt bouncing against her rounded backside with each step. Tempest's lips curved upward slightly. Cherise might come across as shallow, but underneath the rich girl exterior was a truly loyal friend.

TEMPEST GLANCED around Cherise's bedroom. It looked much as she remembered. Lots of evidence of the spoiled little rich girl. Pictures, frills, ribbons and lace... everything spoke of a pampered princess who had never quite grown up. "When are you expecting Stella?"

"About seven." Cherise deposited the suitcase near the door and then flopped down on the bed. "Something about shipping some boxes back home to Texas."

"Moving can be a lot of work," Tempest offered.

"I guess. Anyway, she should be here in time for dinner." Cherise rolled onto her stomach. "Imagine! Stella with a Master's degree! She's probably the smartest person I know. Present company excluded, of course."

"Of course." Tempest pulled out a pink satin covered chair from under Cherise's dressing table.

"What do you do with a degree in 'Environmental Studies,' anyway?" Cherise asked.

"I'm not sure exactly. Field work? Environmental testing?"

Cherise sat up and patted the bed. "Come sit here! You need to tell me everything that's been going on since last time I saw you."

Tempest let out a small laugh, but got up and moved to perch on the edge of the bed. "That was only yesterday at Stella's graduation."

"I know, but we didn't get much time to talk. It seems like ages since we had any girl time together." Cherise sighed dramatically. "I just don't know how I ever got to be friends with you two. You're both just so smart! What in the world did you ever see in a bimbo like me?"

"You're not a bimbo," Tempest defended. "You're smart, too. About lots of things."

Cherise laughed, that flippant tinkling sound that Tempest had come to know so well. "There you go, always trying to make people feel good about themselves. At least that's one thing about Stella. She's honest."

"Well, I just meant -"

"Forget it." Cherise waved a dismissive hand. "I don't mind, you know. Being a bimbo."

"You shouldn't call yourself that," Tempest chided, her voice soft.

"Why not? I don't mean it in a bad way. Actually, playing the part has its advantages." Cherise raised a brow and smiled. "Guys seem to go for it."

"And you've never had trouble in that department," Tempest commented wryly.

"My point exactly," Cherise replied, flipping her blonde tresses. She lowered her voice to a conspiratorial whisper. "Just wait until I tell you about Roberto."

"Roberto?" Another in a long string of boyfriends, no doubt.

"He is an absolute dream!" Cherise flopped back onto the bed and flung her arms above her head. "He's Italian, and you know what they say about Italian lovers."

"Um, right." Tempest focused on the bedspread's stitching, tracing it with her index finger.

"It's all true." Cherise sighed. There was a moment of

awkward silence until she sat up abruptly. "So, anyone new in your life?"

"Nope," Tempest replied.

"Still pining for what's his name?"

"Ron," Tempest supplied curtly. "His name is Ron, and no I am not pining. We only dated for a couple of months and it was a perfectly logical decision on both our parts. Our paths were going in different directions. It was for the best that we end it before things got too serious."

"Oh please!" Cherise groaned and rolled her eyes. "Our paths? That sounds like a cop out if ever I heard one. Admit it. He was just running scared."

"Well -"

Cherise cut her off. "Seriously. I thought he was supposed to be a Christian or something. How dare he string my best friend such a line?"

"I'm a Christian, too," Tempest defended. "He's going into the mission field. A long distance relationship is just too hard. It makes sense."

"Phooey on that. If it's right, it doesn't matter where in the world you go." Cherise pinned Tempest with her eyes. "If you want to know what I think, Ron is probably secretly gay or something. Why else would he dump you like that?"

"Cherise!" Tempest shot back. "That's not true."

Cherise raised a brow. "How do you know? Ever sleep with him?"

"Of course not. I don't believe in sex before marriage and - and neither does he." Tempest blinked rapidly and pushed her glasses up. It was mostly true.

"Oh right. Something I never did understand." Cherise flopped down on her back again. "I'm glad you're the one who got religion and not me. I couldn't handle it."

"You might be surprised." Tempest shrugged.

Cherise shook her head. "No way. I mean, I'm happy if you

are, but don't expect me to change. And as for Ron, I say good riddance. There are plenty of other fish in the sea." Cherise giggled. "Who knows? Maybe you'll fall for some hotty and change your mind about the celibacy thing."

"I doubt it." Since becoming a Christian eighteen months ago, Tempest had given up on casual relationships. Not that she'd been licentious or anything before her conversion, but now she had a legitimate excuse for avoiding men. She'd only had sex that one time in college and well, she'd rather forget all about that. It was possibly the most embarrassing moment of her life.

"It could happen."

Tempest frowned and looked over at Cherise. "What?"

"It could happen," Cherise repeated. "You falling for some hot guy and give up on becoming a nun."

"I'm not becoming a nun. I'm not Catholic."

"Whatever. You know what I mean."

Of course she did. Cherise had a one track mind. Tempest straightened her spine. "When the right person comes along - the person God wants for me - I will be more than happy to engage in... well, you know. Once I'm married, of course."

"But how will you know if you're even compatible?" Cherise asked. "You know... in *that* way?"

"Is that all you care about?" Tempest stood up and crossed back to the chair. *Lord, give me patience with Cherise. She doesn't know any better.* She took a deep breath before turning around. "Sorry. I didn't mean to snap at you. Tell me more about Roberto instead."

The hurt look in Cherise's eyes melted almost instantly. "Roberto," she repeated the name softly, like a mantra. "He is so perfect. Charming, good looking, great build and well, I already mentioned that other part." She sighed. "I would literally follow him to the ends of the earth."

"That good, huh?"

"In every way. Of course, my parents don't see it that way.

They are always so out of touch. I think they expect me to marry someone from their pre-approved lineup."

"What do you mean?"

"Oh, you know. Old family friends. Someone with connections. The right bloodlines and all that. But I'm not having any part of it."

"Good. It's your life."

"You're not going to lecture me?"

"Why would I do that?" Tempest asked.

Cherise shrugged. "I don't know. The religion thing? I know you don't approve of my choices."

"Have I ever lectured you?" Tempest blinked, tamping down the hurt that had risen in her breast. It was a topic that struck a nerve. Sometimes she felt like a bad Christian for not being more enthusiastic about witnessing to her friends. True, she'd shared her faith, but the last thing she wanted was to alienate them, so she avoided leading conversations, opting for the 'friendship evangelism' model instead.

"Well, no," Cherise admitted. She looked down at the bedspread and traced some stitching. She looked up again abruptly, her eyes shining with unshed tears. "But sometimes I feel it. Like you're such a good person and I'm, well… not. One of these days you're going to just jump ship and leave me to my own devices."

"Cherise!" Tempest bolted from the chair and bent to envelop her friend around the shoulders. "I'll never abandon you. You or Stella! You know that. Friends forever, right?"

Cherise sat up and they hugged properly. "Friends forever." When they pulled apart, Cherise examined Tempest closely. "But do you think I'm crazy? Falling so hard for Roberto, I mean?"

"Well… How would I know? I've never met him." Tempest smiled.

"Exactly!" Cherise gave Tempest another big squeeze. "I'm so glad the two of you agreed to come over for one last girl's night before we go our separate ways. I'm going to miss you so much."

"You make it sound like we might not see each other again. I mean, I'm not that far from Boston."

"Oh, I know. But who knows where Stella might end up? I know she's planning to go back to Texas for awhile, but after that, who knows?"

"True." Tempest wished she could add a 'who knows' to her own future. Right now it seemed pretty stable. And pretty dull. But there were bills to pay...

"Anyway, let's go see what Cook is making for dinner tonight," Cherise suggested, rolling off the bed.

Tempest followed. It was hard to mull over life's bigger issues with Cherise around.

CHAPTER 2

*T*he silence that dominated the dining table was interrupted only by the clink of silverware on china plates. Cherise's parents were outwardly hospitable; the dining room was large and beautifully furnished, the meal itself resplendent. Still, there was an awkwardness that permeated the atmosphere beneath the sparkling chandelier. Tempest focused on the morsel of meat that she had speared with her fork. She was a vegetarian, but somehow refusing to eat at least some of everything that had been placed before her seemed ungrateful.

At the head of the table sat Byron Hillyer, Cherise's father and lord of his manor. He was an attractive man for his age, probably in his mid to late fifties. He had a tanned face, sported a full head of steel grey hair, and had clear blue eyes the color of Cherise's. His children flanked him, Cherise on one side and Dirk on the other. Wilma Hillyer took up her station at the opposite end of the table from her husband; a platinum blonde beauty queen who was well preserved as only the wealthy can be. There were a few lines around her mouth, but her eyebrows arched perfectly over carefully made up eyes. A string of understated pearls adorned her pale shift dress. Invited guests filled in the gaps – Tempest, Stella, and one of Dirk's friends, Alistair Montgomery.

"Congratulations, Stella," Wilma Hillyer directed at the third member of her daughter's trio. "I understand you just completed your Master's Degree."

"Yes. Thank you," Stella replied. Her voice still held that characteristic Texan drawl, even after all the years of schooling outside of Texas. She was the smallest of the three friends, with shining shoulder length black hair, dark snapping eyes, and a feisty personality to match. She had arrived around seven, as expected, leaving Cherise only enough time to share the minutest details about the dashing Roberto before they were all called down to dinner.

"I propose a toast," Cherise's brother Dirk piped up, raising his glass of wine. He had Cherise's good looks, only in male form, and his hair was slightly darker than hers, probably because her particular shade of blonde was boosted with a bit of help from a salon. Otherwise, there was no denying the family resemblance. There had never been any love lost between Cherise's older brother and her chosen group of friends, but tonight he seemed willing to bury the hatchet. "To Miss Stella Crayton on a job well done."

"To Stella," everyone present reiterated, lifting their glasses.

"A Master's in Environmental Studies," Byron Hillyer mused. "What does one do with that exactly?"

"I'm especially interested in the impact of large scale industrialization on ecosystems outside their direct vicinity," Stella replied.

"Do you have work lined up somewhere?" Wilma asked conversationally, taking another sip of wine.

"I'm going home to Texas for awhile first," Stella replied. "To my father's ranch. But I do have a couple of offers which I'm looking into."

"It seems to me most environmentalists are concerned about

cutting down on corporate profits and little else," Byron huffed. "I'd hate to see what happens if we shut down the system like most of these tree-huggers want. Chaos, that's what we'd have."

"I'd like to think fiscal and environmental responsibilities can go hand in hand," Stella offered.

"Most of them aren't thinking logically, if they're thinking at all." Byron's blue eyes pinned Stella in her spot. "We can't just shut industry down. Going back to an agrarian lifestyle is impractical on a large scale and I doubt that even the environmentalists would want to give up electricity and running water. People still want to drive their cars and wear their leather shoes. As it is, corporate America has been labeled the bad guy, but the fire is being fueled by stooges who know very little about the practical aspects of an industrialized economy."

"Exactly what I hope to rectify," Stella said. The color had risen in her cheeks, but her voice remained calm. Her gaze did not waver from Byron's.

"Would anyone care for more wine?" Wilma piped up cheerily. "Crosbie, bring another bottle of wine, please." The stoic butler, who had been hovering on the perimeter, bowed and made his exit. Tempest found the corners of her mouth turning upward ever so slightly. It was like something out of a movie.

"I see you've been well indoctrinated," Byron continued, ignoring his wife's attempt at changing the subject. "The truth is, most environmentalists with any real influence are lining their own pockets while preaching restraint. In my experience, altruism is a myth."

"I sincerely hope you're wrong, Sir," Stella rebutted, her voice hardening ever so slightly. "I understand that economically we can't just stop the industrialized world in its tracks, but the planet can't sustain unchecked greed forever."

"Where is that wine?" Wilma flustered. "More meat, anyone?"

The tension in the room was electric. Tempest kept her gaze focused on her plate. The meat she was trying to swallow felt like shoe leather in her mouth. She jumped when someone touched her leg and the meat stuck in her throat like a mouse in a snake's craw. She reached for a drink of water and felt the food squeezing its way down centimeter by centimeter. She glanced over at Dirk Hillyer. His eyes were twinkling beneath hooded lids, a smirk on his face. Apparently he was enjoying the show.

"You're young." Byron's voice was laced with condescension. "It's good to be starry-eyed for a time, but I'm sure your bubble will burst soon enough."

"Let's not talk shop this evening," Wilma interrupted more forcefully. "We can't solve the world's problems in one night."

"I don't know," Alistair Montgomery jumped in. "Stella's got a point. When do we stop putting the needs of the corporate few over the needs of our future generations?" He smiled over at Stella and offered her an almost imperceptible nod. Alistair was good looking, in a polished upscale kind of way, with streaked blonde hair that was styled to perfection. He was dressed with just the right amount of casual elegance that could only be achieved with practiced attention and the budget to match.

"And since when do you have an opinion on the subject?" Dirk directed at his friend with a grin. "Last time I checked you were more concerned about your tennis score than saving future generations."

"I resent that," Alistair replied, lifting his chin. "I think that Stella's ambitions are admirable." He offered her another winning smile, his teeth white against his perfect tan.

"And exactly what do you know of my ambitions?" Stella turned her attention to Alistair. "I don't believe I've shared much beyond a general statement."

"So? Enlighten me." Alistair took a sip of his wine, his eyebrows beckoning over the rim of the glass.

"Yes, do," Byron agreed.

Stella sat up straight. "I'm just saying there's a need for collaboration, that's all. Between corporate America and those with concerns over the health of the planet."

"Here, here," Cherise said, raising her glass of wine.

Dirk gave his sister a withering look. "When was the last time you checked your makeup bag to see which products were tested on defenseless animals? Hm?"

"What does that have to do with anything?" Cherise asked, her wine glass still in mid air.

Dirk laughed. "Exactly my point. Neither you nor Alistair really care one way or the other, just as long as your own conveniences remain intact."

"I resent that," Alistair repeated, the air of smug superiority still in place. The practiced smile had never left his face and he lifted his wine glass to his lips once again.

"So you said already," Dirk countered.

"Dirk, please!" Wilma interrupted. "Your provocation is not helping. We do have guests." She turned to Stella. "Don't be intimidated my dear."

"Intimidated?" Stella repeated. Her voice had risen slightly as if she'd just been challenged.

"I'm sure you are very well versed in whatever it is," Wilma continued. "But I, for one, can't abide talking shop over dinner."

"I thought we were having quite a stimulating conversation. Don't you agree, Miss Crayton?" Byron Hillyer directed his gaze at Stella.

"Absolutely," Stella agreed. Tempest could see the snap in her friend's dark eyes. Stella was gearing up for a fight. She was never one to back down when challenged.

"Miss Crayton probably appreciates the opportunity to express her opinions freely, as do I," Byron continued. "After all, she's sure to encounter far greater opposition than what little I've expressed here. She'll need to get used to it. Toughen up, so to speak."

"Get tough or die," Dirk snorted. "The family motto." He took a long swig from his wine glass.

Byron glared at his son. "If you have a real opinion on the subject perhaps you'd like to share it?"

"What's the use? You never listen anyway." Dirk shrugged. Byron clamped his mouth shut in an angry line, blackness shrouding his features. Dirk looked around with an artificially hopeful expression. "I'm with Mother. Where is that next bottle of wine?"

Byron muttered something indecipherable and drained his own glass before pushing back from the table.

"Where are you going?" Wilma demanded.

"To my study," Byron responded coolly.

"But dessert hasn't been served," Wilma said.

"Can a man not go to his own study when he pleases?" Byron asked, the quietness of his voice frightening.

Wilma's eyes were wide, but she kept her mouth shut.

Byron nodded civilly toward Stella and Tempest. "It's been a pleasure," he drawled and stalked from the room.

Wilma Hillyer expelled a small frustrated breath and motioned to Crosbie. The elderly gentleman barely had time to replenish her wine glass before she snatched it from him and took a long swig.

"He was right, you know," Alistair said, leaning toward Stella and Tempest conspiratorially. "My friend has me pegged. I really was only trying to impress you ladies. I don't actually know much about what's happening on the environmental front. But I'd be willing to learn."

"I've already warned them about your womanizing ways, Alistair, so you might as well relax," Cherise chided.

"Cherise, darling, I'm hurt!" Alistair pouted. "You doubt my sincerity? What if I really do wish to learn more on the topic? Your friend seems like quite the knowledgeable teacher."

"As if you care." Cherise flipped her hair back off her shoulders.

"You should talk," Dirk threw in, raising a brow in her direction.

"At least I can admit it." Cherise shrugged. "And what about you, brother dear? You're a fine one to be pointing fingers."

"Who's pointing? I never said anything to contradict the fact. I actually am more concerned about myself than any future generations." He turned to Alistair as if to prove his point. "Did you see my tennis match at the club this afternoon? Alarming! I'm going to need an extra session with my serving coach."

"You don't say," Alistair drawled with amusement.

"I'm sick to death of you both," Cherise informed both young men. "Come on, girls. It's time for some girl fun." She rose with mock haughtiness and turned.

Tempest took another swallow of water and then scrambled to her feet, straightening her clothes as she rose. If this was family, maybe she wasn't missing much.

"Enjoy yourselves, girls," Wilma Hillyer offered as the three friends exited. Crosbie was already refilling her wine glass.

CHAPTER 3

*C*herise giggled as she bounced onto the king-sized bed, sending her two friends into a counter bounce. "This is sooo like old times!"

"Frighteningly so," Stella noted. The three women were clad in their pajamas. Tempest wore two piece, button up flannels and large matching fuzzy slippers. Stella was in what looked to be an over-sized football jersey and Cherise had on a pink short set.

"Don't be mad about earlier, okay?" Cherise pleaded. "You just need to ignore them. They don't mean to be rude – Mother and Daddy, I mean. They can't help it. It's just their way."

"I'm not mad," Stella denied, perhaps too forcefully. "Your Dad is entitled to his opinions. It's his house, after all."

"Good! So just forget about it. I don't want anything to spoil our fun. Not them, or Dirk, or Alistair."

"Speaking of Alistair," Stella mused, "What is his problem? I felt like he was staring at me all through dinner. Like there were eyes boring through my clothes every time I wasn't looking."

Cherise waved her hand dismissively. "Alistair is, well... he's just Alistair. He thinks he's God's gift to women and likes to flaunt his money to get what he wants. He's got a little problem with tact, if you know what I mean. Just ignore him."

"Kind of creepy if you ask me. What'd you think, Temp?" Stella turned her attention to Tempest.

"Hm? Oh yeah," Tempest agreed, not looking up from the magazine she was reading.

"What are you reading that's so interesting?" Stella cocked her head and bent over, trying to see the cover.

"Oh, just this magazine I found on the nightstand."

"I didn't think you liked fashion magazines," Cherise noted.

"I don't, usually."

"Are you kidding?" Stella turned to Cherise. "You haven't forgotten that Tempest will read almost anything. Even the instruction manual for her curling iron."

"I don't own a curling iron," Tempest said absently, still perusing the magazine.

"No reading on our last night together," Cherise exclaimed as she whisked the periodical out of Tempest's hands.

"It was a very interesting article on how pets can actually add years to your life because of the companionship they provide," Tempest explained. She was only slightly irritated. She was used to acquiescing to her friends. It was only a magazine, after all. Not something important.

"So what's next? Manicures or pedicures?" Cherise asked.

Stella shrugged. "You're the boss of this party."

"Okay. Tempest, come sit in this chair. I'll do your fingernails and Stella can do your toes."

Tempest frowned and pushed her glasses further up on her nose. "Why me?" Being non-confrontational was one thing, but she wasn't sure she wanted to be the guinea pig for Cherise's fashion experiments.

"I get my nails done at the salon," Cherise explained. "But you, my dearest, need some help." She lifted one of Tempest's hands.

"Just look at this! You've bitten them down so far we'll have to apply tips! Good thing I keep an emergency supply on hand."

Stella smirked. "You never know when you might have a nail emergency."

"Exactly." The jibe seemed to go over Cherise's head as she examined Tempest's fingers further.

Tempest snatched her hand away from Cherie's grasp. "Why not do Stella's nails? Hers won't need fake tips."

Stella shook her head. "I'll be mucking out stalls in a day or two, so there's no point."

"Oh, quit being such a baby!" Cherise chided. "This is supposed to be fun, remember?"

"Fun for you," Tempest muttered, but she let her hand go limp as Cherise began buffing the tops of her nails in preparation for the adhesive.

"One of these days I'll convince you to get contacts," Cherise said. "Don't you agree Tempest should get contacts?" she directed at Stella.

"If she wants to." Stella sat cross-legged on the floor in front of Tempest. "Off with these monster slippers."

Tempest kicked off her slippers and propped her feet on the small footstool Cherise had placed there for her.

"Oh, my goodness!" Stella suddenly exclaimed. "Is this still the same friendship bracelet on your ankle?"

Tempest looked down at her ankle. "Yeah," she responded hesitantly. "We were never supposed to take them off, remember?"

"But it's so faded!" Cherise exclaimed, leaning forward to take a closer look. "Is it even sanitary?"

"I guess I just got used to the feel of it," Tempest said, her voice taking on a slightly defensive pitch.

"It's flattering, although a bit weird." Stella surveyed the faded bracelet.

"What you really mean is childish," Tempest stated. She could feel the heat of embarrassment rising in her cheeks.

"No, I think it's cool. I took mine off when I got home to Texas so I wouldn't wreck it and just never remembered to put it back on," Stella explained. "But I still have it somewhere in one of my drawers as a keepsake."

"Really?" A rush of relief enveloped her. "I thought you probably thought it was stupid to still be wearing it after all this time, but… I just couldn't seem to get rid of it."

"I have no idea where mine went," Cherise said. "I guess I lost it somewhere."

"Hey, that's what we should do tonight," Stella suggested. "Make new ones."

"Good idea." Tempest sat up fully. "But out of what?"

"Not till after I finish your nails," Cherise said, a warning look in her eyes.

"How can I weave a bracelet with big fake nails?" Tempest asked.

"You're just trying to get out of it, I know," Cherise said, but she smiled. She paused for a moment in thought. "Now, I suppose I could get Crosbie to go to a store for supplies."

"It's kind of late for that, don't you think?" Stella stated.

"It was your idea." Cherise paused. "I know! We can unwind a sweater or this throw I never use… maybe use the tassels from my drapes."

"Are you sure?" Tempest frowned and surveyed her surroundings. "Most of your stuff is kind of expensive."

"Who cares? Nothing is more important than my two best friends!"

Stella shrugged. "You heard her. Let's do it. The nails can wait."

∾

It was just like old times, only this time they weren't kids anymore. It must have been quite a sight - three grown women sitting cross-legged on the bed, laughing and talking as they wove various strands of colored thread together. Too bad life wasn't always this easy; this carefree. Sometimes the colors of one's own tapestry were not so bright.

Cherise reached over and jostled Tempest's knee. "You are just way too quiet. What are you thinking about?"

Tempest shook her head and laughed. "Oh, just how Aunt Rose would think how absurd this is. Impractical."

"Pooh on Aunt Rose!" Cherise exclaimed.

They all laughed.

"She's been good to me," Tempest conceded. "Without her taking me in after my parents died, I'd never have gone to Parkview and I never would have met you two."

"Too true," Cherise agreed. "But it seems to me she tries to keep you just a bit too close now that you're out on your own. Tries to control your life."

"She's good to me. And she paid for my education."

"She 'guilts' you, that's what," Cherise stated. "You're young and you're a reporter. You should be traveling the world - seeing new places!"

"Well, I have been thinking..." Tempest responded hesitantly.

"Spit it out, girl," Stella piped up, barely looking up as she continued to intertwine the threads.

"Well, I have been thinking about moving back to California," Tempest admitted in a rush of breath. All three of them stopped weaving.

"Really?" Cherise asked, wide-eyed. "California? That's perfect!"

"Well, nothing's been settled. I mean -"

"Just think of all the beaches full of cute, tanned, muscular guys!" Cherise interrupted.

31

Tempest tried not to smile. Of course that was the first thing Cherise would think about.

"When are you thinking of moving?" Stella asked.

"Nothing is settled, like I said," Tempest hedged. "I mean, I haven't been back there since, well, you know. Since my folks passed away. Things have probably changed, you know? But I've always longed to go back. To try to capture some of what it must have been like."

"Always the romantic," Stella mused, not unkindly. She went back to making her bracelet.

"I suppose," Tempest admitted, looking down at the strands of colored floss in her palm. A sudden pang of loneliness stabbed at her heart. *Lord, I thought I'd come to terms with their deaths...*

"So what's holding you back?" Stella asked.

"I don't know." Tempest shrugged. "Fear, maybe?"

"What's to be afraid of?" Cherise asked. "If you don't like it, just move back."

"You seem to be forgetting that I don't have the same monetary freedom you do, Cherise. Aunt Rose took me in and paid for my education, but she doesn't give me an allowance now that I have a job and am out on my own. It's just not that easy to pick up and move across the country on a whim when you don't have a job or an unlimited disposable income."

"Sorry. It would just be the perfect solution, that's all." Cherise started crossing the threads once again, rather forcefully.

"Solution to what?" Stella asked.

"Oh, nothing. Argh! A knot. I give up!" Cherise tossed her half finished bracelet onto the bed.

Tempest sighed. She usually wasn't so blunt. "I'm sorry for snapping, Cherise. I'm just uptight. Excited and scared, you know? I really want to do this. But I'm still working out the details."

Unphased by the small burst of drama, Stella tied off her

bracelet and picked up Cherise's discarded one. "What about your pets? What would you do with them?"

"That's part of my dilemma. It's not that easy to relocate with two dogs and a cat and I know Aunt Rose wouldn't take them in. But I just can't imagine giving them up."

Cherise threw up her hands. "Don't look at me. I've never been good with animals. What about you, Stella?"

"Good with animals? Sure, I was raised on a ranch. But I'm not sure how practical it would be to move them all that way."

"No, silly! I mean what are you going to do now that you're finished school?" Cherise clarified.

"Oh!" Stella laughed. "Once I get back to Texas I'll check out my options, like I said. I'd like to get on at the local university; do some research and still hang out at home. I miss my family and friends back there." She stopped talking for a moment and licked the threads into place, then tied the second bracelet off. "Here you go. I finished two in the time you did one." She reached over to tie the bracelet around Cherise's ankle.

"Hm," Cherise mused, watching as Stella secured the bracelet in place. "There wouldn't happen to be a long, tall Texan that's drawing you back by any chance?"

Stella laughed. "You're the man-tracker, not me." She sat up, reached for the other bracelet, and began the same procedure on Tempest.

"I distinctly remember more than one conversation in the past about some boys back on the ranch with names that sounded like dogs. Rex and Buddy, or something," Cherise said, frowning. "You talked about them nonstop every time you came back from summer vacation."

"That was Zane and Blue," Tempest corrected. She was good with names. Details of any kind, really. She knew exactly what her mother was wearing the last time she saw her… Tempest cleared her throat and forced her mind back to the matter at hand. She had just finished making her bracelet. "Give me your foot, Stella."

Stella stretched her foot out on the bed toward Tempest. "Thank you, Temp. At least someone got their facts straight. And for your information, Zane and Blue are like brothers to me. There's no way I'd ever think of them in that way."

"There! All finished. Now we all have new ones." Tempest sat back on her heels and let a satisfied smile cross her face.

Cherise inspected the new ankle gear. "With names like that, I might have to check them out for myself."

"Their dad is a fan of old westerns. Zane Grey is his favorite author and there used to be some TV show that had a character named Blue in it. At least that's what my dad said," Stella explained. "But enough about them. I know you're just dying to tell us more about the mysterious Roberto. Besides the fact that he's every inch Italian, you haven't said much."

Tempest's smile deepened. Stella knew exactly how to deflect attention away from herself, but Tempest was grateful for the conversation's redirection away from her own dreams about California, too. Stella and Cherise were her best friends, but it was hard, even with them, to express the deepness of her pain - even after so many years.

Cherise's eyes lit up. "Well, I met him through Alistair, of all people. I guess that guy is good for something after all. Anyway, we instantly had this connection, you know – I mean other than the sex thing. Like a bond."

"He sounds too good to be true," Stella teased. "You should have invited him over for our approval."

"That's the problem," Cherise moaned. "He had to go back to Italy. It was so sudden. I begged him not to go, but he wouldn't listen. I think Alistair had something to do with it. They have some kind of business together. Anyway, he left and I'm dying without him!"

"So pack a bag and go to Italy," Stella suggested.

"Not as easy as you might think. My parents don't like Roberto at all. In fact, they think I broke up with him, which is what they told me to do – well, my father did anyway, or he said he would cut off my allowance for a month. So, I lied to them and told them I broke it off when I was really sneaking around with him behind their backs."

"I see." Stella nodded and raised a brow. "Daddy was going to close the purse strings if you didn't break it off. And?"

Cherise hesitated for a moment and then blurted the rest out. "I've already scheduled my flight to Italy, but my parents don't know. I've put enough money away in a separate account that Daddy won't be able to access that should last me at least a month and by that time, if he finds out, he's sure to cool off because he always does. But in the meantime, I've got to get to Italy without them knowing."

"Isn't this a little bit drastic?" Tempest asked. "I mean if the guy loves you like you say he does, won't he come back for you? You're the one who said it shouldn't matter how far apart you are if it's right."

"But it could be months! I'll die!" Cherise wailed.

"Maybe it feels like it right now, but we've all seen you in this state before. Remember Tad, the hot shot race car driver? Or Ritchie, the supposed business exec who turned out to be a parking lot attendant?" Stella reminded.

"That was different!" Cherise's pretty face was marred by a scowl.

"How so?" Stella asked.

"Well, it just was," Cherise said, flipping her hair. "You just don't know what it's like! Neither one of you have ever really been in love. Not like this!"

Tempest swallowed hard. It was true. Her love for Ron had been stable and safe. With God's help she'd finally decided to trust again and when he pulled the rug out from under her, it felt like her whole world had imploded. Even her faith had been shaken, but only momentarily. But there had been no screaming. No ranting. She had just internalized it, squeezing the pain into an unreachable corner until its existence seemed normal.

"Hold it," Stella interrupted. "Are we not adults here? This is borderline juvenile – like an episode of some teen reality show."

"Thanks, Stella! I thought you were my friend!" Cherise scooted to the edge of the bed and stood, crossing her arms over her chest.

"I am your friend," Stella sighed in exasperation. "And as your friend it has often fallen to me to save you from yourself."

Cherise blinked in surprise, digesting the truth of what her friend had just said.

"Listen, Cherise," Tempest said soothingly. "You just need to work with your parents on this. Tell them the truth. When they realize how serious you two are, they'll come around."

"You don't understand. It's way past that. I need an alibi. I need them to think I've gone to visit one of you. They won't come looking for me all the way in Texas. Or, I could say I'm going to California with you, Temp, just to scope it out." Cherise looked from one to the other hopefully.

Stella slowly nodded her head. "So that's what's so perfect."

"I'm not ready to go to California yet," Tempest put in quickly.

"So Texas it is, then." Cherise turned her gaze toward Stella.

"Whoa, whoa, whoa! You're getting way ahead of yourself here," Stella exclaimed. "I'm not totally comfortable with this."

"Fine!" Cherise clipped, flipping her head away from Stella. "Tempest? How about a trip to California? All expenses paid."

"But you said you were going to Italy." Tempest frowned. Her mind felt suddenly muddled.

"Of course I'm going to Italy," Cherise explained with an exasperated sigh. "But I'll pay for your trip to California if you do this for me. You can go and my parents will think I'm with you. Please? Please just do this one thing for me?"

"I don't know..." Tempest hesitated. A paid trip to California?

Maybe this was her chance to make a break for it. Maybe God was making a way for her to go.

"You're not thinking of doing it?" Stella turned an accusatory stare on Tempest.

"Well..."

"Oh, thank you, thank you!" Cherise cried, jumping back on the bed and hugging Tempest. "You're the best friend ever!"

"Hmph," Stella muttered under her breath.

"This is so great! You have literally saved my life! Now there's just one more thing," Cherise continued.

"Here we go!" Stella rolled her eyes.

"I'm supposed to escort some friend of my Dad's around the city tomorrow. You know, show him the sights and all that."

"And?" Stella prompted.

"My flight leaves before the time I'm supposed to meet him. I was just wondering if one of you could pretend to be me – just for the afternoon. If he calls my folks he'll be able to report that I did, indeed, meet him as planned and then I'll be gone to help my friend pack for California and no one will be the wiser. I'll have done my duty and my parents will be off my back."

Stella threw her hands in the air. "Wow, this just keeps getting better and better. Well, you can count me out right now. My Texan accent will blow your cover. Besides, I'm heading home tomorrow."

"Temp? Please?" Cherise looked at her with pleading eyes.

"I don't feel good about this." Tempest's frown deepened. "What if he's seen a picture?"

Cherise shrugged her pretty shoulders. "So, I've changed my hair color. He'll never notice."

Tempest hesitated. "I don't know. It's lying."

"No it isn't!" Cherise countered. "You're just helping a friend."

"As much as I love a good prank, for the record, let it be known that I do not approve of any of this," Stella stated.

There was a light rapping at the door. Cherise scurried off the bed and answered it without any regard for her scant attire.

"What do you want?" she demanded upon seeing her brother Dirk in the hall.

"That depends," he replied, rubbing his chin. "I'm not sure what it's worth to you."

Cherise's eyes widened and she swatted at him. "You pervert! Were you listening at the door?" She leaned forward to peer down the hall. "Where's Alistair?"

"He's long gone," Dirk replied, swinging into the room uninvited and shutting the door. He perched himself on the chair that was nearest the bed. "I always wondered what you girls did at one of these all night pajama parties."

Despite the fact that her attire was anything but revealing, Tempest felt decidedly uncomfortable wearing her pajamas in front of a man she hardly knew, especially a man like Dirk Hillyer. She inched further back against the headboard.

"How much did you hear?" Cherise demanded.

"Enough to know that you're planning a little forbidden get away and have enlisted the help of your oh-so-compliant friend." He winked at Tempest. "I'm surprised, actually, but I guess not every book can be judged by its cover."

"Please don't tell, Dirk. Please!" Cherise begged. Her eyes suddenly hardened. "If you do, I'll tell Mother and Daddy about all the money you've wasted on your backroom gambling habit. Not to mention the trouble you got Sidney Fletcher in. You wouldn't want it getting out that you paid your sleazy little underaged girlfriend to have an abortion, now would you?"

Dirk's eyes matched his sister's. "That was low, even for you. Especially in front of present company." He turned to Stella and Tempest. "Which, by the way, is all a lie. She's nineteen and got pregnant long after I'd already broken it off."

"Whatever." Stella shrugged indifferently.

"You are such a sleaze!" Cherise spouted.

"And you're not? Weren't you just planning your little rendezvous with Mr. Italy behind our parents' backs?"

"That's different!"

"Why? Because you're 'in love'?" Dirk let out a condescending grunt. "We've all heard that one before."

"Dirk, please," Cherise tried to sound reasonable. "We both do things behind their backs and we both know it. Let's just be friends for once. Why can't we just be happy?"

Dirk considered this for a minute. "You don't mention Sidney or the gambling and I'll go along with your 'California' scam."

"Thank you!" Cherise cried, throwing her arms around her brother's neck.

Dirk patted his sister's back with one hand. "See? Who says sibling rivalry is insurmountable? Heck, if you throw in your Porsche while you're away, I'll even help with tomorrow's tour around town."

"You'd do that?" Cherise asked, eyes wide.

"Why not?" Dirk shrugged. "It might be fun, as long as Tempest doesn't mind." He looked over at Tempest and caught her gaze.

Tempest lowered her eyes, focusing on twisting her hands in her lap. *Oh Lord! What have I gotten myself into?* "I never actually said I'd do it yet," she reminded quietly.

"Please?" Cherise turned doleful eyes on her friend. "It will be easy now that Dirk is going to help."

"I suppose it would make things more believable," Tempest acquiesced. A twinge of guilt stabbed at her gut. *Lying about your identity was not something a good Christian should do. Ron would be mortified.* The thought of his pious reprimand brought a heated anger to her chest that she hadn't felt in months - maybe ever - and a sudden desire to do something rash came over her. She looked up. "Okay, I'll do it."

"Hooray!" Cherise squealed. "You're the very best ever!"

"It's a good thing Mother and Father are both blasted and

39

probably asleep by now. With all this noise, they'd be sure to know something was up," Dirk chided. His smile, however, was disarming. "Well, until tomorrow, then." He stood and took one step toward the door, then stopped and turned back. He winked at Tempest. "You know, I think I am going to enjoy our little outing very much indeed!"

CHAPTER 4

"So, 'sister dear.' You ready for this?" Dirk smiled across at Tempest as they waited at a stoplight. She dropped her gaze. He was driving Cherise's white Porsche, on their way to meet the family friend. Tempest twisted her hands together in her lap. She didn't dare peek at his perfectly mussed blonde head. Why, oh why had she agreed to any of this? It was a mistake, plain and simple and she should just jump out of the car right now and hail a cab. Somehow the devil on her shoulder had won out and she needed to stop the lie before it went any further. But how, without betraying one of her best friends?

"Don't worry," Dirk assured, patting her knee. She flinched. "You're way too tense. There is absolutely nothing to worry about. Especially now that I'm playing along. Old man Clarke will never suspect a thing. Besides, it might actually be fun."

"I doubt it," Tempest replied under her breath. She glanced out the window.

Dirk laughed. "Think of it as a game."

"I don't know. I don't feel good about this."

"Look. It's not like we're doing anything illegal," he reasoned. "Just showing a family friend the city."

Tempest couldn't see his eyes beneath his dark glasses. Was he laughing at her? Making fun of her naïveté? She felt the color rising in her cheeks. What a fool she was. Always the gullible one. She was thankful for the sunglasses that covered her eyes. At least he wouldn't be able to read her mind quite so readily.

"By the way," Dirk said, pulling off the main street and into a reserved parking lot. "You look extremely hot in that dress."

Tempest stiffened. "It's Cherise's."

"Still looks hot."

She stole a glance his way. His neck was craned around and his eyes fixed on the rear window as he expertly backed the vehicle into a stall. Still, he wore that characteristic smirk of his. She felt like sinking into the depths of the leather seat. She wasn't used to compliments and wasn't sure what to make of it. *Oh Lord, get me out of this!* The last thing she needed was a come on from Cherise's brother. But he and his friends always did that sort of thing. They were players. It was just the way they rolled and it probably meant nothing.

Last night, after she'd acquiesced to getting her nails done after all, she'd spent an hour trying on clothing from Cherise's ample closet. At first it had been embarrassing, then it became kind of fun – like searching for buried treasure. Finally it got just plain tedious. But they eventually found "the one." When she'd first seen herself in Cherise's full length mirror, she couldn't believe how attractive she felt. Empowered, almost. The dress was a form fitting knit in a luxurious copper shade that brought out some red highlights in her chestnut hair and contrasted beautifully with her green eyes. It was far too revealing and far too short to be comfortable. But it was something that Cherise would wear, and that was the point – to look like Cherise. A little help with makeup and hair this morning, minus her glasses, and she had to admit it. She did look hot.

Before she knew what was happening, Dirk was coming

around to her side of the car and opening the door for her. The length of bare leg she was sporting was painfully obvious as she emerged with his help. She tugged the dress down and avoided his gaze. Dark glasses or not, she knew exactly where his eyes had been.

They reached the restaurant where they'd set up the rendezvous and entered the upscale establishment. Tempest willed her eyes to adjust more quickly to the contrasting dimness after being outside in the sun and let out a deep sigh. Face it, this was going to be tough. She couldn't see a thing without her glasses. The white linen and luxurious upholstery seemed to mock her and she focused instead on the way Dirk's shirt stretched across his well proportioned back as he spoke to the maitre'd. The Hillyer children had definitely been blessed in the looks department. She felt like a mouse in comparison. The maitre'd nodded and gestured for them to follow.

Dirk smiled her way. "Chin up. No need to look so worried." He took her elbow and propelled her through the maze of tables until their guide stopped at one occupied by a lone male.

Tempest felt her insides jump. This was not the middle-aged man she was expecting. Sitting at the table, nursing a cocktail, was a very good looking man of about thirty with short, dark hair and very blue eyes. A hint of stubble shadowed his well defined features. He stood as she and Dirk approached.

"You must be the Hillyers," the man offered, holding out his hand.

Dirk took the proffered hand. "I'm Dirk Hillyer and this is," he hesitated only slightly, "my sister, Cherise."

"Pleased to meet you. I'm Ryan Clarke," the stranger said. "Won't you sit down?"

They did, Dirk holding out the chair for Tempest as she seated herself. It was hard not to feel self conscious in such a form fitting dress and she wasn't used to the necessary restriction in movement that went with it. Any confidence she may have felt earlier fizzled under the new man's electric blue gaze. She was sure he could see through her ruse. She felt nothing short of the biggest fool on earth. She sent up another silent prayer for forgiveness.

"Is everything okay?" Ryan Clarke asked. "You look nervous, Miss Hillyer."

Before she could speak Dirk took over the conversation. "We were expecting... well, someone a bit different," he began. "Dad said we were to meet an old friend of his from college."

The other man nodded. "Ah. That would be my father, Michael Clarke. Our fathers were friends back in the day. But I specifically told Mr. Hillyer - your father - I was the one coming to Boston. My father suggested I look him up, and I was actually surprised when he offered to show me around town."

Dirk shrugged. "Sometimes the old man doesn't communicate clearly. He probably just didn't think to explain it was his buddy's son coming to town, not the buddy himself."

"Sorry for the inconvenience."

"No inconvenience," Dirk interjected.

"We could just skip the tour," Ryan said. "I've actually been to Boston before, but I hated to disappoint your dad. He seemed so – adamant."

"That would be our father. Adamant." He looked at Tempest. "Right, Sis?"

"Hm? Oh, right," Tempest agreed, sitting up straight.

Ryan frowned. "Do you always wear your dark glasses indoors?" He gestured to the sunglasses that still rested on her nose.

Her eyes darted to Dirk. He'd taken his off as soon as they'd entered the restaurant. "Oh. Um..."

"She has a headache," Dirk supplied. He leaned forward and lowered his voice. "A little too much champagne last night at her friend's going away party."

Tempest frowned and shook her head. "No, that's not true -"

Dirk interrupted her with a laugh. "Now, come on, Cherise." He enunciated the name. "I'm sure Ryan, here, has had occasion to celebrate once or twice in his life. Isn't that right?" He winked at Ryan.

"And how," Ryan agreed. He squinted, surveying Tempest more closely. "I must say, though. You don't look anything like your picture."

"You've seen a picture?" she asked too quickly.

"You know women. Always changing their hair. What color was it last week, Sis? Blonde?"

"Um, right."

Ryan nodded. "I've got a sister myself." He looked around the room. "Where's our waitress? Service seems kind of slow."

Dirk raised a hand and the hostess scurried over. "We're ready to order."

"Of course, Mr. Hillyer."

Tempest squinted at the menu. No glasses - and sunglasses to boot - was making the task almost impossible.

"The usual?" Dirk suggested, leaning slightly in her direction.

She nodded, relief flooding her body. "Yes. That would be fine." Maybe Dirk Hillyer wasn't so bad after all. She snuck a peek at him. His tanned good looks and blonde hair would turn any lady's head. He was totally opposite of the other man sitting at their table with his almost jet black hair and brooding countenance. Actually, either man would turn a few heads.

Tempest blinked back to the present. Wearing Cherise's clothes was making her think like her, too. *Forgive me, Lord - although why would You when I'm caught in a lie?*

Every nerve was on edge as they ate their meal. Ryan seemed to know way too many personal details about Cherise. It almost felt like he was baiting her. She had to rely on Dirk more than once to bail her out. She was thankful when the ordeal was finally over and Dirk had paid the check.

"Well? Ready for the tour?" Dirk asked, placing his napkin on the table top.

Ryan shrugged. "If you really want to. As I said, I have been to Boston before."

Tempest cleared her throat. "I, um, I don't think I'm coming."

Dirk swung his gaze sharply in her direction. "What do you mean? It was part of the – well, you know. Dad is expecting it."

"I can't," Tempest said, fiddling with her napkin. "I forgot I was busy this afternoon."

Ryan's eyebrows rose. "I'm sorry if the prospect of time with me seems like such an ordeal." His voice was cool but unmistakably laced with well contained offense.

"No, it's not that -"

Dirk cut her off. "My sister just doesn't like driving in traffic that much. Will you excuse us for just a second?"

Ryan nodded and Dirk helped Tempest out of her chair. She was still trying to pull the skirt down to a half decent length as he maneuvered her a safe distance away from Ryan's ears. "What are you doing? This is part of the plan, remember? In fact, if I remember correctly, this was supposed to be your job in the first place."

"Cherise's job," Tempest corrected.

"Fine. But as Cherise's stand-in, it was your job. I only offered to help out. There's no way I'm getting stuck alone on a boring tour of the city."

"I just don't think I can do this," Tempest wailed. "He already suspects something. You heard him."

"Who cares? After today you'll never see him again. What could go wrong?"

What indeed. "Aunt Rose might worry if I'm gone too long." Another lie. How far could it go?

Dirk rolled his eyes. "You're making excuses." He surveyed Tempest's distraught face and then gently lifted the dark glasses off her nose and looked directly into her eyes. "Please? Don't make me do this alone."

Tempest couldn't speak, working her jaw furiously.

"Please?" he repeated. His eyes reminded her of one of her dogs. All sad and doleful.

Why was she such a wimp? Why couldn't she just stand up for herself? She didn't want to traipse around the city in a too short borrowed dress, worrying that at any moment Ryan Clarke would see her for what she really was – a fraud. And Dirk? Well, he just plain made her feel uncomfortable. She closed her eyes but heard her own voice, barely above a whisper. "Okay." Inwardly, her heart sank.

"That a girl." Dirk gave her arm a quick squeeze.

After collecting Ryan at the entrance, they headed to the parking lot where Cherise's Porsche sat waiting. "Nice wheels," Ryan commented.

"Cherise's wheels," Dirk clarified.

Ryan raised his eyebrows and looked at Tempest. "Really? Owns a Porsche but doesn't like driving in traffic. Seems odd to me."

"Women." Dirk laughed, raising his hands helplessly. "So. Where to first? I'll drive."

"I've actually changed my mind," Ryan said. "Thanks for lunch and give my regards to your father." He nodded a good-bye and stalked away.

Tempest watched as he unlocked what she presumed was a rental and got in. It wasn't until he drove away that she realized she'd been holding her breath. "That was a disaster," she breathed, taking off the dark glasses and putting them in the Gucci purse she carried – also one of Cherise's.

Dirk shrugged. "Whatever. It was good for a laugh."

"Easy for you to say," Tempest said, putting her hands on her hips. "You weren't pretending to be someone else."

"Are you kidding? I think I put on quite a good show. I'll bet Clarke thinks I'm a respectable socialite with a conscience. Although..." Dirk grinned. "I must admit, it was hard to keep up the brotherly front with you in that dress. Ow!" He whistled a cat call.

She followed his gaze down the length of her body, her face flooding with color. She'd almost forgotten what she was wearing.

Dirk chuckled outright. "So? What should we do next?"

"I need a lift. To my car," Tempest clarified, avoiding his gaze.

"I could just drive you to your Aunt Rose's."

"No, I need my car," Tempest insisted. "It should be done at the repair shop. You can just take me back to the spot where we met and I'll take a bus from there."

"No need. I'll take you right to the shop." He turned and started walking toward the Porsche, then stopped, looking back over his shoulder at her. "Will you be around tomorrow?"

Tempest hesitated before answering. What was Dirk Hillyer up to? She narrowed her eyes. "No, I need to spend time with my Aunt Rose before heading home." This time it wasn't a lie.

Dirk shrugged. "Too bad. Who knows? I might just show up on your doorstep someday." He reached for the passenger door handle and opened the door, waiting.

"Pardon me?" Tempest stopped at the open door without getting in.

"I've been looking for a change of scene. Small towns must have some nightlife. Maybe we could check it out together."

"I don't think... I mean, what would Cherise say?" Tempest stammered.

"Just because you're my sister's friend doesn't mean we can't be friends, too," he reasoned.

"Oh, well..." Tempest fidgeted with Cherise's watch. This was becoming more than just uncomfortable. Dirk Hillyer was obviously hitting on her and she didn't know what to do about it.

"Come on," Dirk continued, gently lifting her chin with his cupped hand. She kept her eyes fixed on his Adam's apple. "You don't think I offered to come along today simply to help Cherise, do you?"

Tempest's eyes flew to Dirk's. "What... what do you mean?"

Dirk laughed. "Do I have to spell it out, oh so naïve friend of my sister?" He was staring at her lips.

Tempest's hand flew to her mouth.

"You're kind of cute when you get flustered, do you know that?" A slight smile curved the corner of his mouth and he was still touching her face, tracing his finger along her jawline.

Tempest shook her head, forcing him to drop his hand. "No. I mean... Oh! I'm so embarrassed." She scrambled into the car and grabbed for her seatbelt. The incident was bringing back unpleasant memories.

Dirk allowed a full blown smile to grace his lips as he walked around to his side of the car and got in. "Today wasn't that bad, was it? Who knows? You might even like me, if you gave me a chance."

"It was terrifying." She dug in Cherise's purse for her own glasses' case and slipped the spectacles onto her nose. There. That was better. She relaxed into the seat.

"Come on. You can't tell me you didn't feel a little rush of adrenaline. Even once?"

"Well... It was kind of exciting, sort of." Tempest kept her eyes fixed on the windshield in front of her. There was a smudge on one of her lenses.

"That's a start. Although I hope it wasn't Ryan Clarke that you found exciting."

"Um..." Tempest gulped. If the truth be told, she did find Ryan Clarke rather attractive in a dangerous sort of way. But that was too many romance novels talking. She'd been reading some of late and should probably stop. She opened the borrowed purse again and found the lens cloth she used to polish her glasses.

"If you must know, the whole afternoon was a set up," Dirk stated. "So don't get too dreamy over him."

"What do you mean?" The circular motion of the lens cloth stilled as Tempest brought her gaze up to meet his.

"My father was more than happy to set up a meeting with one of his cronie's sons. He'd like nothing better than to marry Cherise off to someone suitable."

"Oh! That's terrible!"

"And I didn't want him to be too taken with my pseudo sister. Now, if it had been Cherise that was scheduled to meet him as planned, well, that would have been a different story. But what if he liked you and wanted to see you again? We couldn't have that, now could we?"

Tempest blinked, heat creeping up her neck. "You should stop this talk, Dirk. It's making me uncomfortable."

"Sorry." He sat back against his own seat for a moment until a grin spread across his features. "I usually don't have to try this hard, you know. To get the girl, I mean."

"Maybe I don't want to be 'got'," Tempest responded.

Dirk laughed. "Fair enough. Look. Forget everything that just happened and let's start again as friends, okay? It'll give me time to prove that I'm not the jerk my sister has made me out to be."

"Why should I?"

"First of all, as the only double agent in the whole scheme, I think both you and Cherise owe me a big thank you."

"Well..."

"Second, Cherise is pretty lucky. I wish I had a friend like you. Not many people would put themselves through what you did today."

It was probably true, and right about now, Tempest wasn't sure it was such a virtue. "I really need to go now, please." She positioned the now spotless glasses on her nose. She could see clearly - and not just with her eyes. Dirk Hillyer was toying with her and the sooner she got back to her own quiet life the better.

"Right." Dirk started the engine and revved the motor. "Remember what I said, though. Don't be surprised if I show up on your doorstep someday."

empest sat cross legged on her futon, half watching a show on her near obsolete 14" TV. The rhythmic purr of her cat Zoe brought some comfort as she stroked the feline's silken coat. One of her dogs, a Yorkshire Terrier named Paddy, lay on the floor where her feet should be, while the other, a Great Dane by the name of Jupiter, rested his chin on the futon itself, opening an eye now and again to make sure his mistress was still within sight. It would have been a perfectly relaxed and homey scene, except for the unrest inside Tempest's chest.

The past weekend had been a pivotal point in the lives of her two best friends, and although she was happy for them, it also left her feeling melancholy. It seemed as if both Cherise and Stella were moving forward and she… well, she was kind of standing still. Like a stagnant mud puddle.

Lord, forgive me for feeling this way. For being ungrateful.

Sure, Cherise had offered to pay her way to California, but she still wasn't sure if she'd take her up on it. The open ended ticket was sitting right on her dresser. Despite the "deal" they'd made, using it felt unethical. Like taking a bribe. Friends didn't need to be bribed in order to do a favor. She'd helped Cherise out because they were friends, not because Cherise had offered to pay for a plane ticket. Still, the ticket was there. Waiting.

Or maybe she was just scared. She needed a change – wanted a change, but change was also a very frightening prospect. It was easier to stay in her little apartment where any silly notions about moving would be crucified with familiarity. Besides, using it might make her feel guilty all over again. She'd already prayed and prayed for forgiveness because of lying.

Unless this was God's way of opening a new door…

After all, she had ambitions, too. Dreams. Maybe not the same kind of 'save-the-planet' dreams that Stella had, or the hormonally based spur-of-the-moment variety that Cherise seemed to embrace. But dreams, nonetheless.

Dreams about becoming a journalist. Moving to California. Finding love. Having a family. All of these were part of the future that she hoped and prayed would be hers someday. But none of them seemed to be any closer to reality.

She sighed heavily. Why did she always do this to herself? Over analyze. Worry over nothing. If she wanted to go to California, she darn well would! She had some vacation time coming. She could go and scope it out. Who knows? Maybe just going for a vacation would be all she needed to shake this dissatisfied feeling that had encroached on her soul.

She closed her eyes and said a prayer out loud. "God, help me to make the right decision. And forgive me again for being dissatisfied. Oh - and for lying."

The telephone rang and her eyes flew open. Zoe jumped from her lap and landed within millimeters of Paddy's sleeping form. This in turn disrupted the terrier, who barked his disapproval, making Jupiter lift his head. "Paddy! Be quiet!" Tempest scolded, unfolding herself from the low futon and padding to where her cellphone rested on the counter.

"Hello?"

"Hi, Tempest. Dirk Hillyer here."

Tempest raised her brows and hesitated. What on earth did he want? To warn her that the jig was up?

"Hello?" Dirk repeated. "You there?"

She swallowed hard, willing her vocal chords into action. "Hi, Dirk." She waited.

"Just thought I'd call and see how you were doing."

"Fine. And you?"

"Great. Actually, I'm in town and thought maybe we could go out for a drink."

Tempest's eyes widened in alarm. "You're here? In *this* town?"

"Yeah. Who'd have thought, huh?" He chuckled into the other end of the line.

"Well, I'm not really dressed for going out." That sounded lame, even to her.

"So change," Dirk suggested. "And you can't tell me you were doing something better. I won't take 'no' for an answer. I can be very tenacious when I want to be."

Tempest had heard as much from Cherise. And why not? She'd been just sitting here, alone, moping about her life. A little company might be nice for a change. "I guess so," she heard herself say.

"I'll be right over." He clicked off before she could respond any further.

She stared at the now dead phone for a second before setting it down. She had never paid much attention to Cherise's brother until very recently. More like he had never paid her any attention. It was funny how he was suddenly being so friendly. A small warning bell went off in her brain, but she dismissed it. This was Dirk Hillyer. It wasn't like Dirk was a stranger. He was her best friend's brother, for heaven's sake, despite the fact that he was a spoiled, rich, self-acclaimed ladies' man.

She was just about to go to her closet to look for something to wear when the doorbell rang. Frowning, she went to the door instead and peeked through the security hole. "Dirk?" She stepped back, unlatched the safety chain, and unlocked the door before opening it for him to enter. "How did you get here so fast?"

"I was right outside." He grinned and stepped across the threshold.

Paddy let out a string of frantic barking. "Paddy! Be quiet!" Tempest scolded in her sternest voice. She turned back to Dirk and gestured to her attire. "I'm not ready yet, as you can see."

"I'll wait." He sauntered further into the room then stopped in his tracks as he spotted Jupiter for the first time. The Great Dane was standing now, beside the futon. "Whoa! That's one big animal!"

"He's harmless. If he sees that I approve of you, he'll be fine." She walked toward Jupiter, gesturing for Dirk to follow. "Jupiter, this is my friend, Dirk," she said in that voice reserved for animals and small children.

"Hi Jupiter," Dirk said, his voice sounding nervous.

Tempest addressed the large dog again. "Good boy. This is Dirk," she repeated. She patted Jupiter's head several times, then turned to Dirk and reached for his hand. "Now you pet him."

Dirk held out a tentative hand to pat Jupiter's massive head. "Hi fella." Jupiter let out what could be interpreted as a contented moan.

Tempest smiled widely. "There. See? He likes you." Dirk continued patting Jupiter's head. "Sit down and make yourself comfortable for a few minutes while I figure out what I'm going to wear."

"Okay." When Dirk sat on the futon, the dog's head was now towering over him. "Uh, Tempest? Can you make him sit?"

She laughed. "Of course." None too gracefully, she pushed on the dog's behind until his hindquarters were on the floor. "That better?"

"I guess it'll have to do, although I'm feeling a bit like Dr. Doolittle."

Tempest laughed again. "Welcome to my world." Zoe and Paddy had both jumped up on the futon, and were now sitting on either side of Dirk, with Jupiter still sitting on the floor enjoying the ministrations around the ears that Dirk was providing. Tempest took the sight in with a grin, then sighed and turned to a small upright closet that was in the corner of the room. "Now, what am I going to wear?" She slid several options along the rail. "Just where are you taking me?"

Dirk shrugged, continuing to scratch Jupiter under one large ear. "You know this town better than I do. Any clubs? Where do people hang out?"

"Who knows? I don't go out much." She pulled out a pair of pants and a blouse. "I guess this will do. And since you're also in my bedroom at the moment, I'll just head to the bathroom to change."

Dirk looked around the room in surprise. "This is it?"

"What you see is what you get." She pushed her glasses up and then tilted her chin.

"Wow," was all he said, still looking around.

"It's called a bachelor's suite, in case you didn't know," Tempest informed. "I don't have the same privileges you're used to."

She turned on her heel and shut the bathroom door with a decisive click. What kind of game was Dirk Hillyer playing, anyway? She knew enough about him and his reputation to know he wasn't in the habit of seeking out the company of nobodies like her, whether she was Cherise's friend or not. She had half a mind to stay home after all. Only half a mind. But if she was going to go on a date with Dirk Hillyer, he needed to get a few facts straight.

Dirk was standing up when she emerged from the bathroom. "Sorry if I offended you," he said.

"It's okay," she lied. "But let's just get one thing straight. I'm not exactly sure what's going on in that head of yours, but I am not interested in becoming one of your conquests." She snapped her fingers and Jupiter bounded to her side. "I'm not that kind of girl."

Dirk grimaced. "Ouch. My reputation precedes me."

"Yes, it does."

"Would you believe me when I said I was just looking for some genuine friendship? Nothing else?"

"Why should I?" She stroked Jupiter's silky head, letting his strength seep into her; give her confidence.

"Believe it or not, I'm kind of tired of the superficial life." Dirk opened his palms in a shrug. His handsome face looked sincere enough, but then again, he was a practiced con artist when it came to getting what he wanted.

"Fair enough. Why me?" She continued stroking Jupiter.

Dirk furrowed his brow, thinking for a moment. "The other day when we met up with Ryan Clarke you were so uncomfortable, where as for me, it was just a big game. I realized then that I tend to mingle with people who are quite comfortable pretending to be someone they're not. They do it on a daily basis. It's just part of their - our - real life." He laughed self deprecatingly. "I feel ready for a change. I thought maybe you could teach me how it's done."

"How to be genuine?" Tempest repeated, raising an eyebrow.

Dirk nodded. "That's it." He put his hands in his pants' pockets and rocked back on his heels.

"How do I know you're not just playing a game right now?" Tempest asked.

"Good point. Guess I'll just have to prove it."

"I guess so."

"Well, now that that's settled..." He looked around cheerily. "Are you going to let go of your guard dog and come with me for a drink?"

Tempest smiled in spite of herself. "Jupiter, sit!" she

commanded, pointing for the dog to go back to his spot near the futon.

"I take it that's a yes," Dirk mused with a twinkle in his eye. "Now, where does one go for some nightlife in this town?"

"I'm afraid the options are fairly limited, or so I'm told. Besides, I can't stay out long. I work in the morning." She grabbed her purse from the kitchen counter and joined Dirk near the door.

"Oh." Dirk frowned. "That is tedious."

"This is the real world, remember?" Tempest reminded.

He nodded, grinning. "Right."

"And another thing," Tempest added. "I'm driving."

Dirk grimaced. "Now you are kidding. You mean I have to be seen in your little – what do you call it?"

"It's a car, Dirk. Just a car. Unless you let me drive yours?" She cocked her head to one side expectantly.

"Hm." Dirk rubbed his chin. "Would that convince you? That I'm serious about wanting to be friends?"

She held out her hands for the keys. "Maybe."

Dirk sighed and dropped the keys for his Ferrari into her palm. "You drive a hard bargain, lady."

CHAPTER 6

*D*espite her earlier doubts, Tempest found she was
having fun with Dirk. They went to a pub, and Dirk
seemed to be genuinely enthusiastic about this "local" experience.

"So this is how the other half lives," Dirk mused, taking a swig
of his beer as he looked around. The pub was crowded, its amber
interior enhanced by the dim lighting. The wail of a country tune
strained to be heard over the general talking and laughter. Dirk
grimaced and set the tall glass down, shaking some of the foam
off his hand. "I never did understand what people see in beer.
Nasty, bitter drink."

"All part of the local experience," Tempest reminded. She
sipped her ginger ale. They were sitting at a high table somewhere in the middle of the establishment – a good vantage point
for people watching. And there were plenty of people to watch,
even on a weeknight. Most of the patrons were under thirty-five,
if she judged correctly, some paired off intimately, while others
were in larger, more boisterous groups.

There were five women sitting together, all dressed in their
shortest skirts and lowest tops, or so it seemed to Tempest,
making quite a racket. One of them was wearing a tacky looking

veil. Obviously a "stagette" party. Not far away, a similarly rowdy group of young males were playing some kind of drinking game that also involved arm wrestling. The way some of them were flexing their muscles in the women's general direction made her wonder how much longer the two groups would be separate.

"And I can't believe you won't even join me," Dirk sulked, sipping his beer a little more delicately. He grimaced again. "Don't you drink?"

Tempest smiled and shrugged. "I don't need to experience how the other half lives. I am the other half. Besides that, I'm driving, remember?"

"Right. Well, at this rate, I won't be having more than one myself." He lifted his glass and downed another few ounces, squinting all the while as if in pain.

"Why not get something else if you hate beer so much?" Tempest suggested, watching his obvious distaste as he tried to drink his beverage.

"Too stubborn," Dirk replied. "Besides, I'm trying to impress you with how down to earth I am." He gestured with his head toward the arm wrestlers. "If those he-men can drink it, so can I."

"Believe me, those guys don't impress me," Tempest said with a slight snort.

"No? Then what type of guy do you go for?" Dirk leaned forward, resting his crossed arms on the table as he did so.

"The wrong type, apparently." The words were out of her mouth before she even knew she'd said them. How embarrassing! The last thing she wanted to do was spill her sorry guts to a guy like Dirk Hillyer.

Dirk raised his brows. "Do I detect some feminine angst? Lost recently at love, have we?"

"Actually, I don't want to talk about it." Tempest's eyelashes fluttered downward and she reached for her glass and took a drink. After she'd swallowed she added, "I mean it." There was no way she was going to talk about her disastrous forays into the world of romance, limited as those experiences were.

"I can see you're quite serious, so consider it taboo from now on."

"Thanks." There was silence for a few seconds between them, although there was plenty of activity around them to keep them entertained. One of the "he-men" had convinced one of the "short skirts" to come over to his table. She was flirting and giggling like a schoolgirl, despite the fact that she was probably past thirty and he looked barely old enough to be of legal drinking age. Tempest turned her attention back to Dirk, seeking his eyes with her own. "Can I tell you something?"

"Fire away." He'd managed to down his entire beer. A quick nod to a passing waitress sent her scurrying for a replacement.

Tempest watched the other woman's retreating figure then turned her gaze back to Dirk. "I'm thinking of going to California. To check it out."

Dirk shrugged his shoulders. "So? I knew that. Cherise bought you a ticket. It was part of the deal."

"I know, but I hadn't really planned on following through." Tempest hesitated, frowning down at her own empty glass. "Well, I kind of did, but not really. Oh, I don't know!"

"Sounds like you're scared," Dirk observed. The waitress returned and he nodded up at her with a ready smile as she placed their second round of drinks on the table. "Thanks," he directed at her and handed her a fifty. "Keep the change."

"Thanks, good lookin'," the waitress cooed and strutted away.

"That was an awfully large tip," Tempest observed. "It might blow your cover."

"Whatever." Dirk grinned. "Now, back to you. What are you so afraid of? Life is to be lived. Experienced."

"Like you're doing now?" Tempest raised an eyebrow.

"If going to a local watering hole with a genuinely nice person counts, then yes." He reached across the table and took one of her hands.

Tempest stared at their hands for a moment before gently withdrawing hers and putting it under the table. "I know you think I'm silly and naïve. Why not just jump at the chance for a free trip to California? But I'm different than you. Than Cherise."

"That's what I like about you, remember?" He reached over and tilted her chin up with his finger so that she was forced to look directly at him. "And you're not silly. Timid maybe, but not silly."

Tempest's eyes fluttered downward and she sat back so that he had to drop his hand. "This is making me uncomfortable. And I'm not timid!"

"Yes you are. You're timid. It's time the bird learned to fly."

"You're full of metaphors tonight," Tempest quipped, trying to sound witty. If the truth be told, she was feeling more than just uncomfortable. Dirk was obviously trying to charm her and she had mixed feelings about that. On the one hand it was flattering to have such a good-looking and well-to-do guy vying for her attention. On the other hand, she'd known him – or at least about him – long enough to know he was a player. This was probably just a new and elaborate game to him.

"That's me. Poetry embodied." Dirk winked. "Seriously, you should consider taking that trip. A nice 'vaca' in sunny California is probably just what you need. I'll even go with you if you want."

"Gee, thanks," Tempest responded wryly. "Even if I did go to California for a vacation, I couldn't afford to move there. It'd be like tempting myself when I know there's no way for it to happen. I don't want to get disappointed."

"Now you're making excuses."

"Easy for you to say. This is the real world, remember? I'd need to find a job," she reasoned. "I couldn't just move without a job."

"So say, just for the fun of it, that none of that mattered. Money was no object. What would you do then?" Dirk asked.

"Hm." Tempest tilted her head to one side, considering it. "If money was no object, I'd find a nice place on the beach. Nothing too big. Just a nice quiet spot with a view where I could take the dogs for a walk and where I could smell the ocean."

Dirk nodded his approval. "So far it sounds very nice. And?"

"I'd still want to write. Be a journalist. Maybe investigative reporting. Something like that." Tempest leaned back in her chair, a tiny smile playing on her lips, her eyes far away.

"You? The one who doesn't like going undercover?" Dirk laughed.

Tempest sat up straight and joined in his mirth with a grin of her own. "Maybe you're right. Anyway, some kind of writing would be part of the equation. Even the society page if that's all that was available."

"The society page?" Dirk repeated. "In California? Again, I'm not sure that's really your forte either."

"Hey! Whose fantasy is this anyway?" Tempest gave Dirk a playful swat.

He ducked to one side trying to avoid the hit. "Ow!" When their laughter subsided, he cocked his head and surveyed her closely. "I'm thinking more the arts and culture scene. You know, like what's playing at the symphony or what's showing at the art gallery."

Tempest blinked, all merriment subsiding from her features. "How did you know?" Her voice had gotten very quiet.

"Know what?" Dirk looked at her over the rim of his glass as he took another swallow of beer.

"That I might be interested in the symphony."

"I didn't." He set his glass down. "What is it? Did I say something?"

Tempest shook her head and tried to smile. "It's okay. I assumed you knew."

"Knew what?"

"About my parents."

"I know that you used to live in California before they died. That you came to Boston afterward to live with your Aunt Rose. What else?"

"My father was a writer and my mother played cello in the symphony. They were very 'artsy.' Eccentric, in some people's minds."

"Ah." Dirk nodded his head knowingly. "That explains the name. I've wondered what kind of people would name their daughter Tempest." He smiled mischievously.

"Are you making fun of my name?" She couldn't help the smile that was forming on her own lips.

"Not really. I like it. It's different, that's all. Tempest," he repeated her name slowly. "Unpredictable and potentially dangerous. Like a tropical storm."

His gaze was suddenly seductive, drawing her in, and her lashes fluttered downward. "Stop it. You're making me nervous."

"Sorry, Temp. So, back to covering the arts scene. It's a brilliant idea, if I do say so."

"I've always had an interest in that type of thing," Tempest admitted. "I'd love nothing better than writing about the arts. And I never said you could call me Temp." Her eyes rose to meet his once again, the playful smirk back on her lips.

Dirk's eyebrows rose and then he laughed outright. "Okay, Tempest." He pronounced her name with deliberateness. "You'd be good at it, I think. Covering arts and culture. And I didn't mean to make you uncomfortable," he added.

"I'm not." Tempest picked up her glass and swirled the ginger ale around, keeping her eyes fixed on the mini-whirlpool. "I think maybe it just seems like an unrealistic dream."

"It doesn't have to be." There was a space of silence before Dirk broke it with a grin. "Does this mean we're friends?"

Tempest looked up at him and smiled. "Official."

"So can I call you Temp now?"

"I'm thinking about it."

"I meant what I said, too," he continued. "About going to California with you if you want an escort. No strings."

"Thanks. I'll think about that, too."

And for the first time she really was – seriously.

CHAPTER 7

The next day, Tempest sat in her tiny cubicle at the newspaper office, staring at the blue tweed covered divider that was her only real privacy. The click-click-click of fingers on keyboards provided an underlying rhythm for the murmur of one-sided conversations and the odd ring of a telephone. She picked up the framed picture of herself, Cherise and Stella that sat on her desk. It was of their graduation from Parkview Academy, when life's possibilities seemed boundless.

If money was no object, she'd be out the door and on her way to California that afternoon. But she was too practical to throw away a good job on a whim. She would return the plane ticket as soon as Cherise got home from Europe. If and when she made her way west, it would be on her own terms. Her cellphone bleeped and she picked it up, scrutinizing the number on the display. She didn't recognize it, but sometimes she got follow up leads on stories, so she pressed 'answer' and put the device to her ear. "Tempest Ross."

"Temp! Dirk here. How are you? Think any more about that vacation we talked about?"

"Um, no. Not really," she lied. It was all she'd been thinking about. "Listen, Dirk. I can't really talk right now. I'm at work."

"I thought you were a reporter. For all they know you're following up on a lead."

"Well..." She pushed her glasses up on her nose.

"Aren't you glad to hear from me?" She could hear the teasing in his voice.

"No, it's fine. I just wasn't expecting you to call again so soon." She took a deep breath and forced herself to relax.

"Really? Why not? I thought we were, like, buds now."

"Whatever." She smiled. Having a good looking guy for a friend wasn't so bad. Too bad the other employees at the newspaper office couldn't see him. They'd never believe it. Tempest the mouse with a handsome socialite.

"Listen. We need to meet somewhere. Right after you're done work."

Tempest's eyebrows rose slightly. "You mean you've driven all the way over here two days in a row?"

"No, it means I'm on my way," he clarified. "I've got an amazing proposition for you. Seriously, it's too good to be true and you can't pass it up."

Tempest let out a nervous titter. "Hold on. Now you're scaring me. What kind of proposition?" She glanced around the small office to see if anyone was within earshot.

"About your trip to California." He laughed into the receiver at the other end. "What did you think I meant?"

Tempest felt the color rising in her cheeks and was glad he couldn't see her reaction. "Nothing."

He chuckled. "Anyway, think of somewhere we can go for a decent meal and we'll talk about it. Oh – and how soon can you book some vacation days?"

"Now you *are* scaring me."

"Never mind. When you hear what I've got to say, you'll be quitting altogether, not just booking a vacation."

Before she could protest further, he hung up. Tempest glared at her cellphone for a moment before ending the call on her end. The nerve! Dirk was used to getting his own way and hadn't even considered whether she wanted to meet him again or not. She should just ignore his request and go about her own plans.

Except, she didn't have any plans. That was part of the trouble – that and the carrot he'd just dangled in front of her nose. He said he wanted to talk to her about going to California, and if there was one thing she was a sucker for, that was it.

TEMPEST PULLED into the parking lot of the restaurant and scanned the other vehicles for Dirk's Ferrari. The place was a middle of the road type of establishment; not too fancy, but not a drive-in diner either. She spotted the brilliant red vehicle and pulled in beside it. The contrast between his expensive sports car and her well used Chevy brought a smile to her lips. The cars were about as different as the people who owned them.

The interior of the restaurant was cool and dim and the hostess promptly escorted her toward a secluded booth where Dirk sat waiting. A sudden feeling of inadequacy enveloped her. Dirk was devastatingly handsome as always, his clothing impeccable and his hair glinting like a halo under the light fixture that hung over their booth. She, on the other hand, hadn't bothered to change after work but drove straight to the restaurant. Her black pants felt baggy after a day's wear and her blouse was wrinkled.

He stood up when he saw her approaching and waited until she was seated before sitting back down himself.

"My, we are chivalrous tonight, aren't we?" she quipped, hoping she sounded confident and in control of her emotions.

"Always. Did you expect anything less?"

Tempest's eyes fluttered downward as the color rose in her cheeks. Darn the genes that made her reactions so evident! "Of course. Sorry." Even after all her years at an expensive boarding school, she was always saying the wrong things. Of course he was chivalrous. As a rich member of the upper class, he was raised that way. She, on the other hand, was well aware that she would never fit into high society. Sometimes she wondered if Cherise had befriended her as a project. Like what Dirk was doing now.

"Hey." He reached across the small table and tilted her chin up. "No apologies necessary. What are friends for if they can't even tease each other?"

She sat up straighter and tossed her head as Cherise might do, determined to shake off the insecurity as well. "Exactly. Now what's this 'too-good-to-be-true' proposition you're so eager to tell me about?"

Dirk laughed and sat back against the cushioned seat. "Not so fast. First we order, then I tell you while we wait."

Their server came to take their drink orders. Dirk opted for a martini while Tempest went with ice water.

"Okay, what's your excuse this time?" Dirk asked as soon as the waitress left.

Tempest shrugged. "I just don't drink alcohol. Is that a problem?"

"I guess not. Any particular reason?"

"My parents were killed by a drunk driver," Tempest replied. "I vowed to never drink the stuff and I haven't."

"Fair enough."

Tempest could feel the butterflies of tension rustling in her gut, the way they always did when the subject came up. She knew she sounded defensive, but even after all these years the anger and pain of losing her parents so senselessly made her feel anxious inside. Dirk didn't say anything else but busied himself with studying the menu. She took his lead and perused her own, not really caring what she ordered since she'd lost her appetite anyway. The reappearance of the waitress was a welcome relief from the awkward silence that had enveloped them and they placed their order.

"Now are you going to tell me?" Tempest asked, striving to sound disinterested. Whatever it was, she was determined not to like it. She had her life here, and California was an unhealthy pipe-dream with too many painful memories.

Dirk leaned forward into the pool of light cast by the low hanging light fixture, resting one arm on the table top as he toyed with the stem of his martini glass. "Are you ready?" A grin was spreading across his face.

Tempest frowned. "Just tell me."

"Remember you said if money was no object you'd want a place near the ocean? Well, I have a friend who has a place in L.A. It's not right on the ocean mind you, but not far, and he's looking for a house-sitter for a few months. It's close enough that you could take your dogs down there for walks."

Dirk continued talking, but somewhere along the line, Tempest's mind had gone numb. A tingling sensation, like an electric current, was traveling up the base of her spine. What had she thought earlier about refusing to like whatever Dirk had to say? She blinked and forced herself to take a breath. "I couldn't afford that."

"Weren't you listening?" Dirk surveyed her closely. "I said my friend is looking for someone responsible to look after the place while he's in Europe for three, maybe four months. He's not asking for rent, just the security of knowing someone will be there while he's away. Plus, he's a dog lover, so he doesn't mind pets."

Tempest's nostrils flared as she tried to breathe normally. Three months. That was more than enough time to look for a job. "I... what if I don't like it?" Her mind was reeling. Of course she would like it! Her practical side was just grasping at straws, trying to think of any excuse in case it was too good to be true.

Dirk laughed outright. "Not like it? How could you not like it? It's a perfect set up."

"But what about when your friend comes back? Then what? I'd be out on the street."

"You've got three whole months. Enough time to find a job and another place to live."

"What about my pets? How would I get them there?" Her chin jutted forward, daring him to come up with an answer for that one.

"I'll loan you the money to have them flown out."

"I couldn't allow you to do that!" she cut in.

"Why not?" When she didn't answer, he continued. "Or, if you insist on being stubborn, you could sell your car to pay for their flight. My friend is leaving his car behind as part of the deal, so that wouldn't be a problem, and I dare say, his wheels are a bit classier than yours."

"Thanks," Tempest shot back. "I happen to like my car. And what about my job? I can't just up and quit. What if it doesn't work out?"

Dirk shook his head, the light above their table catching his blonde highlights. "Look, it seems to me you're just trying to think of every possible excuse not to go. If you want a change in your life, then make it. Otherwise, stay put. But this is a great chance for you to spread your wings. You've got the plane ticket, the place to live, and I'm willing to help with any other incidentals. A resourceful, smart girl like you won't find it difficult to find a job. This is your golden ticket, Temp. Don't throw it away."

Tempest sat for a few moments, almost unable to take it in. She blinked a few times and then looked up at Dirk, locking her bewildered eyes on his intense blue ones. "Why would you help me like this?" Her voice was low.

"I told you. I want to be friends." His gaze didn't waver. "And this is my way of showing you."

"You don't just buy someone's friendship," Tempest said.

"Maybe not where you come from, but I'm used to getting what I want." He smiled disarmingly. At her scowl of disapproval he added, "Okay, maybe that was in bad taste, but I'm rich, okay? I can't help it and for once I want to do something nice for someone else instead of just thinking of myself. I want to make you happy. Is that so bad?"

"But why do you want to make me happy?" Tempest persisted, afraid of the answer. "I told you already, if you see me as some kind of a challenge, then our friendship is off."

"Are you trying to get me to admit that I'm interested in you?" Dirk asked. "Okay, maybe I am, but I don't want you to get the wrong idea. I don't see you as a challenge, Tempest. I see you as a smart, sensitive, interesting woman who is on the verge of discovering just how awesome she really is. And if that's bad, then I'm sorry. I don't want to scare you away because of my past reputation, so I'm willing to go the friendship route for now and see where it takes us. If we just stay friends, then I'm okay with that. Like I said, I haven't had too many genuine friends before. And if something else develops, then I'm open to that, too." The intensity of his blue eyes dared her to look away. "Is that honest enough for you?"

Tempest looked down at her lap, unsure how to respond to his candor. Did she find Dirk attractive in that sort of way? There was no doubt he was good looking. And he had been very charming of late. She could use a friend right about now and with his wealth at her disposal, she'd be a fool to turn him down. But was it ethical? What would Cherise and Stella think?

The waitress came with their food and the conversation came to a standstill until their plates were settled and their drinks replenished.

"Indulge me," Dirk said once the waitress was gone. "Consider this a gift from a friend and nothing more."

It was the chance of a lifetime and she'd be a fool to refuse. Tempest took a bite of her entrée, chewed and then swallowed before answering. "I've got some vacation time coming and I'll see if a short leave of absence is possible instead of just quitting my job." Actually speaking the words sent her whole body into a thrill of vibrations - despite the slight warning bell sounding at the back of her brain.

"Good girl!" Dirk grinned. "When do we leave?"

"We?" Tempest blinked, fork in mid-air.

"I'll only stay long enough to help you get your bearings. It is my friend's house," he added. "Unless you want me to stay longer that is."

"Okay. I would appreciate that." She took a deep breath and sat up straighter. "As soon as my boss gives the green light, we're off." She raised her glass in a toast. "California, here we come."

God did work in mysterious ways, after all.

CHAPTER 8

*C*alifornia. Land of dreams. Land of opportunity. Land of painful memories.

Who would have imagined that only nine days after Cherise and Stella had taken off on their adventures, she would be here now, on one of her own?

Tempest leaned her arms on the balcony railing and looked out over the view. Terra-cotta tiles mingled with palm branches and other greenery in the valley below. Just a short distance beyond that, was the blue surf and white sand of the beach. She was here and she was ready to face whatever the future had to offer – for better or worse.

She wasn't quite sure how a person like her got to stay in a villa like this. It wasn't exactly palatial – no Hollywood mansion – but it certainly was much larger than her bachelor suite. And the view! There was no way she could afford a place like this on her budget.

The thought of Dirk Hillyer, and all he had done for her recently, sent a quick pang of guilt through her gut. He'd dropped everything to make sure her trip went ahead smoothly. To her surprise, her boss simply asked that she finish out the week, which she did while scrambling to pack her belongings and look after all the other incidentals that needed attention. Without Dirk's assistance, she wasn't sure how she would have managed.

She and Dirk caught a late flight to L.A. on Friday night. Then on the weekend, they got her settled into the villa, did some sightseeing, and went out for dinner each night. It had been a hectic, tiring, whirlwind week and she was more than glad to see him off this morning. If it weren't for the fact that he had another commitment in Boston, he might have stayed longer. Not that she wasn't grateful, but there were some things she needed to do on her own. Plus, she needed some solitude to examine her feelings.

After a week of daily contact with Dirk, she was pretty sure he was sincere. She knew he was interested in more than just friendship - a fact she still couldn't quite wrap her head around - but he had maintained his distance and was nothing but a gentleman. It made her feel guilty after all he'd done, although she'd warned him, so it wasn't like she was totally playing him. The thought of her playing "the player" brought a smile to her lips. If Cherise and Stella could see her now!

That last thought brought her up short. On second thought, it was probably best that they couldn't. Dirk was Cherise's brother, after all. Not that she was leading him along, exactly, but still, she had caved in to his offer to help her financially. Without it, there would have been no way to get her beloved pets out here. She'd taken his advice and sold her car, but she needed that money to live on. Even if she wasn't paying rent or utilities she still needed to eat.

Oh Lord, I hope I'm doing the right thing. Help me to keep a clear head when it comes to Dirk.

The wind whipped a few stray tendrils of hair across her face, catching in her glasses. She disentangled the hair and breathed in a lungful of the salty air. It was calm, serene and breathtaking and she would not allow any lingering vestiges of doubt or guilt to spoil her time here.

She shook her head and turned to go back indoors. She opened the sliding glass door with a swish and bent to pick up Paddy on the other side. The living, dining, and kitchen area were one large open concept room. The color palette was light and airy and there were lots of windows. With a contented sigh she made her way to the sofa and flopped into its depths.

Three whole months. Enough time to find a job, a new place to live, and reconnect with her past. The latter was what she craved most, but it was also the most frightening. It was time to face the deep hurt that she still felt at the sudden loss of her parents. Time to let the wounds heal so she could start a new life. She'd prayed about it more than once, but maybe now that she was here, God would finally answer.

She checked her cellphone for any new messages. Stella had been keeping her up to date on the latest happenings in Texas, but Cherise wasn't quite as good at communicating.

Cherise's parents had called once looking for her and Tempest had to make up an excuse about Cherise being at the spa and her cellphone being out of order. It sounded plausible enough. Maybe. But she couldn't go on lying indefinitely.

Good thing she had Dirk on her side, deflecting some of the attention, although he seemed to be more amused by the whole fiasco than anything. Tempest hated the web of lies that was developing. She prayed for forgiveness every night, but didn't quite know how to make the guilt and worry stop. Sometimes it felt like she had no one left in the world.

Zoe jumped up on her lap as if to remind her that her melancholy musings weren't true. "I still have you," Tempest cooed and stroked the feline's soft fur. Paddy barked. "And you," Tempest called with a laugh. "And Jupiter. Is it almost time for our walk?" Paddy barked again as if he understood every word, while Jupiter affirmed the question with the thump of his tail. "Okay, okay!"

Their outings to the beach were already the best part of her day. She stood up, allowing Zoe to jump gracefully from her lap.

She found the dogs' leashes and clasped them to their respective collars. Jupiter was stoic, although she knew he was just holding his anticipation at bay. With an animal his size, she'd be no match if he ever decided to take off on his own. Paddy, however, was not quite as disciplined. He jumped and barked in agitation, anxious for his frolic in the great outdoors.

They exited through the sliding glass doors and followed the deck to the set of steep steps that led down to the ground. The property was situated on a hill, perfect for the view it afforded, but not allowing for much outdoor space. What little yard there was, was completely enclosed by an eight foot fence. She locked the gate that led onto the property, and set off at a brisk pace toward the open beach. It was only three blocks away. If it wasn't busy, she might even let the dogs loose to run.

Unfortunately, there were several other people out jogging, walking their dogs, or just sauntering along the shore. She moderated her pace a bit to accommodate Paddy's little legs, which meant poor Jupiter would have to settle for a slower pace than he liked. Maybe later she could take him out separately and really let him go.

Looking off to the left, she watched as a seagull swooped several times and then snatched something up from the sand. Probably a bit of garbage or other tasty morsel that some human had dropped. Too bad people weren't more responsible when it came to littering.

She turned her gaze back to the front and let out a small squeal as she almost bumped into a man coming from the other direction. "Sorry," she offered, stepping to one side. Instead of moving on, he'd mirrored her movements, blocking her path. She frowned and reined Jupiter into her side. If he came any closer, she'd give the Great Dane some slack. There were advantages to having a monster for a dog.

"Cherise Hillyer?"

Tempest was about to shake her head when she actually looked up. A cold rush of fear washed over her as recognition dawned. "Mr. Clarke?" Her voice came out in a squeak. She pushed her glasses up on her nose.

"Ryan," he corrected.

"Yes, Ryan." She blinked, trying to smile with confidence. But panic was setting in as her stomach started to roll. Now what was she supposed to do? Run? Sick Jupiter on him?

"I almost didn't recognize you with glasses on."

"Oh. Right. I left my contacts in the house." Tempest grimaced. More lies.

"What are you doing out here? In California, I mean? Besides walking one heck of a big dog," he added with a raised brow.

She clutched the leash more securely, not sure where to rest her gaze. She was sure he could see right through her. "Meet Jupiter," she finally said nervously. Paddy barked. "And Paddy. He doesn't like to be left out." She turned the corners of her mouth up in what she hoped looked like a normal, friendly, smile.

"Hi fella." Ryan squatted down to pet Paddy on the head. The dog responded by wagging his tale furiously. Ryan kept his hand away from Jupiter. "So? Are you visiting?" he asked again, looking up at Tempest as he continued to scratch Paddy behind the ears.

"Um, yes. Kind of. You?"

Ryan stood up, smoothing his pants. "I keep a place out here. I come on business a lot. How are your parents?"

Tempest blinked, another wash of painful remembrance hitting her like a wet blanket. "Um, fine," she managed to mumble.

Ryan nodded. "And your brother?"

"My brother?" She frowned. "Oh, Dirk. Of course. He's fine, too. He was here visiting. He just left today."

Ryan looked out over the waves to his left. "Very scenic down here." He turned back to Tempest and offered a smile. "What are the odds that we'd run into each other like this, eh?"

"Yeah. What are the odds," she repeated. That panicked feeling was returning with a vengeance. Maybe Cherise's parents had sent Ryan Clarke on a mission to find their daughter and report back. Or maybe Dirk was taking his "double agent" status a bit too far. It would be just like the old Dirk to go to such lengths for some amusement. She could feel anger rising in her chest - most of it directed at herself for being so gullible.

"You okay?" Ryan asked. He was wearing dark glasses, but she could see his eyebrows dipping below the rims with concern.

"Fine." She tossed her hair back, like Cherise might do.

"Well, now that we've run into each other - literally - we should get together sometime." He was smiling at her with those white teeth and that perfectly shaped mouth and his nearly black hair was blowing off his forehead in a way that made him look windswept and –

Tempest gulped a sharp intake of air. Now what kind of game was her mind playing? Had she been staring? She could feel the color rising in her cheeks. "I doubt it. I mean, I'm not staying. I mean, I'm busy most of the time." Oh brother! How lame. She was totally tongue tied around the man.

"I see."

"Listen, I've got to go." Her voice came out in a rush. She turned on her heel, tangling herself in the leashes. Paddy started yelping, setting off a baritone response from Jupiter. Ryan took a step back.

Once she got herself righted, she looked up to see an amused smile on his lips. "Bye," she said, averting her eyes as she set off at a trot in the opposite direction.

~

ONE CHANCE MEETING on the beach became two when she ran into Ryan for a second time the next afternoon. By the time she'd recognized his sturdy frame coming toward her it was too late to turn and run. Instead she took a deep breath and trudged forward, Jupiter and Paddy in tow.

Ryan slowed to a stop a few yards away and waited with his hands thrust casually in his jean's pockets until she reached him. "Fancy meeting you here again," he said in greeting. He flashed a disarming smile.

It was the first time Tempest had seen him in jeans and she rather liked it. She fumbled for words, her mouth suddenly full of marbles. "I walk the dogs here every day." She frowned. Now why had she said that? What if he started waiting for her every day?

He reached down and patted Paddy, who fairly quivered with delight. Ryan was smiling when he stood up. He flipped his sunglasses onto the top of his head and turned to Tempest with a questioning gaze. Her breath caught in her throat at seeing the blueness of his eyes. "Is it safe to pet Jupiter as well?"

"Of course. He's actually a big baby." Focusing on the dogs seemed like the safest thing to do at the moment.

"Hi, fella," Ryan said to the large dog. Jupiter's tale wagged, happy to finally be the recipient of some attention.

"Would you like to take over his leash?" Tempest asked, holding the leash out to Ryan.

He looked surprised but pleased and nodded his head. "Sure."

They walked for a space, Ryan getting the feel of the dog's rhythm. "I didn't realize you were such an animal lover." He looked over at her and smiled that disarming smile of his. White teeth against a backdrop of tan and dark stubble. He'd repositioned his dark glasses, but she could see the skin crinkle at the corners of his eyes, inviting a response.

Tempest smiled back. "That's me. Always taking in strays." She wondered if it was something Cherise would have said, but decided she didn't care.

They walked for about half an hour, chatting about nothing in particular. Tempest was very aware of the fact that she needed to be careful, but talking about school days was a safe topic since it was an experience both she and Cherise had shared. When the time came for them to part ways, she felt disappointed.

"Maybe I'll see you again tomorrow," Ryan offered in parting.

Tempest's eyebrows shot up in surprise. "Maybe." She knew she should probably never come this way again, but there was something magnetic about Ryan Clarke and she ignored her better judgment.

When she got home she decided against phoning Dirk again. She could handle Ryan on her own.

CHAPTER 9

Two chance meetings began to take on the semblance of routine. Ryan and Tempest met the next three days in a row in the same spot and took the dogs for a walk together. She no longer felt tongue tied in his presence, but had taken on a new persona - a combination of herself and Cherise which she actually liked. It also helped that she'd bought a couple of new athletic outfits - things she was sure Cherise would approve of. The Tempest part of her could talk about things like the arts, philosophy, or current affairs, while the Cherise part was outgoing, confident, and maybe even a bit flirtatious. Tempest found herself settling into the role. Any feelings of guilt were shoved way back into her subconscious. She was carrying on the charade out of loyalty to her friend. That was all.

"I was thinking," Ryan said as they walked. "We should go out for dinner while we're both still in town. That is, if you're free?"

"Oh." Tempest was taken slightly off guard. "Yes."

"How about tonight?" He looked her way, waiting for a response.

"Tonight?" Tempest raised her eyebrows.

"I may have to leave tomorrow," Ryan added.

Tempest nodded. "Tonight would be perfect." She tried for her best Cherise smile. Careful. It was one thing to walk and talk about nothing. Things she could make up because she was not in her own surroundings and she was pretending to be someone else. Someone interesting. But to actually go out on a date?

They said their goodbyes and she watched him stroll away, while she was left frozen on the sand with two dogs milling around her legs, tangling themselves in their leashes.

"Sit!" she commanded a little too harshly. The dogs both sat obediently and she began untangling the mess.

What in the world was she thinking? Ryan Clarke was a rich aristocrat. Although he didn't come off as a snob, he was certainly out of her league. And a relationship could go absolutely nowhere. He thought she was Cherise Hillyer, and she had done nothing to dispel the myth. In fact, she had cultivated it. To admit the truth now would be mortifying. She was nothing but a big, fat fake and if she ended up burning in hell it was nothing she didn't deserve.

The fact was, each time she caught a glimpse of Ryan standing on the beach, her heart lurched. She'd never felt quite like it before, even with Ron. Definitely not with Jake. She pushed that memory to the very back corner of her mind.

She had loved Ron – or she thought she had, but maybe he'd just filled the role of the male lead in her fantasy about having a family. He was a security blanket. A proper boyfriend with the same beliefs who elicited very few sparks. But Ryan was different. He was handsome in a rugged sort of way, with dark hair and blue eyes and an athletic body. His looks, coupled with his easy going personality, were perfect. Except she was living as an alter ego. This wasn't the real her.

With a sigh she finished untangling the dogs and the threesome continued trudging through the sand on their way to their temporary abode.

She realized she had nothing appropriate to wear on a date

with Ryan. He would be expecting Cherise to wear something flamboyant – and expensive. She didn't have that kind of thing in her closet. A shopping trip was definitely in order - even if she couldn't afford it.

The thought flitted across her mind that she could take Dirk up on his offer and use his credit card. She stopped in her tracks, bringing both dogs up short. No! That was too low, even for the likes of Dirk. He still hadn't called her back and she was still mad at him, but somehow it didn't seem like such a big deal anymore.

She would just have to bite the bullet and shell out for another new outfit. She didn't even bother praying about it. The guilt was already too much.

Ryan picked Tempest up and they went to an upscale restaurant. Small talk wasn't as difficult as she'd thought. She just allowed herself to fall into the new character she'd created and they ended up talking and laughing freely, just as they had at the beach. She almost believed in her own performance. Ryan was making her feel interesting and alive in ways she'd never thought possible.

Buzzing interrupted their conversation. Tempest glanced down at her purse for the source of the sound. It was her cellphone. "Oops. I guess I forgot to turn it off."

"Aren't you going to get it?" Ryan asked.

"It can wait." Her elbows were propped on the table and she rested her chin on one fist. Their plates had already been cleared away and they were enjoying an after dinner coffee.

Her phone went off again. "Maybe it's important," Ryan suggested.

With a sigh, Tempest reached into her bag and pulled out the offending device. She squinted at the number on display. It was hard to see without her glasses, but she figured Cherise would have worn her imaginary contacts. It brought new meaning to the phrase 'blind date'. The thought made her smile.

"Good news?" Ryan asked.

"What?" She blinked up at Ryan. "Oh. It's just Dirk - my, uh, brother. Whatever it is can wait till later." She turned off the ringer and deposited the phone back in her bag.

Much too soon, the evening was over and Ryan was standing at the bottom of the steps that led up to her terrace. "Thanks for a wonderful time," he said. He was looking into her eyes and the way the moonlight was reflected in his made Tempest feel giddy. If only he was looking at her – Tempest – and not a woman who didn't really exist.

If she really was Cherise, she would be inviting him into the house. For a split second she considered it. But she wasn't Cherise. She was Tempest and she'd made a vow, to herself and to God - even if she wasn't on the best of terms with Him right now. "I'd invite you in, but my friends might not appreciate it," she said, hoping that would be an acceptable excuse.

"That's fine. I'd better be going anyway. I'm leaving in the morning."

"Oh yes. You said that." The weight of her disappointment surprised even her.

He nodded. "But I'm sure we'll catch up with one another again. Thanks for making my time here bearable." Before she knew what was happening, he leaned in for a kiss. It was quick and gentle, yet it sent her senses into overdrive and left her wishing that she really was Cherise, even just for this one night.

Paddy came rushing to greet her when she closed the outer door, jumping in a frenzy at her feet. More subtle in her vie for attention, Zoe brushed against her legs. Tempest leaned on the door for a moment then stooped to fluff Paddy's ears before picking up Zoe and heading for the couch. She buried her face in the feline's silken fur. When she reached the couch she plopped down and deposited Zoe beside her and then dug in her purse for her phone and her glasses. She should at least check out Dirk's message. Maybe he had some news about Cherise.

The message simply said. "Call me about Ryan."

Calling Dirk about Ryan was the last thing she wanted to do, especially after such a wonderful evening. Still, duty won out and she punched in his number.

"Sorry, I didn't get back to you right away," Dirk said on the other end of the line. "The other day when you called you left a message about Ryan. You sounded cryptic."

"Cryptic, huh?" Tempest laughed. "More like mad. And maybe a little confused."

"How so?"

"Did you know Ryan Clarke keeps an apartment right here in L.A.? Very near the place I'm staying, in fact?" She wished she could see his facial features so she could gauge his reaction.

"I didn't know." Dirk's voice sounded genuine, but she could never be sure with him. He was a very experienced con-man, after all.

"Yeah. In fact, we went out for dinner together. I just got home." Tempest smiled. There. See how he liked that. There was a moment of silence on the other end. Good. It had surprised him. Or maybe he was jealous.

"That's really strange," Dirk said. "His father Michael actually showed up here a few days ago and he said his son Ryan was in Europe. London, to be exact."

A sense of foreboding crept up Tempest's spine. "Then who did I just have dinner with?"

"Don't panic. Maybe he's pulling a Cherise. Telling the parents one thing and doing another. It happens all the time, as you well know."

"Or maybe this is all part of some elaborate game you and he have going. A way to humiliate your sister's naïve friend." She knew her voice was rising and that horrible fluttering feeling was starting up in her stomach again.

"Now, wait just a second." Dirk's tone sounded genuinely hurt. "Is that what you really think of me? I wouldn't do that to you."

She regretted her words already. She was a terrible person for getting involved in any of this in the first place. "Sorry, Dirk. Really. Just forget I said that. Maybe your parents hired him to spy on me. I mean on Cherise," she corrected.

"Maybe, although somehow I doubt it. Listen, there is definitely something fishy going on. Whatever you do, don't see him again, okay? I'm flying back out there as soon as I can."

"When?" She hated the way her voice suddenly sounded weak - like a desperate female. But right about now she felt a panic attack coming on.

"It might be a day or two. Just hang tight." He let out a curse. "I knew I shouldn't have left you so soon!"

"I'm fine. Everything is fine." She squeezed her eyes tight. No it wasn't.

They said their goodbyes and Tempest clicked off her phone. She felt numb. Who was this Ryan person anyway?

Oh God! Please forgive me for getting myself into this mess in the first place! If you help me get out of it, I'll never do anything stupid again!

After a moment, she stood up, upsetting Zoe from her lap, and strode to her computer. With a few deft clicks she started a search on the Clarke family. Originally from Boston, Michael Clarke was a well known lawyer who was now a judge. It was so easy to bring up the information, she wondered that she hadn't done it sooner. She scrolled further, seeking anything on his extended family, especially children.

Suddenly Tempest froze. She pushed her glasses up and then squinted at the screen. It showed a family picture with the judge, his wife and their two children, Ryan and Krista.

The real Ryan Clarke looked a whole lot different than the man she had been introduced to. There was no possible way they were the same person... which meant she wasn't the only one pretending to be someone else... which meant he must have known the truth all along. A new wave of anxiety washed over her. Who was this mystery man she'd been foolish enough to dream about and why was he masquerading as Michael Clarke's son?

Tempest reached for her cellphone. It had been far too long since she'd confided in someone other than Dirk and right now, she needed to hear the voice of reason.

"Stella? There's some crazy stuff going on and I'm scared."

Stella

*S*tella stifled a yawn as she shuffled into the kitchen. The warmth of the morning sun filtered through the large windows that rose all the way into the "V" of the vaulted ceiling, creating slanted stripes of light against the gleaming wood of the floors. The room was spacious, combining a large open concept kitchen with an informal eating area. A long ranch style table with benches on either side sat directly under the highest peak in the ceiling. Wood, granite, tile... everything felt warm and homey and Stella felt a comfortable wave of nostalgia wash over her body. It was good to be home.

"Good morning, sleepy head," Gabriella Santos, long time cook and housekeeper, directed her way.

"Morning," Stella said through another yawn. She was still wearing her sleeping attire, an old T-shirt and a pair of flannel shorts. "I was up late talking to Tempest. I think I'm still getting used to the time change."

"Excuses, excuses," Gabriella teased, her dark eyes twinkling. "What would you like for breakfast?"

"You don't have to spoil me," Stella protested. "I'll just grab a piece of toast." She sat down on one of the high stools that lined the granite covered island in the middle of the kitchen.

"Tut, tut!" Gabriella pointed her spatula in Stella's direction. "I'll spoil you all I want. It seems like forever since you've been home under your own roof. Besides, you could use some fattening up. Look at you! Wasting away!"

"Hardly."

"I'll make a nice poached egg, hm?"

Stella grinned and nodded her head. There was no arguing. Gabriella's idea of wasting away was obviously measured against her own rounded physique. But she meant well.

Stella sipped from the steaming cup of coffee that Gabriella placed in front of her and watched as the older woman worked. Her black hair was smoothed into a bun at the nape of her neck; only a sliver or two of silver streaked across its shining surface. She was humming. Always humming. Stella smiled and tried to identify the tune. It brought back so many memories.

Gabriella had been Stella's principle caregiver in the early years after her mother's death. She remembered well snuggling into Gabriella's ample bosom for comfort; sitting still while Gabriella braided her hair; or "helping" alongside her in the kitchen as she prepared a meal. Her own mother had been Mexican as well, and even though Stella couldn't remember much about her, she knew Gabriella had been more of a friend than a servant. For that, Stella felt a special connection to her. In every way, Gabriella was the mother Stella never really had. Then Helen came along.

"Good morning, Stella." Speak of the devil. Her stepmother, Helen Crayton, strode into the kitchen. Every coppery brown hair was in place, her make-up was done, and she was dressed in a casual yet fashionable pair of slacks and a blouse. Helen kept herself in shape for a woman of her age and although not a pretentious dresser, she liked to be in style. "Gabriella, I have a list of things that need to be accomplished today."

Gabriella nodded. "Yes, Mrs. Crayton. As soon as I finish up the dishes and prep the stew for lunch I'd be happy to help you do it."

"Good." Helen turned her attention to her stepdaughter. "Did you sleep well, Stella?"

Stella nodded. "My old bed is still the most comfortable." She took another sip of her coffee.

"You certainly seem to enjoy staying in it."

Stella cringed, but maneuvered a plastic smile into place anyway. The older woman was wearing a smile of her own, but it didn't fool her. They had long ago agreed, silently of course, that they didn't like one another.

Stella glanced down as Gabriella set a plate of eggs and toast in front of her. "Thanks, Gabriella." Stella picked up her fork and began eating. With her mouth full she wouldn't have to carry on a conversation with Helen. Her stepmother was always looking for ways to belittle her. Oh, she never did or said anything blatant, and certainly not when Stella's father was present, but Stella could feel the undercurrent of disapproval. Helen wore it like a mantle.

The other women continued to discuss the day's chores. Stella listened with one ear, not really caring what Helen had planned for the day and trying to think of a way to avoid her as much as possible. Once she'd eaten enough to satisfy Gabriella's watchful eye, she took her plate to the sink.

"Thanks for breakfast. It was great." She placed a quick peck on Gabriella's plump, brown cheek. She turned to meet Helen's gaze. "Think I'll go for a ride. Unless you'd like me to stay and help?"

"Of course not," Helen dismissed with a wave. "You go for your ride."

Stella figured as much. Helen was no more eager to spend time in her company than she was.

~

IT DIDN'T TAKE Stella long to get dressed in jeans and a western shirt – clothes she hadn't worn in a while but which still resided in her closet. She was gradually getting back into the rhythm of the ranch – and feeling the awkwardness of her absence. This was her home. Yet for more than half her life she had spent only vacations here. That was going to change. At least, if she had her way about it.

She stepped off the front veranda and shielded her eyes from the brightness of the Texan sun that already beat down upon the earth. The house was a rambling one story ranch style with a covered veranda that ran around three sides of the building. The front yard was mostly grass with some flower beds and low bushes and was fenced in by low white rails. The backyard was much more spacious, with a large deck, pool, and a higher fence for privacy.

Not that privacy was really an issue. Rod Crayton's ranch was a good hour and a half drive from the outskirts of the nearest city, Fort Stockton. The vast size of the ranch itself precluded too much outside traffic except for what was necessary to service the oil and gas wells on the property.

The rest of the yard was a maze of corrals, fencing, and buildings of various shapes and sizes - a barn, stables, large bunk house, sheds and machine shops, and of course, the foreman's bungalow. It was all nestled in a valley that sloped upward in the distance to a rim of rugged hills.

Stella's boots crunched on the gravel as she strode across the yard to the stables. A ride was in order. That was one thing she'd missed the most while away – her horse Dolly. Now she could ride her every day if she wanted.

Stella stepped into the stable, blinking as her eyes adjusted to the dusky interior of the large building. She inhaled deeply of the familiar smell - horse flesh and hay with the distinct undercurrent of manure. She strode down the center aisle toward Dolly's stall. Dolly let out a snort when she saw her mistress, nodding her head in approval. "Hello, girl," Stella cooed, patting the mare's neck. Dolly responded with a whinny as if to say, "What took you so long?" Stella laughed and unlatched the stall door. Dolly was a beautiful chestnut; a gift from her father on her thirteenth birthday as a way, perhaps, of apologizing for sending her away. At fifteen, Dolly was already past her prime by many people's standards, but Stella still loved her.

After putting on the bridle, Stella led Dolly out into the main area of the stable where the saddles were kept. She hauled her favorite saddle down from its resting place, fingering the smooth leather for a moment before hefting it into place on Dolly's back.

Stella looked up when the silhouette of a male figure was framed in the open doorway. "Hey, Blue," she called, continuing to winch the saddle securely.

Blue Shepherd sauntered to where Stella worked. The horse snorted a greeting as Blue reached to pat her neck. "Going for a ride?"

"Yup. Wanna come?"

Blue laughed. "Love to. But big brother has other plans, I'm afraid." Blue continued to stroke the horse's neck, making kissing noises at Dolly while he did so.

Stella smiled. "Oh? And since when did you ever listen to Zane?"

"True." Blue grinned, showing the small space between his two front teeth. It was one of the things that he hated about himself, but Stella found it kind of cute. It gave him a boyish look that went well with the rest of his features. He had a nose that was slightly turned up at the end, twinkling blue eyes under ridiculously long eyelashes, and wavy sandy hair which he wore far too long. At five ten he wasn't tall, but he had a muscular build. He'd always been a bit of a magnet for the girls, but to Stella, Blue was more like a brother.

Actually, he was closer to a partner in crime. At twenty-four they were the same age and they'd gotten into plenty of adventures together, before and after she got shipped away to boarding school. Leaving Blue behind might have been the hardest part of the whole ordeal.

Stella patted Dolly's front shoulder. "It's good to be home."

"Good to have you home." Their eyes locked for a moment over the back of the horse. Stella found hers fluttering downward.

"Blue!" It was Zane calling from out in the yard. They both turned their heads in the voice's direction.

Blue stretched his arms over his head and then pushed his cowboy hat back from his forehead. "Better get going before he thinks I'm slacking off."

"Too late." She gestured with her head to the open doorway. Zane's silhouette appeared, stopped for a moment and then strode toward them.

Zane was a bit taller than his younger brother; more lean and sinewy, although just as strong. His eyes were the same color as Blue's, but were perhaps even more intense under his dark, brooding eyebrows. His chocolate brown hair curled around his neck under his cowboy hat and a shadow of stubble darkened his slim face. His nose was longer than would be normally attractive, but there was something about the intensity of his presence - the very force of his persona, that attracted people to him and commanded respect. It was why he was the perfect third in command, next to Stella's father and the foreman, Duke Shepherd, Zane and Blue's own father.

He stopped several feet away from Blue, Stella and Dolly and crossed his arms over his chest, directing his icy stare at Blue. "What are you doing?" he asked, his voice sharp.

"What is this? Military boot camp?" Blue countered.

"I asked you to go find Ralph. We've got lots of work around here and I don't need to waste my time looking for you when I've got better things to do."

"Keep your shirt on," Blue mumbled. "I just stopped to say 'hi' to Stella on my way." He looked at Stella and rolled his eyes ever so slightly in Zane's direction. "Talk to you later, 'kay? Have a nice ride." He turned and brushed past his brother as he headed toward the outdoors.

"Hurry up about it," Zane clipped and pivoted on his heel, about to follow.

"And a good day to you, too, Zane," Stella called to his back. He stopped and turned, frowning. "Some greeting." She crossed her arms, but allowed a smile to form on her lips.

"Sorry." Zane took his cowboy hat off with one hand as his other ran agitated fingers through his dark brown mass of hair. He shoved the hat back on his head. "It's just, we're busy this time of year and -"

Stella place one hand on a hip while the other pointed a finger at him. "Since when did you become such a task master? Blue was just taking a minute to say hello." She was scolding, she knew, but hopefully he understood she was also teasing him, trying to lighten his mood.

"We're busy -"

She cut him off. "So busy you can't even say 'hi'? You've hardly even acknowledged my presence since I've been home." She sported an appropriately exaggerated pout.

Zane looked directly at her for the first time, his blue eyes hardening. "Work doesn't stop just because her highness is here." Without another word, he turned and strode from the building.

Stella blinked. She'd only been teasing, even though he was acting a little bit overbearing and probably deserved it. What had happened to him recently? Zane had always been the overly responsible one. As the eldest son of the foreman, he did tend to take things far more seriously than his younger brother. Still, she didn't remember him being this uptight.

She shook her head and patted Dolly's neck. "We won't let his bad temper ruin our ride, will we Dolly?" The horse snorted as if in agreement.

With determination in her stride, Stella led Dolly from the stables into the sunlight.

CHAPTER 11

*S*tella mounted Dolly in one fluid motion, steering her toward the gate which led into some pasture land adjacent to the yard. Despite her decision to forget about Zane's unexpected outburst, she couldn't help wondering about the real cause of it. He'd always been a bit rough around the edges, but never this bad.

The Shepherds were more like family than anything else, but where Blue was her partner in crime, Zane was the ever watchful protector. He was five years older than she and Blue and the fact that they had also lost their mother was another reason for the special bond of understanding between them. Their father, Duke Shepherd, had been the foreman of the ranch since before she could remember, and for all intents and purposes was second only to her father in terms of decision making on the property.

It seemed natural, then, that Zane and Blue eventually took permanent jobs at the ranch. According to her dad, Zane was the best horse breaker in all of Texas. She suspected Zane loved the ranch as much as she did, which was probably the real reason he stayed. It was as much his home as it was hers. Maybe even more so.

Like most families, they didn't always get along. But then that was what made her relationship with the Shepherd boys so special. She knew they would be there if she needed their help and she trusted them unconditionally. She couldn't imagine a life without them in it.

Zane was probably just under a lot of stress. It was no secret he was being groomed to take over as foreman someday, but neither Duke nor her father were near retirement yet.

"Stella!"

She turned her head in the direction of the voice. It was her father. She waited for him to approach, allowing Dolly to step from side to side, impatient as she was to go for a good run.

"Going for a ride, I see." Rod Crayton was a large man, thick around the chest and well muscled from years of hard work. At fifty-five he was physically fit with skin tanned a leathery brown, pale blue eyes, and hair that had turned mostly steel grey.

"Yup. Dolly hasn't been out in awhile, so I thought it was time we both got some exercise." Stella kept a tight rein on the impatient mare.

"If you can wait a couple minutes, I'll join you," he said.

Stella felt her eyebrows rise momentarily, but tried not to react with too much shock. "Sure." What was up? Her father never took time to ride just for pleasure. Certainly not with her.

A few minutes later, Rod arrived on his own horse, a beautiful brown stallion that strutted with coiled strength and power. They went through the gate, stopping to re-latch it on the other side, and headed off toward the ridge of hills to the west.

It was one of Stella's favorite spots. She often went there when home on vacation, just to think. It was a short ten minute ride along several switch backs that led to the top of a high spot overlooking the vista below. The ranch with its corrals, fences and buildings, stretched out before them, surrounded by pasture land and fields, all nestled in a cocoon of rocky outcrops and treed hills. They sat quietly for a few minutes, each taking in the majesty of their surroundings.

"You're a lot like her, you know," Rod finally spoke up. His voice was gruff and full of emotion. "Your mother."

"So I've been told," Stella replied, not taking her eyes off the view.

"Oh?"

"Sure. Gabriella used to tell me that all the time."

"Ah, Gabriella." Rod nodded his head and smiled. "Good having you home."

"Good to be home."

"Helen and I missed you this last time you were gone. Seemed longer than usual."

"It was," Stella replied. She doubted that Helen had missed her, but she supposed her father felt it was what he was supposed to say.

They sat for a few more minutes, letting the serenity of the spot replenish their senses. When he finally spoke, he kept his eyes focused on the scenery beyond. "Now that you're an environmentalist with letters behind your name, I hope you're not going to go trying to change the operation any." He was smiling, but there was an edge to his voice.

Stella shifted in her saddle. "What makes you say a thing like that?"

Rod shrugged, taking his time before he turned his gaze to hers. "I heard you've been asking the men a lot of questions since you've been home. About day to day operations. Things like that."

"I'm interested."

"I also heard that you'd been out taking some soil and water samples. Is that true?"

"Dad," Stella said, letting out a small, nervous laugh. She shifted her gaze away from his toward the view. "You don't seriously think I would do anything to harm you or your livelihood, do you?"

"You didn't answer my question."

There was a space of silence, crackling between them. "I didn't think it would be a problem."

He shrugged. "This operation is an open book. Do what you like. It just seems like a strange thing to do. At least without asking first."

"I'm a scientist, remember? It's what you sent me to school for."

"And that's what you plan to do with all that learning? Upset things here?"

"No! I plan to look for a job. At a university or for an oil company or something. You trying to get rid of me already? I thought I deserved a couple of weeks at home, at least. But if I'm not welcome -"

"Course that's not what I meant," he interrupted. "This is your home. Stay as long as you like."

"Is this why you wanted to go for a ride? To interrogate me?" Her tone wasn't accusatory, but the words held strength.

"Can't I even go for a ride with my own daughter?"

She could see by the look on his face that her words had hurt him. "I'm sorry. I shouldn't have gone behind your back."

"Then why did you?" He raised a brow and waited.

"Curiosity?" She shook her head. "I don't know. I was thinking I'd like to contribute. Maybe use some of what I've learned. Give back."

"Change things," he stated.

"Change isn't necessarily a bad thing, Dad." She scrutinized his worried expression. "And the samples are no big deal. Not if there's nothing to worry about, like you said."

They sat for a few more moments. Rod cleared his throat. "I didn't want to send you away, you know."

"No?" Now they were going to a place that brought on over sensitivity. She'd just as soon skip it.

"Of course not. But it was for the best. A smart girl like you needed a proper education. Helen saw that. If you'd stayed on the ranch you would have become, well, I don't know what. But you deserved better. A chance at something more in life."

"What if I didn't want something more? What if all I wanted was my home? My family?" She could hear the pain in her own voice; the little girl that had asked the same question for so many years without getting a satisfactory answer. She squinted to keep the tears at bay. One thing she would not do is cry. Not now.

Rod grunted his disapproval. "So all the time and money we spent sending you to school was a waste. I thought it's what you wanted."

"I did want it – do want it." How could she explain it to him? "I am grateful, but maybe I needed more time with my family, too. To feel like I had roots. Like I belonged."

"You still have your roots," Rod countered quietly. "And your family."

"Sometimes I feel like I don't really belong here anymore." She glanced over at her father to gauge his reaction. He was still staring out across the expanse below. "But if it's okay with you, I'd like to find my place again. In this family and in the world."

Rod nodded. "This is the place to start, then." He looked at her and attempted a smile. "Just let me know next time you decide to do any more of your scientific sampling and what not, okay?"

"I will."

"I better get back now. You go on and take Dolly for a good gallop." He searched her eyes before turning his stallion back toward the trail and then spurred him into forward motion.

Stella watched the retreating figure of horse and rider. For an "open book" there seemed to be a fair amount of tension over a few soil samples.

～

STELLA BRUSHED Dolly's coat with methodical strokes, thinking about the conversation with her father.

Now that she was home, she felt some confusion about the next step in her life. Logically, she should be out looking for a job, but somehow outside prospects weren't as enticing as she'd imagined. The draw of the ranch - of her own roots - was strong, now that she was back.

She could contribute if he'd let her. She wasn't here to police her father's activities or cause any disruption in the day to day operations, but she was a scientist, after all. Her innate curiosity would not be kept down.

Zane entered the stable, leading one of the horses. She felt her back stiffen. After their last encounter she wasn't sure she was up for another. She kept on working, ignoring his presence as he removed the horse's saddle, stowed it, and tended to the animal itself.

Finishing her own job, Stella patted Dolly's neck. She took a deep, cleansing breath and squared her shoulders. If Zane Shepherd thought she would just excuse his earlier behavior he had another thing coming. Head high, she walked with purposeful steps toward the exit.

"Stella." Zane's voice brought her to a dead stop, but she didn't turn. "Sorry for snapping at you before."

She waited another beat before turning slowly to meet his gaze. "Darn rights you should be sorry." She raised a brow but allowed one corner of her mouth to turn upward in a sign of reconciliation. She sauntered to where he continued brushing the mare with brisk strokes. "How are the new horses working out?"

He never looked up. "Why? You planning on offering some advice?" To the untrained ear he sounded curt. To Stella, it was the return of the old Zane. Crusty on the outside, but soft in the middle.

"If you want it."

He grunted, never taking his eyes off his work.

"What's that supposed to mean?"

"I never said anything," Zane replied.

She stuck her thumbs in the belt loops of her jeans. "So what was with you earlier? I should have slapped you for being so rude."

"As if I'd let you."

"Seriously. What's going on that's got you so uptight?" She leaned her frame against one of the stalls, her stance showing him that she was willing to wait indefinitely, if need be.

"It's nothing."

"Not buying it."

"It's all you get."

"Stubborn."

"Maybe."

There was silence. "Okay," Stella finally said, pushing off the wall. "I'll just go ask Blue. He'll tell me."

"Stop," Zane commanded before she could turn around.

Stella met Zane's steady blue eyes with her own brown ones. She raised her brows expectantly and waited.

He shifted his hat and expelled a breath, then set the brush on a nearby ledge. "I wasn't going to say anything to you, but... There's been some talk."

"What kind of talk?"

Zane shifted his stance and looked down briefly, before raising his gaze to hers again. "About you."

Stella's eyes widened. "About me?" she repeated.

He nodded.

"What about me?"

Zane sighed. His jaw worked for a moment as he considered his words. "Just, now that the boss's daughter is back, with all her university learning, things might change around here." He surveyed her for a moment and then picked up the brush.

"That's ridiculous." She dismissed the comment with a haughty wave. "Besides, change can be a good thing."

He continued brushing the horse. "It can be. If the person doing it actually knows what they're doing."

"Oh? Meaning I don't."

"I didn't say that."

"But you implied it."

"I'm just saying there might be things you know nothing about. Things you might be better off not knowing..."

Stella expelled a disgusted snort. "If that's not an invitation, I don't know what is. What's going on around here, Zane?"

"Nothing."

"I don't believe you."

"Until your dad decides otherwise, it's the best I can do. In the meantime, stop acting like you know more about how to run this ranch just because you've been to school."

"Is that what you think?" she asked.

"I haven't decided what I think, yet," he replied.

"Meaning?"

For a few moments there was only the sound of the bristles on the horse's hide as Zane continued grooming her. Stella waited and finally he spoke. "I can't quite put my finger on it. But you've changed, Stella. That's what I think."

"I've changed?" Stella fairly squeaked. "What about you? You've turned into a slave driver. I've seen the way you keep tabs on Blue and the others."

"Blue." Zane fairly snorted. "I'm not sure why he's still here. If it wasn't for my father – and yours – I'd have turned him out on his ear long ago."

"How can you say that? He's your brother."

Zane took one last stroke and then gathered the grooming tools in his hands. He stood up straight and looked her right in the eye. "He's an employee. I don't believe in favoritism."

"Oh, really."

"Exactly. And just because you're back from the east doesn't mean you're better than everyone else around here." He closed the stall and without another glance her way, he stalked from the stable.

Stella blinked. So much for their reconciliation. Exactly what were people so worried about?

CHAPTER 12

"*S*tella? Stella!"

Stella held the mug of steaming coffee with both hands and brought it to her lips, determined not to cringe at the sound of her stepmother's voice. Perched on her usual stool at the kitchen island, she briefly made eye contact with Gabriella.

The matronly cook raised an eyebrow but continued sifting flour into a large mixing bowl. A moment later, Helen entered the kitchen. "There you are. I just got off the telephone with someone who says he's with the press. He said he's going to call back later. You're not in some kind of trouble, are you?"

Stella widened her eyes in surprise. "The press? What did he want?" Immediately she thought of the soil samples. Surely the lab wouldn't leak any unfavorable information before sending her the results first?

"He was asking all kinds of questions about you and your friend from Boston - Cherise Hillyer? I told him I didn't know anything beyond the fact that you two were school friends. What's going on?" Helen waited expectantly, her hands on her hips.

Stella shook her head. "Beats me." A rush of relief engulfed her. At least it wasn't about the samples.

"Well, I for one do not have time to field questions from the paparazzi."

"The paparazzi? What was his name?"

Helen frowned then shook her head. "Ryan something. He made it sound like you were involved in something... unsavory."

"Forget it. It's probably just a prank. If he calls back, I'll handle it."

Helen sniffed. "You do that. It makes me wonder what kind of friends you keep." She turned on her heel and clicked out of the kitchen.

"It was her idea to send me to boarding school," Stella said just loud enough for Gabriella's ears.

"Miss Helen means well. She's probably just worried," Gabriella offered.

Stella expelled an unladylike snort. "How can you say that? You know how things are. How they've always been."

Gabriella shook her head. "I know lots of things. Like the fact that you got a big chip on your shoulder that's weighing you down. Now, tell me more about this friend of yours. Just what kind of trouble you two in, hm?"

"I'm not in any trouble." Stella stared into the coffee cup nestled between her palms.

"But...?" Gabriella prodded.

"It's kind of complicated and very stupid. Cherise took off to Italy after some guy. Her parents didn't approve of him and were about to close the purse strings, so she made up a story – lied actually – in order to get away without them knowing."

Gabriella stopped mixing and waited without saying anything else.

"I was against it, but Tempest helped her pull it off," Stella continued. "She pretended to be Cherise for a day to fool this old family friend who was coming into Boston. In return, Cherise paid Tempest's way to California. Cherise told her parents she was going to California with Tempest, when in fact she went to Italy. Now Tempest found out that the old family friend isn't who he says he is. It's kind of complicated, but I'm sure it's nothing serious."

"Liars never prosper," Gabriella stated. She said a few words in Spanish and then made the sign of the cross over her chest.

"It sounds worse than it is."

"Then why is the press calling? Hm?" Gabriella asked.

"Maybe it wasn't really the press. Maybe her parents found out and hired someone to look for her." Stella looked across at Gabriella. "You won't tell anyone, will you?"

"If you're as innocent as you say, what is the harm?"

"Please? I just think I should talk to Tempest again, first."

It was exactly what she planned on doing - right after she did a little other investigating.

"HI, BLUE," Stella greeted as she entered the machine shop, a motorcycle helmet under her arm. The place was crowded with tools and machinery and smelled of grease and engine oil.

"Hi." Blue looked up from the ATV he was tinkering with, wrench in hand.

She stopped and peered over his shoulder. "Working hard, I see."

"You know it." He straightened from the half crouching position he was in and grabbed a rag to wipe his hands. "Checking up on me?" He gave her one of his winning smiles.

"Maybe." Stella smiled back.

"Since I had a bit of time on my hands, I thought I'd make a few adjustments on my quad." He gestured at the helmet she carried. "You going for a ride?"

"I was going to." Her brow furrowed slightly. "I thought Harry was the mechanic."

"He is. But he's busy and sometimes a guy likes to do something different for a change, you know? Work on his own stuff. Besides, I wasn't that busy, so I figured I'd put my time to good use."

"Oh. So this machine belongs to you?" She pointed to the ATV. Its red paint job had rust spots. It looked a little worse for wear.

Blue nodded proudly, slapping his palm on the handlebars. "Yup."

"So, you think I could borrow one for the afternoon?" She glanced around the shop at the various vehicles.

Blue shrugged. "You're the boss's daughter. I guess you can do whatever you want."

"Not you, too." Stella gave Blue a playful shove. "I'm sick to death of hearing about my status as the 'boss's daughter.' Since when did I quit being just plain old Stella?"

"Plain you ain't never been." Blue winked.

The compliment was masked in playfulness. Still, Stella hesitated for a moment, taken aback. Blue was like her brother. She'd never thought of him in any other way and he'd certainly never tried to flirt with her before. She snatched a quick glance his way to see if she could read exactly what he'd meant. He was still grinning like a school boy. It was probably nothing. "Quiet or I'll tell my dad."

"Now I'm scared."

"Seriously. I need to borrow one of the quads," Stella said, redirecting the conversation back to her original purpose.

"Take your pick." Blue made a sweeping gesture with his arm.

Stella surveyed her options. There were three ATVs parked in the machine shop at present, of various sizes and horsepower. "Maybe I should stick with the 300," she mused.

"It's a piece of junk in my opinion," Blue said. "I'd take the 500."

"I don't want to take something I can't handle."

"You? Not able to handle a 500?" Blue shook his head in disbelief. "You're as capable as most of the men around here. I wouldn't worry about it."

"Okay, fine." She started walking toward the 500 horse powered machine.

Blue followed her. "Where you headed, anyway?"

"Just around," Stella hedged. She checked to see if the key was in the ignition, which it wasn't.

"A secret mission?"

Stella took a deep breath and then turned slowly around to face Blue's grinning features. "You can stop speculating. I'm not on a secret mission to undermine my father's holdings. Despite what your brother or anyone else thinks. So just stop it before I do something I'll regret."

"Like what?" Blue laughed. "Spank me?"

Stella just rolled her eyes.

"What if I like it?" Blue asked with a twinkle.

Stella pursed her lips. He was doing it again. Flirting – sort of. "Blue," she warned.

"Hiding from work again?"

Stella swung around. Zane was standing right there. "How long have you been there?" she demanded.

"Long enough." Zane was rooted to the cement floor with his arms folded over his chest. He turned his gaze to Blue. "You're needed."

"Okay." Blue lifted his hands in surrender. "Have fun," he directed at Stella as both brothers exited the shop.

She watched them go. So different and yet both so dear. Despite the current tension, they were an indispensable part of her life. She just hoped her snooping wouldn't change that.

Stella retrieved the key for the quad from its spot within a small cupboard on the wall. After checking the gas tank, she secured her helmet in place, started the motor and revved the engine a few times. Without a backward glance she squealed out of the machine shop.

~

IN ACTUALITY, she *was* on a secret mission. Sort of. She had noticed a metal building tucked into a ravine on the far reaches of the property while out riding Dolly the other day. She knew this ranch like the back of her hand and didn't recall ever seeing it before. Maybe it had just been hidden in the brush and trees up until this point, but with all the negative talk about her career path, she didn't want to raise any eyebrows by asking around. It was more for curiosity's sake than anything; she wasn't expecting to find anything untoward. But she was a scientist for crying out loud. It was in her nature to investigate.

It was quite a distance to where she remembered seeing the building, which was why she wanted to take the quad. Also, if there were any samples to be taken, she could more easily carry them back to the ranch than in a saddlebag on Dolly's back.

She spotted the blue metal roof in the ravine below as she pulled onto the crest of a hill. It was more of a faded turquoise color and blended in with the surrounding sagebrush, rock and foliage. As she approached she noted that the roof itself was very low – almost right on the ground as if it covered an underground bunker.

She pulled up beside the roof, cut the engine and removed the helmet, shaking out her hair. She furrowed her brows as she approached. What kind of place was this, anyway? She rounded the side of the structure, noting the absence of windows. Then she saw it. A stairway leading down to a small door. There was a padlock on it. And a sign, faded over time.

Suddenly she froze. She felt a sickening wave of nausea wash over her body the moment she recognized the symbol. Biohazard.

CHAPTER 13

*S*tella went straight to her room and flopped down on her bed. The urgency with which she had arrived back at the ranch after her discovery was replaced by uncertainty and fear. She'd taken some samples from around the perimeter of the building, but she needed to think this through. Come up with a plan of action before confronting her father.

She fingered the oval gilt frame which sat on her nightstand. Inside was a picture of her mother, in her early twenties with black hair and dark eyes - very similar to her own appearance, except for the darker timbre of her mother's complexion. She was a Mexican beauty who had married young to a hard working Texas rancher. At the time her father was small potatoes – until oil was struck. Unfortunately, so did tragedy. Not long after their windfall, Stella's mother had been diagnosed with cancer. Within six months she was dead, leaving a three-year-old daughter and a bereaved husband.

Stella's father became the full-fledged workaholic that he'd been bordering on previously. It was surprising that he found the time to remarry. Stella was about nine when Helen came into their lives. From the start, she felt Helen's antagonism. It was obvious, to Stella at least, that Helen's plan was to get rid of her. Helen had family back east and knew about Parkview Girls' Academy. Somehow she convinced her husband that Stella would benefit from going there. It had been horrible, being ripped away from those she loved – her father, Gabriella, Zane, Blue...

But those days were gone. She was all grown up now. Time to leave the past where it belonged. In the past.

With a sigh, Stella set the revered photo back in its place of honor.

Just what kind of contaminants were hiding in that storage shed? What kind of secrets had her father been keeping? From the look of the sign and the state of the roof itself, it must have been there for years. Come to think of it, she'd never been out that far before without someone else tagging along. Someone like her father.

The soft Southwestern colors in her bedroom did nothing to ease the tension and worry that she felt mounting. This home-coming had been anything but the rejuvenating retreat she had envisioned. Emotional turmoil seemed to pop up at every turn. Maybe she should just forget about it – pretend she'd never seen the blue tin roof or read the sign on the padlocked door. Just let the operation continue smoothly without any nasty confronta-tions. Just move to the city and get a job.

No. That wasn't the way she was wired. This was not some-thing she could ignore. But confronting her father? That was not a pleasant prospect. There was someone else she could talk to first, though. Someone far less intimidating.

STELLA FOUND Duke Shepherd crossing the yard with long, easy strides, heading toward his own quarters. Dusk was falling, but she could recognize his lounging gate anytime of the day or night.

"Duke!" Stella called, jogging to catch up with him.

"Hm?" The older man turned around, his face breaking into a smile as he turned. "Hi, girlie. What can I do fer ya?" He pushed his dusty hat onto the back of his head. He was about the same size and build as Zane, probably a replica of him in his younger years, but his face was now a leathery mask, his hair thinned and greyed, and he stooped ever so slightly.

"I, um, I just wanted to talk, that's all." She rubbed the front of her jeans with her palms.

"Come on in, then." Duke gestured to his front door. The foreman's house was a quaint one-and-a-half story structure with shutters and a small veranda. It was a real house, as opposed to the bunkhouse that housed the other workers. Her father had upgraded the facilities in recent years, and no one was without their creature comforts, but still, the foreman's residence was a step up in terms of prestige and privacy. Duke and his family had lived there ever since Stella could remember, and in her mind, the Shepherds had ownership.

They crossed the veranda and Duke held the front door open as Stella entered, stepping directly into the small parlor. The room hadn't been redecorated in decades. The same flowered print sofa took up one wall across from the TV. The wood trim on the windows and doors gleamed with the same cherry-red stain. Odds and ends of horse tack acted like ornaments, while a pair of well worn cowboy boots took their place on the mat by the front door alongside some hooks holding a Stetson. Stella settled into the depths of a gold upholstered armchair, the fabric threadbare along the arms.

Duke took off his cowboy hat and hung it beside the other, smoothing his hair before heading for the sofa. He plopped down on its faded surface with a contented sigh. "So? Shoot. What's on your mind?"

Stella hesitated, not sure where to begin or what to say. She took a deep breath and then plunged in, keeping her eyes on

Duke for his reaction. "It's actually about something kind of odd that I came across. Out in one of the ravines."

"Oh? What's that?" Duke focused on some dirt under his nails, not looking up.

"Well, I wanted to ask you about it first, before I bring it up with my dad. I'm kind of afraid of what his reaction might be."

"Now you've got me curious." Duke smiled his easy grin, the same one that came to Blue so effortlessly. "Just spit it out, girl."

"Okay." Stella expelled a breath, holding her hands steady in her lap. "I came across what looked like an abandoned biohazard storage site." There. She'd said it. She eyed Duke closely, waiting for his reaction.

The change in his body language was almost imperceptible, but she noticed a stiffening of the back, a slight fidget with the fingers, the flash of a frown that was quickly replaced by his easy smile. "So you came across that old storage shed, did you?"

She nodded. "Yes. How long has it been there? How come I've never heard of it before?"

"Hold on, now!" He chuckled and shook his head. "Too many questions at once for an old beggar like me."

Stella sat forward in her chair. "Duke, I get the distinct feeling you're avoiding the answers."

"No, not avoiding, really," he said, cocking his head to one side. "Just considering the best way to go about answering."

"So?" she prodded.

"That storage shed was completely legit and up to code when it was first put up. Your dad did a deal with the previous owner. It's on that same parcel of land where he first struck oil. It's what made him rich. And it's monitored every month. That's the honest truth." He glanced upward. "God as my witness."

Stella widened her eyes. "Then why all the secrecy?"

"It's no secret, really." Duke shrugged his shoulders. "It's just not something that needs advertising."

"Who does the monitoring?"

"Your dad and me."

"But this is exactly the kind of thing I could help you with. I'm trained in assessing environmental impact and -"

"Slow down, there. I doubt your dad would be too pleased about that. You pokin' around that old site."

"Why not? He knows I have an interest in such things. I've been training for years, for goodness sake! If it's up to code and monitored, as you say..."

"Just leave it alone, Stella. That's the best advice I can give."

Stella peered at the older Shepherd through skeptical eyes. "There's more to this than you're letting on. I can tell."

"If you start diggin' things up, the press might get a hold of it. Not that there's anything wrong, mind you. But your dad just doesn't want any bad press. He prides himself on a clean and aboveboard operation. You don't think your dad would jeopardize that, now do you?"

Stella frowned, trying to process everything she'd learned. Duke was sitting comfortably, maintaining eye contact and that smile of his. He certainly wasn't acting like someone with something to hide. "That's it?" she asked, not convinced.

"That's it," Duke confirmed with a nod. "You know I wouldn't lie to you."

"I just don't understand -"

Duke cut her off. "That's all I can tell you. Probably more than I should have."

Stella sighed. "I guess I'll have to get the rest from Dad, then." She challenged him with her stare but he didn't flinch.

"Suit yourself. Although, he has had a lot on his mind, lately. We all do."

It was obvious she wasn't getting any more from him tonight. Stella rose from the chair and nodded. "Well, thanks."

Duke stood as well. "You're a lot like your mother, you are." He smiled fondly in remembrance. "No wonder the boys are fightin' over you."

Stella stopped in her tracks. She swung to look at the older man. "Pardon me?"

He chuckled. "You didn't think you could come waltzin' back here and not cause some kind of stir. I'd say all the single men from sixteen to sixty have their eye on the boss's daughter. Even my own two boys, although Zane wouldn't admit it if you tortured him."

Stella's eyes widened in shock. She'd seen just a hint of flirtatiousness from Blue earlier, but that was just his way - playful and unpredictable. But Zane? She dismissed the thought with a shake of her head.

Footsteps sounded on the veranda and both Stella and Duke turned at the sound. "That's funny. I coulda swore Blue said he was goin' to town tonight."

The doorknob jangled and Zane entered the living room. He gave a terse nod toward Stella then turned to his father. "Just wanted to let you know everything is ready for branding tomorrow. We should be ready to start by 6:00."

Duke nodded. "Thanks, Son. See you then."

Zane left without a backward glance. Stella felt her stomach turn a flip flop. Was Duke delusional, or was Zane really attracted to her in that way? As unlikely as it was, it wasn't a totally distasteful prospect.

Even if it wasn't true, she was sorry that they hadn't been getting along the best lately. She should go after him right now and try to make it right. Instead she stayed rooted to her spot.

They heard the door again. This time it was Blue.

"I thought you and the boys was headin' to town?" Duke directed at his younger son.

"The slave driver won't allow it." Blue gestured toward the door where Zane had just exited. "Something about an early start tomorrow."

"Probably right." Duke nodded his head in agreement. "I'd a done the same when I was in charge."

"What do you mean?" Stella glanced at Duke questioningly. "I thought you were in charge."

Duke shrugged his shoulders. "Of course. He's just helpin' out." He yawned and stretched his arms over his head; an over exaggerated motion.

Stella frowned. Something else was going on around here. It seemed there was more than one secret to which she was not privy. "Well, I guess I better be going, then."

"I'll walk you out," Blue offered.

"You don't have to."

"The coyotes might be howling," Blue said with a wink.

Stella gave him a withering look. "Since when am I scared of coyotes howling?"

"I don't know." Blue shrugged. "You've been gone a long time. I just thought..."

"Nobody seems to be thinking around here these days," she muttered under her breath as she strode to the door. "Good night, Duke," she called and stepped onto the veranda. Blue followed and closed the front door with a click.

They descended the steps side-by-side, Stella's hands deep in her pockets. "Why do I get the feeling that everyone around here is keeping secrets from me?"

"Beats me."

"You're no help at all." Stella released one hand to give Blue a punch in the arm. He just laughed.

Their boots crunched on the gravel path that led from the Shepherd's home to the larger ranch house. Its interior lights beckoned warmly as the rosy glow of the setting sun silhouetted its rambling outline. Without warning, Blue grabbed Stella by her free arm and swung her around. He caught her around the waist and kissed her square on the mouth, releasing her almost as forcefully.

Her utter shock left her speechless for a moment as she stood wide-eyed and blinking, mouth open as she tried to breathe normally. "What are you doing?" she finally blustered, hands on hips.

Blue just stood there grinning, the picture of perfect innocence. "Just a brotherly kiss good night."

"Brotherly kiss my foot!"

Blue shrugged. "I'm just really glad you're home." His eyes came up to meet hers. "Mad at me?"

The initial shock was wearing off a bit and Stella felt herself melting beneath his gaze. "Well..." How could she be mad?

"I mean *really* glad."

"Just stop, Blue. Please? Before you say something stupid." Blue was so familiar; so comfortable. She'd never thought of him – or Zane, for that matter – in a romantic context. But Blue was charming and attractive and a solid friendship wasn't the worst place to start a relationship.

"Sorry. I'm not sure what I was thinking," Blue offered, rubbing the back of his neck.

"That's obvious."

"I guess I just wondered what it would be like. To kiss you, I mean."

"Blue." Stella's voice was calm. Reasonable, although she felt anything but. "You're like my best friend. Let's not spoil that, okay?"

"Okay. Sorry. Forgive me?" He looked at her hopefully.

Stella nodded. "Now I really need to get going. I've got something I need to talk to my dad about before it gets too late."

CHAPTER 14

*S*tella marched straight into her father's study where he was sorting through some paperwork. "We need to talk."

Rod Crayton looked up, his eyebrows raised in question. "Oh? What about?"

She took a stance right in front of his desk where he couldn't ignore her, planting her feet shoulder width apart and crossing her arms firmly over her chest. "I was out on the quad today and came across an old hazardous waste storage site." She waited, watching as a dark cloud crossed her father's features. "Duke said it's being monitored and all the documentation is in place. Why haven't you told me about it?"

Rod worked his jaw, his mouth a firm line of tension. Finally, air whooshed from his lungs. "Sit down," he ordered quietly.

Stella's body tingled with sudden apprehension. This was not the reaction she had expected. An angry outburst, maybe, or even another well tailored explanation that left just as many unanswered questions. Clearly, what he had to say was going to have more impact. She lowered herself into the opposite chair, waiting for his next words.

Rod leaned back in his office chair, as if readying himself for a long story. "Back when I bought my first piece of land, I didn't have much in terms of capital. I needed to do extra work in order to raise the necessary funds. So, I took on odd jobs. Hired myself out wherever I could." He paused, taking a deep breath. "Back in those days, people were just finding out about the hazards of certain chemicals. Sure, there were regulations in place, but they weren't always as strictly enforced as they are nowadays, and sometimes it was easier to just get the job done than go through all the red tape."

Stella could feel the nausea rising in her stomach.

Her father continued. "I agreed to do a job for the owner of the land right next to mine. He paid good to maintain this storage site for chemical waste he had on his land."

Stella closed her eyes.

"It wasn't much work, really. Moving the odd barrel now and again. I didn't know – and neither did he at the time – that the materials we were handling were so toxic."

"Who's we? Did you have a crew?" she interrupted, sitting forward.

"Not a crew exactly. Just me and Duke. He was my first and only hired hand at the time, so he and I worked together on it after we finished our own chores. I bought the land it was on the first chance I got – when the owner died of cancer. I guess that shoulda been a warning. I shoulda known something was up."

"Oh, Dad," was all Stella could think to say. She blinked and looked down at her hands.

"Which turned out pretty well for me in the end." Rod sat forward in his chair and leaned on his desk. "That's where we found our first oil well. And the rest is history, you could say."

"But why the secrecy?" Stella gazed back up at him, trying to understand.

"Not secrecy, exactly," Rod countered. "It's all legal. That site is signed, sealed and approved as safe. One of us monitors it every month and there are no signs of any problems whatsoever."

"Monitors it how?"

Rod shrugged. "Just a drive by. Make sure it's all locked up and secure. That's all."

"You should be testing the air quality. Water supplies nearby. Soil samples. After so many years, contaminants could be leaching into the surrounding area." She looked him squarely in the eye. "I took soil samples today."

He chuckled. "Of course you did."

"But I still don't understand why you didn't tell me about any of this before. I'm your daughter. I have a right to know."

"When you were a kid there just didn't seem any point to it. The fewer people that knew about its existence the better. We didn't need the negative publicity. The oil business takes enough hits from environmentalists as it is." He surveyed Stella closely. "And then you became one."

Stella opened her mouth to protest but Rod put up a hand to stop her. "I'm very proud of you Stella, and I won't ever question your motives. You're a smart girl with gumption and you'll make a success of whatever you choose to do. I've got nothing against environmentalists, generally speaking. Just doing their job, like the rest of us. But I'd appreciate it if you'd not go stickin' your nose where it shouldn't be. Leave well enough alone. The last thing I need right now is for some snoopy reporters to go stirring up trouble."

"Snoopy reporters?" Stella furrowed her brows.

"Helen told me about the reporter that called today. Maybe I'm just paranoid, but if the paper gets wind that there's hazardous waste on my land, it could bring all the wrong kind of attention. Affect our insurance. It's bad enough people don't want to eat beef anymore."

"I already told Helen not to worry about any reporters. It has something to do with my friend Cherise Hillyer, not you."

"And what kind of trouble is she in? One thing can lead to another and I don't want any snoopy reporters on my tail or my daughter's."

"Cherise's life is kind of complicated, that's all. And she comes from a well known family in Boston. If he calls back, I'll just get rid of him, okay?" The truth was, her friends' lives had become far more complicated than she was letting on, if what Tempest said was true. But she wasn't about to share any of that with her father.

Stella reached out and placed her hand on top of her father's much bigger one. "I'm just glad you're okay. Who knows what kind of danger you might have exposed yourself to. You should go for a check-up. You and Duke, both." A slight frown crossed her face. "What did you mean 'affect our insurance'?"

Rod stared down at their hands. His was calloused and freckled, hers smooth and brown. "I just want to make sure everything is in place before... Well, I just need to make sure everything is all straightened away." He looked up at Stella. This time his eyes were soft, like he was pleading with her to understand.

Stella narrowed her eyes. "Dad? What else are you not telling me?"

Rod continued to hold her gaze for a moment and then sighed, looking down. "I wasn't going to say anything just yet. I mean, there's no need worrying you unnecessarily."

"Tell me what?" Her skin was tingling unpleasantly again.

Rod set his sights on the bookcase behind Stella's head, speaking almost absently. "As it is, you and the boys should be set up for life. Just don't want any leaks to the press or otherwise until everything is settled. You understand?"

"Dad!" Stella exclaimed. "What are you talking about?"

He shifted his gaze and looked her right in the eye. "I've got cancer, Honey. Both Duke and me have it."

Stella sat in stunned silence for a moment, hardly able to absorb what he'd just said. "But you seem so... healthy."

"Doing the best I can to stay strong so as not to worry anyone. The only other people who know are Helen and Zane. And maybe Gabriella. It's hard to keep things from her. The doctor says chemo, but I'm still deciding."

"But of course you'll take the treatments!" Stella cried. "You have to."

Rod shrugged. "If it's my time, it's my time. I'm not sure I want my last days on earth to be full of sickness from the thing that might not cure me anyway."

"But if your cancer is linked to the waste site then all the more reason to make sure it's safe."

"Not till after - well, you know. Nobody else needs to go near the place."

"But -"

"No buts! You'll not cross me in this, Stella. It could ruin it for everyone. You, Helen, Zane, Blue - the whole lot who makes a living here."

"But, Dad, that's no solution. We could fix this now - before anyone else gets hurt."

"And risk losing the whole kit and caboodle?" He shook his head. "Besides, the risks are minimal. Duke and I didn't know enough to take precautions back then, but no one else needs to get sick. Especially if they stay away until… well, you know."

"You don't know that, Dad. That the risks are minimal, I mean. Once we get those samples back -"

He cut her off. "Did you send them already? From the waste site?"

"No, not yet. I was going to do it first thing tomorrow."

"I want those samples, Stella. You'll not send them, hear?" He was sitting forward in his chair, his steely gaze that of an oil baron, not her beloved father.

"But -"

His eyes suddenly softened. "No more worrying about it

tonight. And that's an order. In the meantime, I'd appreciate it if you didn't do any more fishing around. Understand?"

Stella nodded. How could she deny a dying man's wish? Especially when that man was her own father.

～

STELLA OPENED the door as slowly as possible and stepped onto the veranda. She turned and closed the door just as quietly. Who in their right mind could sleep after tonight's revelations? Her beloved ranch secretly harbored hazardous waste and she was bound by a promise to keep it silent. Worse yet, her father was dying of cancer. She clutched the light sweater she'd donned more closely around her form and stepped down onto the gravel path.

The sky was a velvety indigo above her head; the odd star stubbornly twinkling like a jewel against its inky darkness. It was a still night. The sound of her own feet crunching on the gravel seemed loud next to the hoot of an owl and the distant cry of a coyote.

She'd cried after her father told her the news. All the tears of frustration she'd been harboring for so long just seemed to spill over in one giant burst. Her other worries seemed pale in comparison to the ominous portent of her father's death. He'd held her for awhile, patting her back like the little girl she had suddenly become, always the strong father. Then he'd shooed her to her room without giving any more details. As if a good night's sleep was the answer. If only it were true.

Her steps took her to the path leading up to the Shepherd residence. The porch light was off. Everyone in the world was getting some rest except her.

"Couldn't sleep either?"

Stella gasped, her hand instinctively covering her mouth. "Blue! You scared me!" She could just make out his form, sitting on the porch steps. She picked up her pace, skipping up the steps and plopping down beside him on the landing. "I thought you had an early morning."

He grinned. "Getting earlier all the time."

"You should be in bed."

"As should you." He cocked his head and peered at her. "So what's your excuse?"

She sat for a minute and then sighed. "I got some upsetting news tonight."

"Care to share?"

She shook her head. Her father had implied that Blue knew nothing about his own father's illness and it wasn't fair for him to hear it from her if he didn't know. "No. Sorry. I don't want to cry anymore."

Blue shrugged. "Suit yourself."

"I could use a hug, though."

"Done."

Stella scooted closer and Blue held up his arm until she had settled herself into the warmth of his side. They sat that way for several minutes. The steadiness of Blue's heartbeat was calming to her own uneven equilibrium.

"Sorry about earlier," Blue finally spoke. "Kissing you, I mean. I'm not sure why I did that. It was just a crazy urge and I went with the feeling. I didn't mean to freak you out."

"It's okay. Forget it."

There was more silence, then, "What if I don't want to forget it?"

Stella adjusted her head so that she could look at Blue's profile. "Blue..."

Their eyes met, his asking silently for permission. She knew she should refuse, but for some reason, she didn't. His mouth descended slowly, their eyes still locked until their lips finally touched.

Blue's lips were warm and inviting. Stella closed her eyes and allowed all the hurt of the day to melt away. It was a soothing balm to her frayed nerves and not at all unpleasant.

When Blue moaned and pressed his lips against hers more urgently, her eyes flew open and she pulled back. "Whoa! Slow down."

Blue blinked and then grinned, straightening. "Sorry." He let his arm drop from her shoulder.

Stella's heart was suddenly pounding in her chest, not from desire, but from fear. What had she just done? What if she'd just ruined her friendship with Blue? He was her best friend in the world next to Cherise and Tempest, and in some ways he was even closer. He knew her inside and out, even the not so likeable parts. "Look, Blue. Don't read too much into it, okay?"

He frowned. "What do you mean? I thought you liked it, too."

"I did. But I just don't want to spoil anything. I'm upset. Not myself. And you're my friend and, well, this could change things. Please don't go and get all weird on me."

He sat forward with his elbows on his knees. "Don't worry. Nothing will ever change the way I feel about you."

The characteristic smile was not in its usual place and Stella felt her heart sink to her toes. The pin-prick of unshed tears threatened and she raked in a breath.

"Hey, don't sweat it, 'kay? I'm more patient than you think." He planted a quick kiss on her forehead before standing with an exaggerated stretch. "I'm ready for bed after all, though."

Stella stayed put until she heard the click of the front door. If she could somehow turn back the clock, she would. The hazardous waste, her father's illness - even that kiss. Life had just gotten way more complicated than she had ever imagined.

CHAPTER 15

Several days passed, all of them surreal in their normalcy. Everyone acted like there was nothing wrong - her father, Helen, Duke, Zane - even Gabriella. Day to day chores continued uninterrupted. It was like if no one talked about it, the terrible sickness that hovered over their lives would just go away. Stella found herself buying into the charade. It was easier to pretend that her dad was as healthy and fit as he appeared on the outside. At least she told herself so.

She'd gotten the results back from the first soil and water samples she'd sent, and fortunately all toxin levels were well within normal parameters. She itched to send the samples from the waste site, too, but knew she couldn't keep the findings from her father or the outside world if they weren't up to snuff. Somehow she needed to make him see sense. Maybe getting Duke and Zane on her side was the answer.

As for her relationship with the younger Shepherd males, it was definitely strained. With Blue, it was just plain awkward and Zane seemed perpetually out of sorts. At least she knew the reason why, now, but it didn't make matters any easier. She found herself avoiding both of them if at all possible. Her own home had suddenly become a place of isolation.

She snatched up her cellphone from her nightstand, considering a call to Tempest just to talk. She'd gotten so caught up in her own troubles that she'd kind of neglected the fact that Tempest was going through a hard time right now, herself. She was about to punch in the number but stopped, finger hovering over the screen. It was probably too late. She'd call tomorrow.

Stella donned a light sweater and slipped out of the house and into the stillness of the night - something that was becoming a habit of late. Her feet carried her down the path to the Shepherd's house as if by their own accord. A lone figure sat in the shadows of the veranda on a wooden bench that resided near the front door. Blue was probably still awake, too. It was time she stopped avoiding him. They needed to have a heart to heart about the awkwardness their kiss had created.

"I'm glad you're still awake. We need to talk," she said from the base of the steps.

"Oh? About what?"

Stella's eyes widened for a second. From the shadows it looked like Blue, but that was definitely Zane's voice. "Oh. I thought you were Blue."

"Sorry to disappoint you."

"Now, why would you say that?" She tried to keep her voice light. "Can I come up and join you?" She had some things that needed airing with the older brother as well. Like how he had agreed to keep a safety hazard a secret.

"Sure."

Stella could hear the shrug in his voice but ignored it. She ascended the steps, crossed to where Zane sat, and perched on the other end of the bench to his right. They were silent for a space, each looking out over the eerie quietness of the yard. Finally Stella spoke. "I guess you have a lot on your mind these days."

"You could say that."

There was silence again. Stella sighed and swallowed. "Dad told me you're taking over as foreman soon."

"Maybe."

"Which is it? Are you or aren't you?"

"Only if needed."

Zane's lack of words was not making this easy. She wanted to apologize. To say she understood, now, why he was so uptight and miserable. But the lump in her throat was suddenly getting in the way of her own speech. "I, um..." she stopped and swallowed again. "I just wanted to say sorry."

Zane sat for a moment before replying. "For what?"

She closed her eyes. Was the man dense? "I get it now. Why you've been so tense." He didn't respond and she pushed forward. "He told me why. He told me about the... the cancer. That both he and your dad -" Her voice hitched and she pressed her lips together in an effort to regain control.

Stella could feel the tears welling up and she sucked in a breath, trying desperately to keep them at bay. She squeezed her eyes tight and then opened them again. "This sucks."

"Yup." He put his arm loosely around her shoulders and rubbed his hand up and down her arm in a comforting gesture. This was the Zane she remembered. Protective Zane. Dependable Zane. She closed her eyes and just allowed the strength of his presence to seep into her. After several shuddering intakes, her breathing began to steady.

She lifted her head and looked up at his profile. There were lines around his eyes and mouth that she hadn't noticed before. A day's growth of stubble darkened the lower half of his face. His eyes shifted and he caught her staring. Their gaze held for a moment until her eyelids fluttered downward. But not before she'd seen the unexpected. Along with the weariness and sadness she'd seen something else. Her stomach did a little flip.

Zane cleared his throat and dropped his arm, sitting up a little straighter. "You okay now?"

She nodded, not trusting herself to speak.

"Good."

More silence. Stella sighed heavily. "I don't want to fight anymore, okay?"

Zane leaned forward on his elbows, his eyes fixed on something unknowable in the darkness. "I'm willing if you are."

"Agreed. But…"

"Always a but," Zane said.

Stella sighed. "Look. I also know the reason for the cancer. Dad seems to think there will be trouble with insurance if it becomes known before… well, before he dies." Her breath hitched again but she carried on. "But I don't agree. It needs to be cleaned up now, before there is any semblance of a cover-up."

"I agree."

She had braced herself for his rebuttal and was taken off guard. Her shoulders sagged. "You… you do?"

"You sound surprised."

"I guess I am. Then why are you staying silent on this? We need to convince them both that it's a mistake."

"It's not what they want."

"Either way there will be monetary repercussions. You know that, don't you?" She searched his profile. "It could go south either way."

"I know. But it's not my decision." He turned to look at her. "Or yours."

"So that's it, then? You won't even try to convince them that they're making a mistake? I mean, if you and me and your dad could make a united front, we might be able to convince my dad that -"

"Nope. I already been down that road and it's no use. Now, I just intend to do my job and make life as worry free for my dad - and yours - as I can."

"So, that's it then?" she repeated.

"Pretty much. That site's been out there for decades. A few more months won't matter much."

"A few more months?" Stella choked out. "That's heartless. They could get treatment. It could be years -"

"It could. They're both stubborn enough. But in the meantime, I'll honor their wishes and let the chips fall where they may."

Stella sat for a few seconds in silence. Then she slapped her knees and stood up. "Well, I guess there's nothing more to say."

"Be careful with my brother." Zane said before she could step away.

Stella sucked in a breath. "What?"

"Blue. He might seem worldly, but he's not really. He's hardly been off the ranch."

"What are you implying?"

"I would imagine you've had a lot more experience. Your higher education wasn't all about books was it?"

"I could slap you." Stella clenched and unclenched her fists, keeping them safely at her side.

"I wouldn't advise it." Zane unfolded himself and stood also.

"For your information, most of my time in Boston *was* about books. I worked my butt off. I didn't have time for relationships."

"Could have fooled me."

"And just where are you getting your information?" Her eyes snapped.

"I saw you," he stated. "Kissing Blue."

There was a sinking feeling in Stella's chest. She felt like crying again and she blinked rapidly, her breath coming in shallow spurts. "That was nothing."

"It didn't look like nothing."

"So what?" She lifted her chin. "It's bad enough you keep tabs on his every move at work. Now you're going to tell him what to do after hours, too?"

139

They stood glaring at one another. The last thing Stella expected was what happened next. Zane reached for her and pulled her to him, his mouth descending on hers with sudden force. She could have fought back; struggled to free herself. But in the split second that it took for their lips to connect, she found herself responding, pressing into him with as much urgency as he was pressing into her.

His cowboy hat slipped off, landing on the wooden veranda with a distant thud as her hands tangled in his hair. His arms were holding her to him in a steely embrace as their mouths danced a heated tango.

"Stop!" Stella finally came to her senses and pulled away. "I'm... this is nuts!" Her chest was heaving and she turned abruptly, shielding her face with her hand.

"What? Not up to your standard?"

She jerked her head toward him. His eyes were still smouldering and he ran an impatient hand through his already tousled hair. He bent to pick up his errant cowboy hat and jammed it back onto his head.

"What kind of thing is that to say?" she bit out quietly.

He shook his head. "Sorry. At least it proves one thing, though."

"What's that?"

"That you're not choosy about who you kiss."

Stella looked at him sharply but she couldn't tell if it was meant as a joke or if he was being serious.

He sighed heavily. "I'm over tired. You should head to bed now, too." He turned and walked straight to the front door. Stella watched as he opened it and went inside without a backward glance.

She blinked back more tears. A melancholy smile played at the corners of her mouth as she ran down the steps and jogged home. It was a perfectly ironic ending to the worst - and best - day of her life.

Cherise

CHAPTER 16

*C*herise sat on the king-sized bed filing her nails, a pout marring her perfectly stained lips. Here she was again, sitting in Roberto's luxurious suite, waiting. Always waiting. A lot of good it did her to be here in Rome. It seemed Roberto was always out on "business." Pooh on business! She wanted to go out. Have some fun. Rome was meant to be experienced at night.

But the last time she'd gone out on the town by herself he had been furious. She'd never seen that side of him before. It was scary. He'd yelled and ranted and even held her arms so tightly that he left tiny bruises. He had apologized and they'd had glorious make-up sex. Still, she wasn't willing to risk it again. He said he'd be here to pick her up and so here she would stay. Waiting.

The door clicked as the lock was disengaged and Roberto entered the suite. Cherise bounced off the bed and ran to meet him. "Hi babe," she gushed, throwing her arms around his neck.

He responded to the kiss but then untangled her arms and disengaged himself from her grasp. "Hang on, hang on," he said in his sultry accent. "I've got a call."

"Let your voicemail get it." Cherise pouted. He already had the phone to his ear and was walking away, talking in hushed tones.

It was always like this. The first few days she had been here they didn't do much other than stay in the hotel room. He seemed genuinely happy to see her. But then, their time together started to taper off. If she wasn't so in love with him, she'd fly back home to Boston. Let him feel the pain of separation for a change.

Except she wasn't sure he would. Not the same way she did, anyway. With a sigh she flopped into a chair and picked up a magazine, absently flipping through its pages until his phone call ended.

"Who was that?" she asked.

"Just business," he replied, heading to the washroom.

"Are we going out tonight?" She inserted just enough whine into her voice to make sure he understood she really wanted to.

"Okay," he called from the bathroom. The water came on and she knew he was taking a shower.

She thought about joining him, but then that might mean they'd spend the whole evening in the suite – not a totally distasteful prospect, but she desperately needed to get out of here. See some of the city. Experience some of the nightlife that Rome had to offer. She stayed put in the chair and waited for him to emerge, towel wrapped around his waist.

"Where would you like to go?" He sauntered over and placed a kiss on her upturned lips.

Cherise smiled up at him. "You decide. You know this city better than I do."

He gave her another kiss and straightened. "Okay. Tonight we celebrate."

Cherise tucked a stray strand of hair behind one ear. "What are we celebrating?"

"A business deal I just closed." He walked toward the one large window and looked out over the city below. Rome at night was breathtaking, its monumental sites unsurpassed when illuminated, standing out like markers against the twinkling backdrop of the city's lights in general.

"That's good news. Does this mean you'll have more time for me?" She sidled up behind him and wrapped one arm around his naked torso.

"I can take as much time as you need." His accent had thickened and he turned around to face her. His lips found hers as he simultaneously slipped the towel off his waist with one fluid motion.

Staying in the suite wasn't such a bad prospect after all, Cherise decided.

CHERISE AND ROBERTO ended up going out on the town - eventually.

Rome was the perfect city for a romantic escapade. All disgruntled thoughts had vanished now that they were riding in the back seat of the cab together. The city was spectacular at night, its iconic architecture and *object'd art* illuminated to showcase the splendor of its history. Cherise secured her arms in the crook of Roberto's elbow and leaned in for another quick kiss. Then she giggled.

"What is so funny?" Roberto expertly raised one eyebrow, a mischievous smile playing at his lips.

"I'm just so happy to be here with you, that's all." She sighed and snuggled in closer.

The cab pulled up to the restaurant; an elegant but unassuming white facade tucked between similar two and three story buildings. It was well lit and violin music greeted them as they emerged from the cab. Roberto's eyes were appreciative as he helped her from the vehicle and Cherise allowed a provocative smile. She knew she looked stunning in the silk dress that clung to her curves. Roberto was just as handsome, in his white shirt and dark suit. She was so proud to be attached to his arm as they entered the upscale restaurant. Afterward, the plan was dancing. She couldn't wait.

The maitre'd led them through crisp white linen and flickering candlelight to their own table. Dinner in Rome was an experience and Cherise was determined to enjoy every minute of it - especially with such a handsome man as her companion. Roberto ordered wine and the waiter made a show of presenting the cork, allowing Roberto to sniff and then taste a small amount before pouring them each a glass. She was just settling in to take a sip when two men approached.

One was built like an NFL football player from back home, his neck wider than his head. His hair was shaved very close to his scalp. The other was equally muscular, but not as large, his black hair slicked back. Both wore dark glasses.

Roberto scowled and said something sharp in Italian. A short conversation ensued, until he abruptly put up his hand. He turned to Cherise. "Excuse me, my dearest," he said. "This will only take a minute." He rose from the table and led the other men away. Cherise watched their retreating figures and took a large gulp of her wine. Both were very shifty, in her estimation. What kind of business associates did Roberto have, anyway?

She downed the rest of her glass and within seconds the waiter was back to refill it. "*Grazie,*" she murmured. She was about to take another sip when she noticed a man sitting alone at a corner table. Had he been staring? She couldn't be sure, since he was now perusing his menu, but she had the distinct feeling that he had been watching her. He looked to be in his early forties, with well groomed brown hair parted down the middle, an outdated moustache, and a bow tie topping off his brown tweed suit. Although quaint, he wasn't altogether bad looking. Italian men made no secret of their appreciation for a good looking woman. It was disconcerting at times, but something she was beginning to get used to. Just the same, she shifted so as to turn her back toward him just a bit more. Hopefully Roberto wouldn't be too long.

Roberto reappeared, minus the two thugs, and settled back into his seat. "I'm sorry," he apologized.

"Business associates?" Cherise asked, looking at him over the rim of her wine glass.

He nodded. "I told them that business would have to wait for pleasure tonight. And believe me, it is a pleasure to be in your company this evening." He smiled that sexy, debonair smile and Cherise felt her heart melt. She could never stay angry with Roberto. Not with those dark eyes staring into the depths of hers.

LATER THAT NIGHT, as she lay entwined in Roberto's arms, some of the doubts came creeping back. "Babe?" she asked, turning so that she could look at him.

"Hm?" Roberto muttered, opening one eye.

"Who were those men that came to the restaurant earlier tonight?" She used her finger to trace a little pattern on his chest.

"Business associates." He closed both eyes again and took a deep breath as if readying himself for sleep.

She frowned, her finger stopping. "What kind of business?"

"Just business."

"They look like thugs."

He chuckled. "Don't worry your pretty head about it."

"No, really," Cherise persisted. "You never told me what kind of business you're in, Roberto." She propped herself up onto one elbow.

"Go to sleep." He pulled her down toward him and kissed her

on the mouth. She frowned, trying to move away from his embrace, but he was too strong.

Soon she didn't want to move away. Whatever Roberto did for a living didn't matter. All that mattered right now was that she was here with him and he made her feel like she was in heaven.

CHAPTER 17

Cherise looked up from her cellphone just as Roberto entered the suite. She stowed the device in her jeans pocket and ran to meet him at the door, greeting him with a lingering kiss.

"What were you doing?" he asked, unwinding her arms from around his neck.

"Oh, it was just a text from a friend back home."

"It is expensive to use your cellphone for overseas calls. I thought I told you this."

Cherise shrugged. "I'm not worried. I've hardly used my phone at all."

"Still, you should limit your contact. The less information you share, the less likely your parents will come looking for you. You don't want your parents to come looking for you, do you?" His voice sounded reasonable, as if talking to a child.

"No. You're right." She looked down at her bare feet. "But how much longer until we can go back to the States?"

"Soon." He kissed his index finger and then touched the tip of her nose with it. "You're the one who came chasing after me,

149

remember? Now you just have to be patient while I finish my business."

Cherise sighed. "Okay." She brightened almost immediately. "I went to the *Piazza di Spagna* today. Do you want to see what I bought?"

"Sure."

She skipped to retrieve some shopping bags from beside the end table and brought them back to where Roberto was now lounging on the sofa. "A new dress, matching heels, and this perfect scarf," she said, displaying each item. "Do you like them?"

"Of course." He looked up briefly with an appropriate smile before turning his gaze back to a text message he'd just received.

"Shall I try them on for you?" Cherise clutched the items to her bosom like a little girl who'd just opened her Christmas gifts.

He frowned slightly. "Later, perhaps. Come sit for a moment." He patted the sofa.

She blinked, lowering her purchases as she sank onto the sofa obediently.

"I know you love shopping," he began, focusing his gaze on hers, "but perhaps you shouldn't be going out alone."

Cherise's eyes widened. "But I'm in Italy, for goodness sake. Rome! Of course I need to go shopping. How can I not go shopping?"

"Hush, hush!" He patted her hand in a calming gesture. "Of course you can go shopping. I just said not alone."

"But why?" she demanded. "It's bad enough you won't let me go out of this blasted hotel room by myself at night, but now I'm stuck here during the day, too?" She put on her best pout.

"I just worry about such a beautiful woman alone on the streets of Rome. I know the hot blood that flows through the veins of all Italian males, and I'm a jealous man. You are mine and I don't like other men looking at you." He leaned in for a kiss that trailed from her mouth to her chin to her neck.

"Oh," was all she could say. "But..."

"Sh, my sweet," he interjected. "I will take you shopping as often as you need, just as soon as I've wrapped up these last few details." He sat back and smiled disarmingly. "Or I'll send one of my associates."

Cherise frowned. "Not one of those men from the other night?"

Roberto studied her earnestly for a few minutes. "Can you just trust me?"

She looked into his eyes – so perfect with those disgracefully long lashes – and searched for a reason to doubt. She saw none. "Yes. I trust you."

ROBERTO WAS true to his word. The next day his "friend" Dominic - the bald headed football player - was waiting in the lobby to escort her on a shopping trip. How conspicuous was that going to be, having her own personal bodyguard underfoot all day? With a nod in his direction, she flounced past and out the double doors to hail a cab. She decided to ignore him as best she could. The man spoke very little, anyway.

The cabby dropped them off at the *Via del Babuino*, one of the premier shopping areas next to the *Piazza di Spagna*. The street itself, like most in Rome, was a narrow corridor with four and five story buildings rising on either side. Awnings, iron-railed balconies, and umbrella covered tables vied for attention among the milling crowd of humanity; well dressed business men talking on cellphones, elderly couples strolling hand in hand, hipsters, 'goths' and homeless vagrants - all intermingled in a cacophony of textures, colors, and languages. At the end of the street, a spire rose above the rest of the architecture, a symbol of calm in an otherwise vibrant and hectic setting.

Cherise took her time browsing through some designer shops, a bookstore and an antique market. She hadn't thought much about buying gifts for her friends back home, but this might be just the place to start.

She stopped in at a jewelry shop, bending over the glass covered countertop to look more closely at the sparkling baubles beneath. "Oh!" Her eyes widened. "Can I see that bracelet, please?" She pointed through the glass at a delicately woven ankle bracelet.

"Certainly," the man behind the counter said with a nod. His black hair was slicked back on top with the sides shaven. He brought out the piece with a flourish. "Very beautiful, yes? For a beautiful lady?"

The bracelet was made of three different metals woven together - copper, gold, and silver. The clasp had a small diamond embedded in it. "I'll take three," Cherise said.

The salesman raised his eyebrows. "Do you not wish to know the price?" he said in heavily accented English.

"It doesn't matter. I want three."

"I will check our stock. One moment." He nodded to the other salesperson, a woman with bright red lipstick, and slipped through a door behind the counter.

"Gifts?" the woman inquired.

"Yes. For my friends back home."

"May I suggest the matching earrings?" She pointed to some diamond studs surrounded by tri-colored florets.

Cherise examined the earrings, but shook her head. "Not today."

The man came back with two small boxes. "It is your lucky day. We have exactly three bracelets. May I suggest the matching earrings?"

Cherise let out a small giggle. "No, thank you. Just the bracelets." She made her purchase, feeling very proud of her restraint when it came to the earrings.

She stepped out of the shop, and shielded her eyes from the

sun. "I don't know about you, but I'm starving," she said to her bodyguard. "Any suggestions?"

Dominic just shrugged.

"Let's try that café, then." She allowed Dominic to carry her purchases as she walked a few feet ahead.

Like so many others, the sidewalk cafe practically spilled out on to the street itself. Tables nestled under umbrellas flanked the entrance. Its brick and mortar facade showed its age but only added to the charm. Cherise motioned for Dominic to set her purchases down on one of the chairs and then sat down herself. Dominic followed suit, albeit reluctantly.

A waiter brought her a menu. She ordered a bottle of Perrier and then began scanning the menu for something light. "Aren't you eating?" she asked her companion, noting he hadn't looked at his menu. He just shook his head. "Fine," she shrugged and took a sip of her Perrier.

The bottle of water stopped midway to her lips. Tucked under an umbrella near the wall of the building was a man she recognized. The same man from the other night at the restaurant. At least she thought it was the same man. Brown suit, bow tie, and moustache, only this time a fedora topped his head and dark glasses shadowed his eyes. Coincidence? Maybe. Rome was a big city.

Trying not to appear alarmed, she took a sip of the water. She was glad dark glasses shielded her eyes so she could take a second look without being noticed. Definitely the same man. Her stomach did a flip flop. Even though she'd accepted Roberto's explanation that he was simply jealous and she therefore needed a bodyguard, she knew in her heart there was more to it than that. He was involved in something. Something that included danger.

She suddenly lost her appetite. "Um, let's go back to the hotel, shall we?" she said brightly. She signaled to the waiter, paid an appropriate sum and took no time in exiting the premises.

~

"WHO ARE YOU TALKING TO?" Roberto demanded. Cherise jumped. She was checking her favorite social networking site and noticed that both Stella and Tempest were on-line at that very moment. It had been ages since they'd communicated and she was longing for their companionship. For someone she could trust. Roberto had slunk up so quietly she hadn't even heard him approach.

"Just checking my messages." A slightly defiant edge had crept into her voice.

"I thought we agreed -"

"I know what we agreed, Roberto," Cherise cut in. "But I'm not your property. You don't own me." She swung around in the chair and faced him. She was at a slight disadvantage since she was sitting and he was standing, but she jutted her chin forward anyway. His control issues were starting to get out of hand, great sex or not.

Roberto narrowed his eyes. "You American women. So independent."

"Yes," she agreed, flipping her hair back. "We are."

"Perhaps you're ready to go home? Fly back to America?" He raised a brow and crossed his arms.

"I, well, maybe," she fumbled for words. "I don't know anymore. I mean, I still love you, but I miss my friends and my home. I feel like I'm in prison."

"Soon. Very soon," he assured. "Things will change."

Cherise's lips went out in a characteristic pout. "You keep saying that. But when?"

"Patience, my sweet." He took her hands in his and gently drew her out of the chair and into his arms.

Cherise rested her head on Roberto's shoulder, snuggling into his warmth and allowing him to stroke her back. "I'm afraid I don't have much patience left," she admitted. "I can't help it,

Roberto. All this secrecy and not being able to come and go as I please... I'm just not used to it." She pulled back a bit and looked at him fully. "I'm starting to get creeped out. When I arrived in Rome I was the happiest woman on earth, but now I'm not feeling safe, with or without Dominic. I think we were followed today."

Roberto's expression changed. His eyes became like steel; his mouth a hard line. He stepped out of their embrace and grasped her by the upper arms. "What do you mean? What did he look like?"

Cherise's eyes became round saucers. "It's the same man I saw at the restaurant the other night. He's about your height. Brown hair, a small moustache. He wore dark glasses and a hat today – like a fedora."

Roberto's eyes narrowed. "Hm, I can't be sure..." He swore in Italian and turned away. "Tell me where you were when you saw him."

Cherise stammered out the location. "What is it? Are you in trouble?" Her voice started to whimper. "Tell me you're not in any danger."

Roberto stopped pacing for a moment and ran a hand through his dark hair. The intensity in his gaze was frightening. "I have many – competitors," he said. "If this man is watching, there could be others."

"Are you... is it something... illegal?"

"What I am or am not involved in is not for you to know," he stated, turning away. Cherise started to cry in earnest. Roberto let out an oath and crossed the room in giant strides. He enfolded her in his arms and let her cry for several minutes. When he finally held her away from him, his face had softened. "Believe me when I say I did not mean for you to get involved."

She finally pulled away completely, and wiped her eyes on her shirt sleeve. "What's going to happen?" She sniffed.

"Nothing," he assured. "As long as I don't have to worry about you, I can take care of myself. I told you, soon everything will be over and we can both go back to America."

"Really?" she asked, searching his face.

He nodded. "Trust me."

She wanted to. Lord knows, she wanted to. "Maybe I should just go home right now?" she suggested.

"I'm afraid that is a bad idea," he said.

"Why?" she squeaked, renewed distress surfacing.

"Sh," he soothed. "Didn't I just say to trust me?" She nodded mutely. "Well, then. You will have to start. And the first item is no more phone calls, emails, or other communication. And no more outings."

She nodded again.

"That's my good girl." He smiled. He leaned in to kiss her. Somehow the physical contact didn't quite have the usual effect.

CHAPTER 18

$\mathcal{I}$f Cherise felt like she was in prison before, it was even more so now. Roberto posted a guard at the suite. If it wasn't Dominic it was Antonio, Roberto's other "business associate" with the slicked-back hair. It seemed the only place she could get away from the prying eyes of Roberto or one of his goons was in the bathroom. She took to having long showers or bubble baths.

"I'm going to soak and read for a bit," she informed Antonio, who was lounging on the sofa, his feet up on the coffee table. She held up a novel, her bathrobe slung over one arm. Antonio just shrugged, and turned back to the TV.

Once inside the bathroom, she turned on the fan and the water, both good sound barriers. Then she took out her cellphone, which she'd smuggled into her makeup bag. She started searching the internet for anything she could find on Roberto Percelli. Nothing. Although, it stood to reason that if he was involved in some kind of drug or mafia ring, he might be using an alias.

If she was going to find anything and be able to get herself out of this mess, she needed outside help. She punched in Tempest's number and got her voicemail. Same with Stella. She considered leaving a message, but decided against it. What exactly could she say that wouldn't sound alarmist? She had no real proof of anything. She sighed heavily. There was always family...

She was just about to hang up when someone picked up on the other end. "Dirk?" she said into the phone.

"Cherise?"

She breathed a sigh of relief. "It's you! You picked up."

"Of course it's me." He laughed. "Who else did you expect would answer?"

"I don't know. Listen, I need to talk to you."

"I can hardly hear you," Dirk interrupted. "You'll have to speak up."

"I can't," she responded. "I need you to check on something for me."

"What was that? It must be a bad connection."

Cherise gritted her teeth and tried again, this time speaking more slowly without raising the level of volume. "I think I'm in trouble. I need to get home."

"You and Roberto have a fight? You know these Italians. Just as passionate about war as they are love."

"Listen, please!" Cherise interrupted. She took a steadying breath. "I think Roberto is involved with something bad. I'm afraid."

"I didn't quite catch that."

"What do you know about Roberto?" Cherise asked, more loudly. She glanced at the tub. She'd have to turn the water off soon.

"I think you just asked me about Roberto? Why? Is something wrong?"

Cherise sighed in frustration. "Never mind! I'll try to call back." She ended the call and buried her head in her hands. What in the world had she gotten herself into?

LATER THAT NIGHT, when Roberto had returned and Antonio had taken his leave, she took the opportunity to hide out in the bathroom once again. How could she sleep with a man whom she now suspected of criminal activity? She had to find a way to get out of that hotel room and make her way to the nearest airport.

She flushed the toilet for effect and then waited an appropriate length of time before placing her hand on the doorknob. She hesitated when she heard Roberto's cellphone ring. Most of the time he took his calls out on the balcony, but with her in the bathroom, he might actually reveal something. She pressed her ear up against the door, trying to hear his side of the conversation.

Roberto laughed - a low, barely audible sound. "Don't worry. She won't be a problem. I'll take care of it." Cherise felt her blood freeze. She? Did he mean her?

She squeezed her eyes tight for a moment. She couldn't remain in the bathroom all night. With a deep breath, she opened the bathroom door – and squealed.

Roberto was standing right there. "Sorry, my dear. Did I startle you?" His voice was smooth as silk.

She nodded and pasted on a smile, placing her hand on her thumping heart.

"Come sit down and I'll pour us both a drink." He led her to the sofa, all attentiveness as he found and uncorked a bottle of wine and poured them both a glass. "It's been a long day for me as well."

She took the drink with shaking hands and sipped, avoiding eye contact.

"You seem nervous tonight," he observed. "Is something wrong?" He sat down beside her and placed his arm along the top of the sofa, behind her back.

"No, no," she denied, almost too quickly. "I just have a

headache is all. I was trying to find some medication in the bathroom."

"I see. Poor darling." His fingers began weaving their way into her hair.

She felt her insides cringe and willed her body to respond normally. By this time she should be reciprocating his advances. She wasn't sure she could pull it off. "I – I'm really tired," she stammered. "Sorry. I hope I'm not coming down with something." She held her fist up to her mouth and forced a cough.

He surveyed her for a moment and smiled. "Well, off to bed with you, then."

"Oh, I'm not sure I feel up to -"

"Without me, of course," he added. "You don't think I'm such an animal as to demand sex from you when you aren't feeling well?"

"Oh. Okay." Her eyes fluttered downward. "Thanks."

He rose and extended a hand, helping her off the sofa. "Tomorrow I have a surprise for you."

A surprise? That could mean anything. On the phone, he'd said he was going to take care of her.

He surveyed her closely, a small frown marring his perfect features. "Why so worried? I thought you liked surprises."

"I… I do," she stammered.

"It's something I think you'll like." He smiled in that familiar way and her defenses melted just a little.

"Oh? What is it?"

He placed a finger over his lips as if to seal the secret. "I couldn't tell you, now could I, or it wouldn't be a surprise." He kissed her on the cheek. "Now off to bed!" He gave her behind a little swat and she squealed, scurrying for the large bed.

She crawled between the cool sheets and pulled them up to her chin. She actually did have a bit of a headache. It was probably tainting her brain function. Maybe her suspicions had been all wrong and she was reading this whole situation in a paranoid light. Maybe he'd been talking about the surprise on the phone when he said he was taking care of her. This was probably all just a giant misunderstanding and she and Roberto would laugh about it later. How could someone so attentive, so warm, so perfect be anything but good?

CHERISE WOKE in the middle of the night, a cool breeze caressing her cheeks. She opened her eyes in the darkness and felt the emptiness of the bed beside her. Roberto wasn't there. She glanced at the clock. Three AM. Then she heard it – a man's voice, talking very quietly and low somewhere nearby.

She was alert now. The breeze she'd felt was coming from the open balcony door. The voice was Roberto's, talking into his cellphone, the hum of traffic a backdrop for his hushed tones. This time he must have assumed she was asleep, because he had neglected to shut the door.

"My American contact is in place," she heard him say. There was a pause. "The goods are ready for shipment." She strained to keep her breathing quiet. She couldn't miss a word. "Enough kilos to make you a very rich man." Another pause. "I told you the girl is no problem. Leave her to me." She froze, her breathing cut off for a moment until she purposely inhaled painful stabs of hot air as she tried to control herself.

The conversation was over and he was coming back inside. She lay still, hoping her breathing sounded like the heavy, peaceful rhythm of one who was asleep. For effect, she stirred slightly but kept her eyes shut. When she felt the weight of Roberto's body as he lay down beside her, she sighed and snuggled into him, as she supposed she might have done under normal circumstances. He kissed her lightly on the forehead and turned over.

Oh, God! Her mind was in a panic as she subconsciously called out to a supreme being she really didn't know or believe in. She waited for Roberto's body to relax - and as soon as she felt his breathing slow down, she knew it was her chance.

CHAPTER 19

*C*herise turned ever so slowly in the bed, sliding her feet out from under the blankets. Then with as much speed as she could muster she flipped the covers and jumped to unsteady feet, charging blindly toward the door in the darkness. She hadn't even unlocked the deadbolt when she felt steely fingers biting into the flesh of her upper arms.

"What are you doing?" Roberto yanked her around to face him, holding her at arm's length.

"Please don't hurt me," Cherise whimpered. Renewed fear was knotting her stomach.

Roberto surveyed her for a second and his mouth tightened. Then his grip relaxed, although he didn't let go altogether. "That you would even say such a thing is why I must do what I'm about to."

Cherise's eyes widened, her voice barely audible. "What are you going to do?"

"I'm not going to kill you, if that's what you think." He continued to survey her features. His eyes were sad. "You were right. I can't let you get involved in my business. I've arranged to send you home." He released her arms, letting his drop to his sides.

Cherise expended the trapped air from her lungs. She blinked, taking it in. "I'm going home? Is that the... surprise?"

He nodded. "I can't take you myself. I'm sorry. But I've arranged for someone else."

"But -"

"No buts. It is arranged and it is for your own good." He ran a thumb over her cheek. "Only know this. That I really did care." He let his hand drop and he turned away with an oath, separating them with several strides.

All of her doubts about Roberto vanished. "But, what if I don't want to go?" She rushed after him, placing a hand on his muscled bicep.

Roberto's lips formed a melancholy smile. "Just moments ago you thought I might be a murderer."

She tried to throw her arms around his neck. "It was stupid. Forgive me."

He held her at bay, clasping her wrists within his hands. "What do you really know about the real me?" His eyes searched her face.

"I know you won't hurt me." She blinked up at him, daring him to prove otherwise.

"You are correct," Roberto confirmed. "I would not do anything to harm you. Intentionally." He dropped her hands and took a step away from her, turning toward the window as he went. "But I cannot guarantee your safety. There are others, perhaps, who would use you to get at me and that I will not have."

Cherise's eyes widened. "You mean having me here might be putting you in danger?"

He nodded. "For your own good – and mine – I have arranged for you to leave tonight. In secret."

She approached him where he stood at the window. The rush of traffic, even at this hour, was something she had become accustomed to in Rome. She watched for a moment, the beauty of the city mocking her current state of emotional turmoil. "Will I see you again?" She wound her arms around his torso as she had done so many times before.

He took one of her hands and brought it to his lips. "Don't think I never cared. I did. Perhaps too much. It's why I let you stay in the first place."

"Just what are you saying?" Cherise felt her body stiffen.

"You need as much distance from me as possible to keep you safe."

She blinked, tears gathering at the rims of her eyes. She rested her head against his back and he leaned into her. "So, this is good-bye?"

He turned in her arms so that he was facing her and took her face between his hands. He brushed a tear away with his thumb as it spilled over. "You will get over me. It is for the best."

She hesitated, not quite sure what to do. It was over, then. Just like that. She had been a fool to rush after him in the first place. But then again, it had been glorious while it lasted. She would cherish these memories forever.

"We must hurry, now," he instructed, pulling away. "Dominic will be here soon to take you to the airport."

"You can't come?" She already knew the answer.

"No, I'm afraid not. Now, you must pack your bags. Quickly."

She leaned into him one last time but could feel the distance already growing, as if he had suddenly placed a barrier between his emotions and business. She straightened and flipped her hair back. "Well, I'd better get changed, then." She stepped toward the closet. If he could shut off his emotions that efficiently, so could she. At least enough to put on a good show.

CHERISE PLAYED the early morning's events over and over again in her mind as she watched the sights of Rome roll past through the car window. The parting moments were surreal. Dominic came to the suite to retrieve her suitcases; Roberto remained by the window, looking out over the rooftops of the ancient city. A small cry had escaped her lips as she pondered one final plea. But he didn't move. Eyes blurred by tears, she swung out the door, only allowing the anguished cry of her heart to escape in full once she'd donned the privacy of the elevator.

Dominic ignored her misery with stoicism as they drove to the airport. By the time they arrived, she knew she looked a mess, all red and puffy and blotchy. Her appearance mirrored her emotional state. A wreck. The first thing she needed was to get to a ladies' room and try for some damage control.

It was still dark out, the first edges of pink rimming the horizon over the city as the cab pulled up in the unloading zone. With a final sigh, Cherise hoisted herself from the depths of the vehicle while Dominic retrieved the suitcases from the trunk.

She surveyed the big man for a moment, as he stood there waiting with the bags. With a flip of her hair, she turned and marched into the terminal, head held high. If Roberto thought she needed a bodyguard then he could start doing his job – and then some.

"Not much time." It was the first thing Dominic had said since she'd set eyes on him this morning.

"I just need to freshen up. I won't be a minute." She breezed into the first ladies' room she saw, catching a glimpse of Dominic as he came to a halt just outside its wide entrance.

Cherise shook her head in frustration. Oh well. Soon this nightmare would be over and she'd be back home. Why didn't that prospect make her feel happier?

The woman staring back at her from the mirror was, indeed, a sight to behold. Cherise took a deep breath and then opened her purse, determined to do something with the havoc that was her makeup. A skillful touch up with concealer and a few strokes of the mascara wand and she started to feel herself again. Misery was an explanation, but certainly no excuse. A final fluff of her hair and a test smile into the mirror and she was satisfied that she looked presentable. She clicked the purse shut and headed for the exit.

She stopped short once she was out of the seclusion of the restroom, glancing to the right and then the left. A frown marred her newly made up features. Dominic was nowhere to be seen. She spun, trying to see if he was lost in the crowd somewhere. Nothing. Some bodyguard. And she needed her bags, too.

She looked up at the signage, deciding which direction to go. She didn't have time to wait and he probably just slipped away to get a coffee or something. Either way, she wasn't about to miss her flight – with or without her suitcases. She started marching in the designated direction, all the while keeping a watchful eye out for the wayward Dominic.

Then she saw him. Her breath caught in her throat as her hand flew to her mouth. It wasn't Dominic, but the other man with the hat. The one that kept showing up everywhere; that Roberto had been so agitated about.

She was sure, for a split second, that their eyes made contact. Panic rose in her chest and she clutched her purse more closely to her side as she spun on her heel, heading back against the grain of humanity in the crowded terminal. She hurried forward, clearing past a few straggling travelers, then glanced back over her shoulder. He seemed to be following – she was sure of it.

A cry of fright escaped her lips as she broke into a run. She looked back again. He was in aggressive pursuit now, pushing his way through the crowd, ever gaining ground. Her heart raced as she rounded a corner. There was a woman's bathroom up ahead near the luggage check. If she could make it there and somehow duck inside without him seeing –

Suddenly a hand came around her mouth and she was jerked

into an alcove. She struggled, eyes wide, trying to scream beneath the pressure of the hand that had been placed over both her mouth and nose. Soon she would suffocate. Die right here among thousands of people, not one of them the wiser.

"Sh!" came a harsh whisper. "Don't move!"

Tears were pricking her eyes now. It felt like the leather from her captor's glove was getting sucked right into her nostrils. She shook her head, trying for a tiny bit of air.

"I said shut up," the voice hissed again. "Are you trying to get yourself killed?" He must have realized her predicament, for he moved his hand from over her nostrils and she sucked in as much air as she could. That voice was familiar. Definitely not the European accent that she would have expected.

"I think it's clear. Are you going to be quiet now?"

She nodded mutely.

"Dirk will hear about this when I get home." He released her mouth and she sucked in a great gulp of air. She turned to look straight into her captor's eyes.

"Alistair?" she squeaked.

CHAPTER 20

*C*herise's head was spinning – not just from a lack of oxygen, but from the identity of the man whose body was squeezed next to hers in the narrow airport alcove. "What -"

"Sh." Alistair raised a finger to his lips. "It might not be safe yet."

"But -"

"Later," he clipped. "Right now we just need to get you safely away from here."

"But Roberto said he was sending me home." Her voice was a little too loud and Alistair put his finger to his lips again in a silent shush.

Alistair peeked around the corner for a millisecond and then turned his gaze back to hers. "Good thing he had a contingency plan."

"What do you mean?" Cherise asked, eyes wide. "You and Roberto planned this?"

"He sent me to make sure you actually got on that flight. If things didn't go as planned, I was to take you elsewhere."

"But Dominic was right there and..."

"Too many questions. First item - get you out of here." He

surveyed both sides of the hallway before slowly emerging from the alcove, drawing Cherise with him. "Just walk naturally. Don't draw any attention. My car is waiting right outside in the loading zone."

She did as she was told, traipsing along beside Alistair, her hand held firmly in his as if they were a couple on vacation. She kept her head pointed straight ahead, only allowing her eyes to dart from side to side at each person they met.

Finally they emerged into the ever lightening outdoors and made a last bee-line for his waiting car. Once inside, Alistair put it in reverse, made a quick check over his shoulder as he backed up, and then slammed it into gear and sped away.

"You almost suffocated me back there, you know," Cherise informed with a pout.

"Sorry." Alistair kept his eyes on the road as he maneuvered his way out of the parking lot.

She waited until he was less distracted and further away from the airport before speaking further. She thought she'd seen the last of Rome, but many of its now familiar sites were rushing past her again as they re-entered the city. "Tell me what you're doing in Rome. Are you and Roberto in business together?"

Alistair relaxed his grip on the wheel. "Not a chance. I think Roberto might be into something... well, let's just say, messy."

"Oh." She sank back against the seat. So it was true. Roberto was involved in the drug trade.

"Sorry to burst your bubble. But we're still friends, which is why I offered to help him out. You're safe now that I'm here." He flashed a grin laced with superiority.

Cherise gazed out her own window at the passing sights. Although it was a relief to be out of danger, she remembered now why she found Alistair so distasteful. He was an old moneyed snob and proud of it. Just like her own brother and father and she hated it. Hated the pretense. Hated the bigotry. Hated the smug self assurance that went with such privilege. It was probably why she had been so drawn to Stella and Tempest. Although Stella's family had money, her family riches came from hard work and sweat. No pretense there and Stella always said exactly what she thought. And Tempest? Well, Tempest was a bit of a project, if the truth be told. A floundering, wounded bird that needed mending and encouragement to fly.

"I'm surprised Roberto never mentioned you might be coming," Cherise said, flipping her hair back.

Alistair ignored her comment with a laugh. "I have a great story about Roberto." He briefly glanced her way before concentrating on the winding streets once more. "Do you want to hear it?"

"Not especially."

"I'll tell you anyway. When he was in Boston last, he looked me up, interested in meeting some local, shall we say, 'quality girls.' I hated to do that to him, so I arranged to have you two meet instead – accidentally of course – at a party. I'm a genius. I should go into business."

"So you introduced him to me rather than a prostitute," Cherise bit out, her eyes narrowing. "Thanks a lot."

"I don't know why you're angry," Alistair responded innocently. "You seemed to be enjoying your time together. I thought you'd be grateful. Especially after what I've gone through today."

Cherise expelled a puff of air. "Of course. Thank you." She was thankful. Who knew where she'd be at the moment if he hadn't shown up. She just wasn't happy about the fact that she would now have to be nice to him. Wait until she got home. She was going to make it her mission to never speak to him again. "So now what's the plan?" she asked, trying to sound civil. "Meet Roberto? Try for another flight tomorrow?"

"It's better if you don't know that much," Alistair replied mysteriously.

"But -"

Alistair cut her off. "No buts. Roberto's orders."

Cherise clamped her mouth shut, folded her arms, and hunkered down in her seat. She'd be perfectly happy to never lay eyes on either man again.

~

THEY WERE DRIVING down a narrow street with just barely enough room to meet an oncoming car without having to pull over. It was a part of the city she had never been to before. It looked to be an older industrial area, with metal warehouses and brick buildings. Alistair pulled over and put the car in park.

"Why did we stop? What are we doing here?" Cherise sat up and looked at the unfamiliar surroundings.

Alistair glanced at Cherise and took a deep breath. "You're not going to like this," he said, eyeing her closely. "But it's for your own safety. Roberto's orders." He reached across her body and opened the glove box, pulling a ski mask out of its depths. He held the mask up, dangling it close to her face.

Cherise pressed back against the seat and frowned. "What exactly am I supposed to do with that thing?"

He gave her a withering look. "I thought it would be obvious. Put it on. Backwards."

"I'm not putting that smelly thing over my head," Cherise announced, folding her arms.

"It's for your own safety," Alistair repeated. "Come on. Don't make me force you."

Cherise sat for a few more seconds, then gave in with a bluster and grabbed the ski mask. She pulled the offensive head-gear down over her face so that the eye and nose holes were in the back. "Satisfied?" her muffled voice asked through the knitted fabric.

"Not exactly the most fashionable." She could hear the humor in Alistair's voice. "If only you could see yourself."

"Just shut up and take me wherever it is you're taking me."

Alistair put the car in gear and pulled back onto the street. Cherise could feel the sway of the car as he took a right and then a left hand turn. Soon, however, she gave up trying to keep track. If Roberto didn't want her to know her whereabouts it was probably for the best. He had asked her to trust him and right about now her options were limited.

The car slowed and she heard the motorized sound of an automatic garage door as it creaked open. The vehicle bumped over some kind of small obstruction – probably the lip of a driveway – and the door whined and shut behind them as they continued to crawl forward. Alistair stopped the car and cut the engine.

"Can I take this horrid mask off now?" she mumbled. "I feel like I'm suffocating."

"Not yet. Stay put." She heard Alistair's door open and shut and the muted clack of his shoes as he came around to her side of the car. Next, her door opened and he was helping her out. "Watch your head," he said, putting a hand on top of her head to protect her from bumping it on the way out. "This way."

Alistair had her by the arm and she shuffled along beside him, trying to see through the knitting with little success. A flight of stairs and two doorways later, they finally entered a room that was definitely warmer than the rest.

"Okay," Alistair said, releasing her arm.

Cherise pulled the wool off her head, sparks crackling as her hair stood on end. She looked around the sparse interior. There were no windows and one lone bulb hung from the center of the low ceiling, casting harsh streaks of light on the otherwise dark paneled walls. There was a worn, brown couch along one wall, an old, tube television set on a stand, and a coffee table with a cracked veneer finish.

"Beautiful," Cherise said flatly. "I take it this is my new suite?"

Alistair nodded. "Bathroom is right through that door. Sorry I couldn't retrieve any of your belongings. I'll see what I can do about getting you some basics."

"How long will I be here?" Cherise cast a sharp glance in Alistair's direction.

Alistair shrugged. "I guess that's up to Roberto."

"I should call him." She opened her purse and started digging through it.

"Ah-ah-ah!" Alistair grabbed the purse right out of her hands.

"What are you doing?" Cherise demanded. Alistair proceeded to dump the purse on the coffee table. "Hey! Stop it!"

"What's this?" He reached for a small velvet jewelry bag.

"Leave those alone. They're gifts for Tempest and Stella."

"Fine. But I'll take this and this and this," he said, snatching up her cellphone, passport and wallet. "It's not safe for you to have a cellphone. It could be traced right to this location."

Cherise placed her hands on her hips. "What about my passport and wallet? Why are you taking those?"

"They'll be safer with me." He pocketed them along with the phone.

"That's ridiculous. You can't just take my passport." Cherise lunged for Alistair's jacket. He grabbed her wrist in mid air and held it in a steely grip. Her eyes widened. "Ow! You're hurting me!"

Alistair's stare was borderline menacing. He practically flung her wrist from him.

"Now you're starting to scare me." She rubbed her wrist and pouted.

Alistair turned without a word and headed for the door. "Where are you going?" she demanded.

"To get supplies. I'll be back soon." His voice was impatient. Hard.

"Well, bring some food. I'm starving." She flipped her hair back and plopped down onto the couch, picking up the remote control. She clicked on the television as Alistair left the room.

She heard the distinct sound of the door being locked from the outside, but she got up and checked it anyway. Just as she suspected. Locked.

What in the world was going on here? It seemed she was a prisoner once again, only this time, the accommodations were anything but five-star.

THE DAY WANED ON. Alistair came back with some take-out, shampoo, soap, a towel, and a change of underwear. She scowled when she saw the latter. He probably had fun picking them out, she mused blackly. He also brought a pillow and a blanket. Apparently she was staying the night. Fortunately, he didn't stay long, although he was frustratingly closed mouthed about the whole situation. "Roberto's orders," seemed to be the catch phrase of the day. Right about now she'd like to have a word with Roberto.

There was only one channel available on the television, and she found herself dozing on the couch between shows. After a while she wasn't sure if it was day or night or if it was even the same twenty-four hours. She consulted her watch and was surprised to find it was two A.M. No wonder she was tired. She had started on this nightmare adventure in the wee hours of the previous morning. Surely Roberto would make a way for her to get out of here before long.

CHAPTER 21

*A*nnoyance turned to anger which turned to despair. Three days in the wood paneled prison. Three days without any word from Roberto. Three days with only Alistair's daily visit to break the monotony. Cherise heard the rattle of the lock and sat up from her lounging position on the couch, trying to smooth the tangled mass which had once been a stylish coiffure. She felt sticky and dirty despite her attempts to clean herself up. This was definitely not the way she wanted to look if and when Roberto did appear.

Alistair. She flopped back into the depths of the lumpy sofa.

"Dinner." Alistair dropped a paper bag onto the coffee table near her face. It blocked the TV. She pushed at it with her arm and it toppled to the floor. A dark stain started to seep onto the worn carpet. "You've spilled it," he barked, grabbing the bag and righting it. "I brought soup for a change."

Cherise stared at the TV. "Who cares? I'm tired of this. How much longer, Alistair? I'm beginning to think Roberto has forgotten all about me."

Alistair shrugged. "Maybe you were just an expensive prostitute after all." He sniffed loudly, and sat down on the edge of the couch next to Cherise.

After a sharp intake of breath, Cherise felt her color blanch from head to toe. "That was cruel. I can't stay here any longer. I want to go home." She scuttled as far from Alistair as possible without leaving the couch herself. The tears welled up and spilled over, unbidden. She swiped at them with the back of her hand.

"I didn't think it would take this long," Alistair said, shaking his head. He bounced one leg in a nervous gesture.

Cherise looked over at the jiggling leg, her gaze slowly traveling to Alistair's profile. She noticed that his eyes were red rimmed. He rubbed his nose vigorously and sniffed once again. She narrowed her eyes. "What's really going on, Alistair? There's something you're not telling me."

He shook his head in the negative. "For your own safety," he said, avoiding eye contact.

"No." Her voice was quiet. "I'm not buying that anymore. Tell me what's going on."

Alistair sat for a moment, a slow grin spreading across his face. "Why not?" He looked directly at her and Cherise felt a shiver go up her spine. She was suddenly more frightened than she'd ever been, despite everything she'd been through.

"Let's see," he began. "It's all my father's fault, really." He smirked. "The old man is just so tight with his money. Never trusted me with any more than the barest allowance."

"You always had everything money could buy," Cherise whispered.

"As did you," Alistair countered.

"I've never denied it."

"Except Roberto," Alistair mused, turning his gaze back to some point on the far wall. "He just didn't fit into your parents' idea of an acceptable boyfriend. Never mind that he was rich, he didn't have the pedigree. And so, they rejected him."

"This isn't about me," Cherise said under her breath.

"Now that's where you're wrong." Alistair cocked his head to one side. "You see, even though our problems are somewhat different, I find an ironic similarity. It boils down to our parents trying to exert control over our lives. Why can't they just accept our choices? Hm?"

Cherise didn't respond. She squeezed her body into a hug, trying to put as much space as possible between herself and Alistair.

"As a senator, my father has to keep up appearances. He doesn't appreciate some of my – recreational activities."

"Meaning?"

Alistair laughed. "For someone who is so worldly in some respects, you are certainly naïve in others. You see, my dear friend, I've taken a liking to a certain white powder that, if my father's opponents found out, would put him out of politics for the rest of his life."

Cherise looked down at her hands. "I see." She'd suspected as much.

"Do you?"

He was staring at her now. She could feel it. Boring into her with his eyes. "I don't see what any of this has to do with me."

Alistair raised his eyebrows. "Don't tell me you still don't know what kind of character your dear Roberto is?"

Cherise swallowed. "He's your supplier?"

"He certainly didn't introduce me to drugs, if that's what you think."

Cherise rubbed her temples and sighed. "You're talking in circles. I'm tired, I stink, and I'm going stir crazy. Just get to the point. What is going on and when can I get out of here and go home?"

"That's up to Roberto," Alistair said with a shrug. "The ball is in his court now. If he wants you back in one piece he better start playing ball."

She was about to retort, but the possible meaning of his words suddenly hit her. She froze. "Just what are you saying?"

Alistair laughed - an almost maniacal sound. "The look on your face is priceless, do you know that? All this time you thought Roberto was the one in charge, didn't you? You knew he was in trouble with someone, but you didn't know who. The mafia? A shady drug lord, perhaps? He thought so, too – until the other day. I played my cards perfectly. I had him running scared. It's what happens when an amateur tries to play above his league."

She didn't dare open her mouth. Fear of what he was saying had paralyzed her tongue.

"I see I've caught you off guard," Alistair noted. "All this time you thought I was your benefactor. The one who had rescued you from the clutches of some evil mafia man out to kill you and your pathetic boyfriend. Fooled you, didn't I?" He reclined against the backrest and clasped his hands behind his neck. His leg was still jiggling.

Cherise swallowed hard. "What have you done?" she finally whispered. "Where's Roberto? And what do you want from me?"

"So many questions." He smiled wickedly, and glanced her way, his eyes straying.

Cherise flinched. "Touch me and you'll be sorry."

He laughed. "You're not exactly in the strongest position to be making the rules, now are you, Cherise?"

Cherise's nostrils dilated as she dragged oxygen into her lungs. She didn't take her eyes off him.

He finally looked away, the smirk still in place. "You'll be happy to know that Roberto is unharmed. As for his sidekick, the square head, not so much."

"What do you mean? You killed Dominic?"

"Don't tell me you were attached to that hulk?" There was amusement in his voice. He patted her leg. "Don't look so frightened. He didn't know what hit him. Probably just ended up with a bad headache. I haven't heard any reports about an unsolved murder at the airport, anyway."

Cherise felt like she was going to be sick. "What do you want, exactly?" she asked, her voice barely above a whisper.

"Money. Satisfaction. And drugs, of course." Alistair gazed at the ceiling, a lazy smile splitting his features. "Although I must say, this is the most fun I've had in a long time. A life of crime can be quite thrilling. I might take it up permanently."

"You're crazy," Cherise said. He had obviously slipped a screw somewhere.

"Perhaps. I think I shall enjoy this. Watching the fear in your eyes every time I come close." He reached to touch her face with his index finger and she slapped his hand away. He just laughed, then stood up and stretched. "In any case, I think you've learned enough for one night."

He strode to the door, turning before he opened it. "Enjoy your dinner." He gestured to the stained paper bag still sitting on the coffee table.

The click of the lock as Alistair closed the door reverberated through her consciousness. Cherise bent over double and began to cry.

CHAPTER 22

*C*herise wasn't sure how much time passed. It could have been one day, it could have been several. Everything blended together in a nightmarish blur. She had never liked Alistair. He was the quintessential rich snob whose very pores exuded superiority. But she'd never dreamed he would be capable of anything like the scenario that was now playing out. He must be deeply entrenched in his addiction to stoop so low. Or maybe privilege and too much money made him bored. Whatever it was, she waffled between wanting to scream and rant and break things, and just lay down to die.

Her mind shifted to her brother Dirk. The last time she'd talked to him on the phone he hadn't been able to hear anything. How much did he know? Was he also involved in the underworld? Maybe the bad connection was a ruse. She shook her head at the thought, as if to banish it from her mind. Surely not her own brother. Then again, drugs made people do bizarre things and they had never been especially close.

She closed her eyes. Curse the day she ever laid eyes on Roberto Percelli! She had been a fool to come chasing after him, halfway around the world. If she got out of this alive, she was swearing off men. At least good looking, foreign types.

She didn't know how much of Alistair's story about his relationship with Roberto she could believe. Alistair had implied he was blackmailing Roberto, but for all she knew, they could be laughing over a drink right this minute, congratulating each other on how easily she had been fooled.

And when she thought of how compliant she was in giving up her cellphone and passport! If she did manage to escape, how in the world was she going to get help?

She heard the lock and her stomach suddenly growled. The sound was her dinner bell. Just like Pavlov's dog.

"Still here?" Alistair greeted, a mocking grin on his face.

She scowled. Oh, how she hated that man. "Where else would I be?"

He threw the paper sack of food her way and she lunged for it, hating herself all the more for her reaction as she tore into the bag. With trembling fingers, she unwrapped the plastic on a ham and cheese sandwich then crammed a giant bite into her mouth.

"A far cry from counting calories, eh?" Alistair observed, raising an eyebrow. He leaned against the opposite wall with one shoulder, watching her. "When you get home you might want to recommend it as the newest craze. 'The Abduction Diet.' What do you think?"

"I think you are an animal," she said through the food in her mouth. She scrunched the cellophane into a ball and threw it at him.

"Don't bite the hand that feeds you." He laughed at his own joke. "Literally."

Cherise could hardly contain the anger that raged inside. "You can't keep me here indefinitely."

"Who's to know?" He picked at some lint on his cuff. "As far as your parents know you're still off in California. And besides your two friends and Dirk, no one else even knows you're in Italy.

Well, except me, of course, and I'm not telling anyone." He looked up and grinned.

She was about to retort but clamped her mouth shut as she took in his words. How did he know about her pretense of going to California? How did he know Stella and Tempest were the only ones who knew her true whereabouts besides Dirk? The thought of where he had gotten his information ripped the last vestiges of hope from her breast. Perhaps Dirk was in on this after all.

Alistair stretched lazily and sauntered to the sofa. Cherise instinctively tightened her body. He hadn't made any designs on her since that one time when he'd first revealed his true colors, but still, if he chose to do anything untoward, she would be no match.

He sat and put his feet up on the coffee table instead. "What's on TV?"

He flipped through grey fuzz, coming back to the only available channel. She sat stiffly, watching him, willing him to take his leave, like usual, so she could bask in her own misery. Instead he settled back on the couch and stared at the TV - some idiotic game show in Italian.

She watched blindly for a few minutes until a plan started to take shape. It was risky, but it just might work.

She sighed, wiping at her neck and upper chest. "It's so hot in here," she complained. "Isn't there a way to turn down the heat?"

Alistair glanced her way, opening his mouth to reply and then stopping as his eyes wandered to her movements. Her hand dipped just below the "V" of her blouse, parting the material just enough to expose more cleavage. Alistair blinked. "I don't know. I could check."

"Thank you," she breathed. "I'd be very grateful."

He smiled. "I'm not stupid, Cherise. I've been around enough beautiful women to know what you're doing. The question is, why?"

"What do you mean?" She batted her eyelashes.

He chuckled. "Okay, I'll play along. I must admit I've often wondered what it would be like with you. You've never been without a man in your life, but unfortunately, it was never me."

"That could change," she said, smiling.

"In exchange for what? Better food?"

"A change of clothes would be nice." She smiled seductively. "A few magazines. Maybe even an outing. I promise I won't scream or try to run away. I could even wear a disguise."

He laughed outright. "The change of clothes I could probably handle. The outing? That may take a lot more than one favor, if you know what I mean."

She shrugged. "Okay. Whatever it takes." She stood up and started to unbutton the blouse, gauging Alistair's reaction. She could see the dilation of his pupils; hear the quickened breathing. She opened the front of the blouse altogether and beckoned with one finger for him to join her. He rose slowly from his sitting position, self assurance in his gaze as his eyes never left her open blouse.

Inside, her heart was pounding in her chest. Could she really pull this off? He reached her and she grabbed his face and started kissing him - a full on tongue invasion of his mouth. It was all she could do not to gag or to bite his tongue off for spite.

Timing was everything. When she felt his reaction changing, becoming more heated, she jerked her leg up to knee him square in the privates.

He gasped and released her, giving her the split second she needed to spin for the door, slam it shut and lock it from the outside, just as he had done so many times to her.

CHAPTER 23

*C*herise stood panting and leaned up against the door for a moment, her head spinning. A moment later Alistair was banging on the other side with such force she was afraid he would knock it down. With a stifled cry she launched from the door and stumbled down a dimly lit hallway.

It had been so long since she'd used her legs for anything that she felt as if they might give out. She lurched through another hall, down a flight of stairs and across a cavernous cement space which appeared to be an empty warehouse. She was gasping now, partly from exertion but mostly from fright. It wouldn't be long before Alistair was on his cellphone calling for help. She had to get out of there – now.

She saw his car parked near the large garage doors. Surely she wouldn't be so lucky to discover the keys in it? She peered inside. Nothing. She bolted away, heading for the door to the outside, and jerked it open with more force than was necessary.

She stumbled from the building and squinted, shielding her eyes with her arm. It was broad daylight – not what she had expected. She stepped forward, searching the street for some familiar landmark. Well worn brick and stucco facades, terra-

cotta roofs, and a winding street that led toward a piazza...
Everything looked the same yet nothing seemed familiar. She
headed down the street, tripping along on the rough cobblestone,
ignoring the pain in her bare feet.

She saw a telephone booth ahead, tucked between two buildings - a wonder to see in itself, anymore, and she let out a little
cry of relief. She reached the rectangular sanctuary and dove
inside. She was disoriented for a moment and blinked,
scrunching her features as she tried to focus on what to do next.
Realization brought another cry. She had no change!

Bolting from the booth, she made a bee line toward a small
shop across the street. The sign above said *"Granaio"* - breadbas-
ket. A little bell rang above the door as she pushed into the shop's
warm interior. The smell of freshly baked bread wafted toward
her and her stomach grumbled. Half starved, she wasn't sure
whether to ask for bread or a phone. Immediate survival won
out. "Phone!" she yelled in English. "I need to use your phone!"

The woman behind the counter looked at her and let forth a
string of Italian. Using a rounded loaf as a pointer, her terrible
scowl matched the ranting tone of her voice. Cherise glanced
down and saw that her blouse still hung open, her undergarments and plenty of cleavage clearly visible.

Cherise fumbled with several buttons and then held her hand
up to her ear in the universal sign for telephone. "Telephone," she
repeated.

The woman frowned. "No - shoo!" She said something else in
Italian, which by her gesturing, seemed to point to the pay phone
outside.

"Please!" Cherise pleaded. "I have no money." She acted out
putting the money in the deposit on the telephone.

The woman sighed and said something else, which by the
tone, sounded derogatory, but Cherise must have looked
desperate enough because the other woman went to her cash
register and gave her a coin. "Shoo!" the woman repeated.

Cherise took the coin and dashed back across the street. With shaking fingers she deposited the coin and waited for the operator. "Police," she barked into the receiver when she finally got an answer. She tapped her foot in exasperation. What in the world was taking so long? There was a click and then dial tone. With an oath, she slammed down the receiver. She closed her eyes and leaned her forehead against the glass of the booth. Now what?

With renewed desperation she scooped the coin out of the change tray and deposited it a second time. It seemed to take an eternity for the overseas operator to come on. Finally, she was connected and she heard the ring of the phone on the other end. "Pick up, pick up, pick up," she recited into her own mouthpiece.

She glanced around just as Tempest's voice answered. "Tempest!" she gasped, relief flooding through her body. "Thank goodness! I -" Tempest interrupted her greeting in the rehearsed mechanics of a recorded message. *"I can't come to the phone right now."*

A small cry escaped Cherise's lips. She glanced out the window pane and froze.

The man. The man in the fedora. The same man who had been stalking her all along. He was a block away, and had not seen her – yet. The last of the message sounded. *"Please leave your message after the beep."*

"Tempest!" she cried into the receiver. "Listen. I'm in big trouble. Roberto's a drug dealer. I was kidnapped but I escaped." Pause. "Oh no! He saw me! I have to go."

Cherise bolted from the telephone booth, the receiver swinging to the final beep on the other end of the line.

Trio

CHAPTER 24

empest's eyes squinted open, searching and finding the digital alarm clock by her head. 4:45 AM. She was normally a morning person, but this was a bit ridiculous. She hit the snooze button just in case, and rolled over, falling back to sleep almost immediately.

Two and a half hours later, she opened her eyes again, this time to Paddy barking. He needed to go outside. Had she been dreaming or had someone called her early this morning? With a grunt, she sat up, rubbed the sleep from her eyes and then reached for her glasses. "I'm coming, I'm coming. Hold your horses."

Paddy circled her feet as Tempest shuffled to the patio doors. She unlocked the sliding glass and opened them with a swish. Paddy dashed out, anxious to do his business.

"Jupiter!" Tempest called over her shoulder. "Come." The Great Dane lifted his head then unfolded his frame, stretching and yawning as he stood up. He preferred sleeping in the living room on the rug, which was fine with Tempest since her bed was already crowded with a terrier and a cat. He trotted to the open doors and obediently went outside to get said business over with. Zoe the cat slipped out the opening under his feet.

Tempest left the door open and went to the kitchen to put the coffee on. Today she was going to take Stella's advice and move on with her life - without any men to complicate things. Maybe God wanted her to remain single. Paul talked about its advantages in the Bible and she was beginning to think she was among those whose lives would be better off singular, not plural. Jake, Ron, Dirk, Ryan… every time she'd gotten close to a guy things turned out badly. It was time she quit relying on others - starting with this condo - and find her own place.

Paddy and Jupiter re-entered almost simultaneously. Tempest waited a few more seconds and then called out to Zoe. Nothing. Cats were much more independent. She'd come scratching when she was ready.

Tempest closed the screen and sauntered to the couch, coffee in hand. She sank down into its padding, Paddy jumping up beside her. Time to check her messages. One new voicemail popped up on the cellphone's screen. Unknown caller. A knot instantly formed in her stomach.

What if Ryan who-ever-he-was had found her number? What if he was calling to see if she was home or not so he could snoop around? What if...

Tempest dragged in a breath to steady her nerves. This was ridiculous. She needed to get a grip. Take charge of her life. That was today's motto, remember?

Her thumb hovered over the icon for a moment as she wrestled with the compulsion to listen to the message. "Not now," she said aloud, striving for resolve. "Later. First, I've got condos to view."

She stood up, went to the sink and dumped the rest of the coffee from her cup. Then she went to the screen door and poked her head out one more time. "Zoe! Here, kitty, kitty!"

There was no response. With a sigh she closed the door and

locked it. Time was ticking and she had places to go and people to see. She wasn't going to put her life on hold for a con-man. Or a cat.

STELLA AMBLED INTO THE KITCHEN, still wearing her night-time jersey and shorts, and plunked down on one of the stools at the counter. Gabriella placed a steaming cup of coffee in front of her. "Thanks," she said through another yawn.

"You were up late I take it?" Gabriella busied herself with wiping the counter, avoiding eye contact. Stella knew it was a ruse. Gabriella was gearing up for a motherly lecture.

"I had trouble sleeping." Stella took a sip of coffee.

"Any particular reason?" Gabriella asked. Wipe, wipe, wipe.

Stella shrugged. "Lots of reasons, I guess."

"You are worried about your papa." It was more a statement than a question.

Stella surveyed the older woman over the rim of her coffee mug. "You know about Dad's illness?"

"Mrs. Crayton has confided in me. She is very worried."

Stella snorted. "Yeah? If she's so worried why isn't she insisting he do something about it?"

Gabriella stopped cleaning for a moment. "Your father. He is a proud man. He wouldn't want to be pampered or to have people think he was weak. He will make his own decision in his own time."

"Except, he's running out of time." Stella took another sip, more to steady her nerves than anything else.

Gabriella continued wiping vigorously. "I was hoping that you would have grown out of your dislike for your stepmother now that you are an adult also. If you plan to stay here, you will have to make peace with her."

"I haven't decided if I'm staying or not. I mean, obviously I will for now..." Stella's voice trailed off. "But after? I'll cross that bridge when it comes."

"I am thinking that there might be another good reason to stay. No?" Gabriella's gaze caught Stella's and she raised her brows knowingly.

"I don't know what you're talking about." Stella let her own eyes stray beyond the dining table to the large window that rose up to a V into the open rafters. Outside the sun was already shining brightly and the poplar leaves were shimmering in the breeze.

"I think you do." Gabriella rinsed out her rag and draped it carefully over the towel bar under the sink. "They are both good men, no? And it would be difficult to choose between them."

The mug stopped halfway to Stella's mouth, but she had no words.

"Now Blue, he is handsome and funny. And a good friend. And Zane? He is headstrong and stubborn, but loyal. I think when he falls for a woman it will be for life."

"Gabriella, I'm not sure what you think you know, but I can assure you -"

The larger woman cut her off. "I see things is all, and I see it in both their eyes. When they think nobody is looking. And I think you've seen it, too. Look me in the eyes right now and tell me you haven't."

Stella sighed and set her mug down on the counter. "Okay, maybe you're right."

"Ah ha! I knew it." Gabriella beamed. "And? What are your feelings?"

Stella stared at the gleaming countertop, avoiding Gabriella's penetrating gaze. "My feelings? I think I am... confused. I never really thought about either of them in that light before, you know? But now..." She looked up into Gabriella's eyes. "What would you do? I don't want to hurt either one, but I can't deny there's an attraction there. For both of them."

"What does your heart tell you?"

Stella let out a small, self-depreciating laugh. "My heart is unreliable."

Gabriella placed her hands on her hips. "This is quite the pickle. I see I will have to say a few extra prayers tonight on your behalf."

"Thanks, I guess."

"There's no 'I guess' about it." Gabriella pointed a finger in Stella's direction. "And it wouldn't hurt for you to do the same."

Stella shrugged. "I haven't taken time to pray much. Not lately. It seems like a waste of time."

Gabriella's eyes widened and she made the sign of the cross over her ample bosom. "Don't you be saying such nonsense. You'll come to the church with me later tonight and we'll light a candle for your father."

"Okay." There was no arguing with Gabriella. Not only did she see things, but she was a force to be reckoned with if crossed.

CHERISE SAT UPRIGHT on the hard, steel bench, hands folded neatly in her lap. The cell, although small in dimension, was next to another and another and another, all lined up like cages in a long row that seemed to go on and on like the mirrors in a fun house. Only this was anything but fun. The cinderblock wall was the only backrest and she felt bone weary. Apparently, she was now a suspect, having been hauled in by the fedora stalker himself. Turns out he was actually a police officer.

It had been silly to run. Futile. She'd barely gotten a block before he'd tackled her like she was a football receiver. The handcuffs he'd used made it impossible for her to resist and she'd been shoved into a waiting car and taken here, to the main precinct downtown, where she'd been waiting in a cold cell for most of the afternoon.

She glanced over at the occupant of the cell next to hers. Bleached blonde hair, too much makeup, and a micro-mini skirt. The woman met Cherise's gaze with hostile eyes and Cherise quickly looked down, but not before the other woman had flipped her middle finger and said something sharp in Italian.

Maybe the prostitute next door thought she was a fellow "working girl." She probably looked every bit as unsightly as she felt. Tangled hair, wrinkled clothing... Cherise felt her stomach growl. When was the last time she'd eaten a decent meal? She couldn't remember.

A door clanked open followed by the click of footsteps on concrete as a uniformed officer approached. The rattle of keys brought Cherise to attention and she stood up as the officer inserted the key into the lock on her cell door.

"Thank goodness," Cherise breathed. "I told them I was innocent. And the treatment in here is deplorable. I'm starving to death and I have to pee like a racehorse." She added for good measure, "I'm an American citizen, you know."

The officer seemed deaf. Either that or he didn't speak English. Cherise harrumphed her disappointment. The man was balding and overweight, and she gauged her chances at escape. Probably not that good considering she was in a building full of policemen. Once she was able to tell her side of the story, everything would be straightened out. At least she hoped so.

A few minutes later she found herself in an interrogation room. The dimly lit interior was sparse and bare. The only furnishings were a steel topped table and a couple of folding wooden chairs. A large two way mirror like the kind on TV graced one wall.

"Wait! I'm an American citizen," Cherise yelled to the retreating officer. The door clicked shut and she was by herself. "And I have to go to the bathroom," she added. She stomped her still bare foot and swung away from the door. She strode to the mirror and stood just inches away. "I need a washroom. Now. Unless you want to clean up the mess."

A moment later, the door opened. It was him. The man who had been her shadow of late.

"You can't hold me. I'm an American citizen and -"

He cut into her rant quite effectively by raising his hand. "You're not in America, *cherie*." There was something about his presence that made her pause. The gravelly yet melodic cadence of his voice. The self assured stance. The penetrating eyes which she could see for the first time without the dark glasses. "Someone will escort you to the facilities and then we will have a chat. *Oui?*" He raised an eyebrow.

The same stoic officer that had led her to the interrogation room reappeared. A few words in Italian and the uniformed officer gestured for her to follow. Cherise did as she was bid. She gave the man in the brown suit her best glare before exiting the room. His eyes barely registered the insult.

Thoughts of escape once again flitted through her mind, but were soon put to rest. At least the man with the moustache was a policeman and not a criminal. Still, by the look of him, her looming interrogation wasn't going to be easy - or pleasurable.

CHAPTER 25

Tempest brought the borrowed Corvette convertible to a stop in front of the garage doors and hit the automatic opener. The door whirred overhead and she rolled the yellow sports car into the cool interior of the underground parking garage. It was attached to the house, built into the basement at the back, and the entrance was almost unseen from the street.

She could already hear the dogs barking furiously from within the house. She'd left them inside while she went on her apartment hunting trip just to make sure one of them - namely Jupiter - didn't jump the fence before she returned. Still, the noise was frantic. They needed a good, long walk to calm them down.

Come to think of it, so did she. Apartment hunting hadn't been as successful as she'd hoped. The realtor was about as condescending as they came. Her budget was too low, her expectations too high. His attitude said he really didn't have time for someone who didn't have connections in his preferred social circles.

"Patience," she scolded, opening the inside door. "I'm coming."

Both dogs were dancing in front of the patio door. Apparently, three hours was long enough without a bathroom break.

Tempest's eye caught sight of something strange hanging down in front of the glass patio doors on the outside. It swung gently in the breeze like a pendulum on a grandfather clock. She squinted, moving closer. A few more steps and her hands flew to her mouth as she stifled a scream.

Zoe's lifeless body swung lazily from the end of a rope tied around her neck.

STELLA TOOK a deep breath and surveyed the yard from her slightly higher vantage point on the veranda. Her father had built it all with his own sweat. Now he was going to risk it all because of what? Pride?

She was dressed in a typical western shirt and jeans, her standard wear since being home. It was funny how easily one could revert back into one's comfort zone. Well, comfort zone at least in that department. The rest of her life was anything but comfortable.

She stepped off the veranda and strode across the yard toward the stables, hoping that both Shepherd brothers were occupied elsewhere. Verbalizing her confusion to Gabriella hadn't really helped sort out her feelings any. She decided her best course of action at present was to purposely avoid either one if at all possible, which wasn't going to be easy.

"Hey," Blue called out in greeting. He'd emerged from the machine shop and was jogging to catch up to her.

"Hi, Blue." Stella slowed her pace but didn't stop. Who would have thought she'd ever feel awkward in his company?

"Taking Dolly out for some exercise?"

"Yup. It's good for both of us."

"I'd join you but the taskmaster wouldn't like it," Blue said.

"It's okay. I enjoy the solitude. It helps me think." They reached the stable and stopped.

Blue shuffled some gravel with the toe of one boot. "Look, about the other night. I was thinking -"

Stella cut him off mid-sentence. "I don't want to talk about it right now."

"But -"

"I mean it. Let's just pretend it never happened."

"Stella. I can't just pretend it never happened." Blue took her by the shoulders and forced her to look into his eyes. "Surely you know how I feel about you. How I've always felt."

Stella shook her head from side to side. "Blue, don't -"

Zane suddenly emerged from the stables, leading his own horse. He stopped short when he saw them. Blue's hands were still on her shoulders.

"Zane!" Stella blurted, stepping away from Blue. "You nearly scared us half to death!"

Zane surveyed each one separately. "Is that so? Hope I didn't interrupt something." His words were laced with sarcasm.

"It's not what you think," Stella began. "We were just -"

"You don't have to explain yourself to me. He, on the other hand," Zane gestured at Blue with his head, "is supposed to be working." He stalked away, leading the mare behind him.

Stella sighed and rubbed her forehead. Why did it matter so much that Zane not get the wrong idea?

"Forget him," Blue said. "He's always got his shorts in a knot. I better get going before he gets real owly." He started walking away from her backwards, still facing her as he spoke. "But we need to talk about this, Stella."

"Blue..."

"I mean it." He turned, loping off after Zane.

Stella closed her eyes. She'd light a hundred candles tonight if she thought it would make life any simpler.

~

CHERISE SQUEEZED her lids shut for a moment, trying to relieve the headache that was now pounding behind her eyes. How long since this nightmare had started? Half an hour? Two hours? She couldn't be sure. The trauma of the last days, hours, minutes crowded her brain and she wondered if she would just pass out right then and there from exhaustion. At least they'd offered her a sandwich, which she'd hungrily devoured. Now she just wanted sleep.

"Once again, who were you phoning when I caught you?" Her shadow, whose name she now knew was Garneault, leaned forward in his chair, mirroring her clasped hands on the table top. The familiar fedora rested near his elbow.

"I told you already. My friend from the States." Cherise rolled her eyes and sat back, folding her arms over her chest.

"And what about the drug ring? Tell me everything you know." He again mirrored her movements and relaxed against the back of the chair. "I'm a very patient man. I've got all night."

Cherise hadn't been sure about his age before, but in these close quarters she judged him to be about forty. His hair was parted in the middle and he had a well trimmed brown moustache to match. His eyes were what startled her the most, however. They were golden with little flecks of green in them. Very cat-like, if she had to compare them to anything, and the man behind them was probably just as cunning. He was not as tall as Roberto, but she suspected that under the horribly outdated suit there was a well muscled physique. She'd felt the strength of his biceps when he'd caught up to her on the street and wrapped his arms around her flailing body, subduing her with ease.

"I am waiting, *cherie*." Garneault twiddled his thumbs, but otherwise didn't move.

Cherise sighed and met his expectant gaze. "I already told

you, I am not involved in this. In fact, I was trying to get to the police when you abducted me. I'm the one who's been kidnapped!"

The one door in the room opened and another man poked his head in and said something in Italian to her interrogator. Garneault nodded and turned to Cherise. "I'll be right back," he informed in his thick accent. Was it French? It didn't have the same cadence as Roberto's, but his voice was melodic none the less.

He exited the room and shortly after she heard some faint yelling on the other side of the door. If only she'd paid attention and learned more Italian. The door swung open. Garneault stalked in followed by another man wearing a rumpled shirt and pants and a loose sweater.

"You are free to go," the other man said in clipped English. She noted the daggers he shot toward Garneault, who for the first time seemed visibly upset.

Cherise raised an eyebrow and looked from one man to the other. Just like that? "Thank you." She rose from the hard backed chair. "But, what about the kidnapping? Aren't you going to do anything about that?"

"We'll look into it," the man in the sweater said, "but I'm afraid there isn't much to go on. We have a lot of cases, you understand."

"But I was abducted. Held against my will by another American -"

"There is always the American Embassy. You can take it up with them," the man said, rubbing the back of his neck.

Cherise was about to object some more but Garneault cut her off. "You heard him, *cherie*." He placed his fedora on his head. "Now, may I suggest you get moving?" He took her elbow and propelled her from the interrogation room.

"My case isn't important enough? Is that it?"

"I'll explain later," Garneault clipped. He ushered her down the hall, past several desks.

Cherise clamped her mouth shut, fuming inside. So much for justice. They arrived at a bank of elevators and Garneault dropped his hand from her elbow once they were safely on their way down. Then he took out his dark glasses and slid them into place, effectively covering his exotic eyes.

"So? Start explaining," Cherise said, crossing her arms. "I heard yelling back there. One minute I'm being treated like an accomplice, and the next I'm being released."

Garneault shook his head. "That's the Italian police for you."

Cherise surveyed him. "That's a funny thing to say seeing as you're one of them."

Garneault straightened his back. "Me? I am not with the Italian police."

"No? Then who are you?"

"I work for the French government," he answered. "Like your secret service."

"Oh!" Her eyes widened. "And you've been following me? Why?"

"All in due time." His profile remained focused straight ahead.

"Meaning?"

"Let's get you safely away from here first, shall we? After all, someone went to the trouble of kidnapping you once. I don't want to let it happen again."

A new wave of anxiety washed over her body. "So you believe me? That I was kidnapped."

"Of course. And now your abductor will be even more anxious to find you and shut you up." The elevator doors slid open. "Come." Garneault placed his hand under her elbow again and maneuvered her out of the elevator toward the front doors.

"Where are you taking me?" Cherise slowed her pace, trying to extract herself from his grip, but his fingers only tightened on her elbow.

"Somewhere safe." They emerged onto the street. To Cherise's surprise it was already dark. Garneault was leading her toward a waiting nondescript sedan. He stopped beside it and pulled a pack of cigarettes out of his suit jacket and proceeded to light one.

"How do I know I can trust you?"

He took a long drag from the cigarette. The smoke formed a cloudy ball as it tried to escape his mouth, but he sucked it back into his lungs and then let it out slowly before he answered. "What are your options? Now, would you kindly get in the vehicle, *s'il vous plait?*"

Cherise blinked. He was right. Her options seemed very limited at the moment. With Garneault's help, she slid into the passenger seat. He clicked the door shut and walked around to his own side. Two more drags on the cigarette and he threw it to the gutter then got into the vehicle. For better or worse they pulled out of the parking lot and onto the street.

CHAPTER 26

Tempest backed up, bumped into a dining chair, and inadvertently sat with a plop.

Zoe. Her beautiful cat. Hung.

Tempest buried her head in her hands, not daring to look at the grisly sight a second time, an inaudible cry forcing her mouth into an anguished "O".

The dogs continued to bark, Paddy ineffectually jumping against the window as if to release his feline friend from her maudlin trapeze. The thought of touching the body – taking her down – was more than Tempest could grasp. She rocketed from the chair and ran to the kitchen sink, just in time.

When the heaving was over, she leaned against the counter for support. What kind of sick person would do such a thing?

The dogs quieted and she glanced their way. They were both sitting, heads cocked to one side as they gazed at their mistress. Somehow she was going to have to do something. But there was no way she was going to take *it* down.

She squeezed her eyes shut for a moment, trying to gather her thoughts. Police. She had to call the police. But first she needed a drink. The acid in her mouth might make her throw up a second time. She turned back to the kitchen sink and ran the tap, then poured herself a glass of water, trying not to choke as she swallowed.

Suddenly the doorbell rang – a chilling sound in the eerie stillness of her sorrow. The dogs launched into another hailstorm of barking. Who could it be? Maybe she shouldn't answer it.

Oh God, oh God, oh God!

Banging was added to the din and then the sound of a familiar voice. "Tempest? Tempest, you in there?"

She closed her eyes for a moment and took a deep breath, then headed for the garage entrance. There was only one other person who had a key for the garage. With trembling hands she released the deadbolt and swung the door wide. "Dirk." Her voice was barely above a whisper.

"Surprised to see me?" Dirk was grinning from ear to ear as if he'd just pulled the biggest prank ever. The dogs were there to greet him with wagging tails. He patted each one and then turned back to Tempest. His smile slowly faded as he surveyed her features. "Tempest? Is everything okay?"

"Um, I…" She didn't know if she could put it into words.

He gripped her shoulders and peered down into her face. "You look like you've just seen a ghost."

"I'm -" She burst into tears, launching herself against his chest. His arms enveloped her body as she sobbed into his shoulder.

"What's wrong? What's happened?"

"Zoe," she managed between sobs.

He rubbed his hands over her back in a soothing, circular motion. "The cat? Something's happened to the cat."

"She's dead. Hung." Tempest leaned back in his arms and looked up into his eyes.

Dirk frowned. "Your cat hung herself? That's surprising. Cats are usually very agile. Nine lives and all that."

"No! She was hung on purpose." She pulled away from him

and gestured in the general direction of the patio doors. "See for yourself."

Dirk walked to the patio doors and peered out. "Oh my."

"Who would do that to a poor innocent animal?" Tempest sobbed. She flopped onto the couch. Paddy immediately jumped up on her lap while Jupiter laid his great head beside her leg.

Dirk ran one hand through his hair. "Is there a note? Anything else suspicious?"

"Who knows? I'm not going anywhere near it."

"You can't leave her there indefinitely."

"I'm not touching her."

"Called the police?"

"I was just about to when you got here."

"Okay. So that's our first priority," Dirk said. "They probably prefer if we don't disturb anything and then they can do the dirty work for you." He joined her on the couch.

"It's just sick. Sick, despicable and disgusting." The agitation in her voice brought Paddy's head up with a jerk. His eyes searched hers for a moment. She patted his head and he laid it down on her lap again.

"You going to call or do you want me to?"

"I will." Tempest pulled her cellphone from her pocket. Her countenance froze.

"What is it?"

"I almost forgot I got a call this morning. From an unknown caller. I was afraid to listen."

"Let's listen to it together."

Tempest put the phone on speaker and hit the message button.

"Tempest! Listen. I'm in big trouble. Roberto's a drug dealer. I was kidnapped but I escaped... Oh no! He saw me! I have to go."

Tempest and Dirk looked at one another with wide eyes.

"Let me hear that again," Dirk demanded.

They listened to the message a second time. Tempest sucked

in a breath. "Kidnapped? This is terrible! Why did we let her go off to Rome? I should have known better. I should have..." She trailed off. "Oh! God is punishing me for lying. I know it!"

"Don't be stupid," Dirk said, a little too sharply. "And don't blame yourself," he added in a softer tone as he placed a hand on her knee. "Cherise is headstrong. She would have gone with or without your help. If anything, I should have checked up on Roberto. I just never thought... especially since Alistair knew him." Dirk blinked. "Maybe I should call him." He reached inside his jacket pocket for his cellphone.

"Wait." Tempest laid a hand on Dirk's arm. "Can you trust him?"

"Can you trust Stella?" Dirk countered.

"Touché."

Dirk tapped in Alistair's number and waited. There was no answer and he clicked off.

"Why didn't you leave a message?" Tempest asked.

"I didn't want to sound alarmist. I'll try again later."

"Alarmist?" Tempest squeaked. "Your sister has been kidnapped and you don't want to sound alarmist?"

"Of course I'm worried. But we both know Cherise. Maybe things aren't as bad as it sounds. She does have a flair for the dramatic, and she tends to exaggerate."

"Let's listen again." Tempest pressed the message a third time and they listened. "She actually sounds afraid. And the message ends so abruptly." Tempest raised her eyes to Dirk's. "Don't you think?"

Dirk sat in silent contemplation for a moment and then nodded. "I have to agree."

"What if she's really in danger?"

"Well, we're calling the police anyway, so maybe we should mention it to them. Let them handle it."

"What if this is related to that Ryan person? We know he's an impostor. Maybe he and Roberto are dealing drugs together. Or maybe they're part of rival gangs and one of them kidnapped Cherise and is holding her for ransom." Tempest stood abruptly, sending Paddy scrambling to stay on the couch.

"Slow down," Dirk advised. "It sounds like you've been watching too much television."

Tempest turned to him with wide eyes. "Who knows what can happen when drugs are involved?" She swung around, pointing at the patio doors. "Zoe's murder was a warning, Dirk. They probably know I'm not really Cherise, but maybe this is a way to warn me to keep my mouth shut. Or worse, what if they come for me next to get me out of the way? Dirk, I'm scared."

"Hold on just a minute." Dirk rose from his sitting position and placed his hands firmly on her shoulders. "You're jumping to conclusions. None of what you just said makes any sense. First of all, Ryan was just here a couple of days ago, and he couldn't kidnap Cherise and kill the cat at the same time."

"He could have hired someone to do it," Tempest said.

"True," Dirk conceded. "Or the cat might have been a prank."

"A prank!" Tempest fairly spat the words. "Who in their right mind plays a prank like that?"

"Well? Maybe the neighbor hates cats?" Dirk offered.

"No! This is serious and I've got to get out of here." She started pacing in front of the couch.

"Okay, okay. As soon as we talk to the police we'll go out for lunch and come up with a plan. Have you had lunch already?"

Tempest shook her head. "I'm not hungry."

"Still, you've got to eat."

"And then what? I... I just don't know if I can stay here after this. Every time I come through those doors I'll see..." Her eyes darted to the patio doors and then down at the floor.

"Hey. I'm here now. It's going to be okay." Dirk forced her chin up with his index finger and searched her eyes. Slowly he enfolded her in his arms and Tempest relaxed against him, resting her head against his shoulder.

Dirk had proved himself a good friend over and over again, and she willfully released any last doubts about his motives. Even though she felt no attraction for him in a physical sense, his arms felt safe, and that was what she needed right now. Especially since it felt like God had abandoned her.

"Why don't you gather up your stuff and we'll check you into a hotel?" he suggested.

Tempest lifted her head. "But what about -"

"No buts." Dirk held her at arm's length. "I'm paying and you can stay as long as you need to." He lifted a finger and placed it on her lips when she was about to protest further. "We'll find somewhere that is pet friendly."

Tempest felt the tears straining to escape. "I couldn't. It's just too much."

"Don't be silly. I can afford it and I want to."

"But I can never pay you back." A tear spilled over.

Dirk smiled down at her and wiped the tear away with the pad of his thumb. "When are you going to get it that I'm not expecting payment? I just want you to feel safe. Happy."

She gulped. "You're sure?" He nodded and then drew her back into his embrace. "Thanks," she mumbled into his shirt.

They stayed that way for several minutes, Tempest simply allowing Dirk's strength to seep into her own depleted stores. Finally, she pulled away and smoothed her shirt with her palms. "I guess we better call the police now."

"I'll do it if you like," Dirk offered. At her nod, he made the call. Tempest lowered herself onto the couch and waited, half listening until he was finished. "Well, they should be here shortly," Dirk said. He sat down beside her.

"Good. I'm glad you showed up when you did." It was true. So much for her resolve to take charge of her own life. She frowned. "What are you doing here, anyway? I had no idea you were in L.A."

"That's because it was supposed to be a surprise," Dirk replied.

"Unfortunately, my little plan to impress you with a romantic evening on the town kind of backfired. *C'est la vie.*"

Tempest internalized the meaning behind his words. Why did she keep fighting this?

She knew the answer without really having to think about it. Dirk wasn't a believer and she didn't really feel any attraction for him. But at the moment she needed someone to lean on and Dirk Hillyer was the only prospect.

CHERISE GLANCED over at Garneault's profile. His eyes were fixed on the road ahead as they maneuvered through narrow streets. A light rain had begun to fall, creating a shimmer of reflected light on the wet pavement. "What am I supposed to call you?"

"Whatever you like, or nothing at all."

She turned her attention to the scurrying pedestrians on the sidewalk to her right, some hunkering into their collars while a few ducked underneath umbrellas. Her own reflection in the passenger window, void of makeup, with unkempt hair and sunken sockets, was a fright to behold. She looked away. "I heard someone call you Garneault. Is that what I should call you? Officer Garneault?"

"I am a detective."

"Oh. So Detective Garneault, then?"

"If you wish."

"Don't you have a first name? I'd like that better." Cherise stole another glance at his profile. He was older, but definitely handsome. The lines around his mouth and eyes gave him character.

"My name is Jean Yvres," he supplied.

"Jean Yvres." Cherise tried it out, rolling it on her tongue in her best attempt at a European accent.

He glanced her way for the first time since they'd started driving. "Correct, but perhaps Garneault is best."

"Okay. So tell me more about what's going on. Why have I been under surveillance?"

"I've been tracking a drug ring all over Europe for quite some time now. Then a new player showed up - your boyfriend – and put the operation in jeopardy." Garneault said something in French, presumably a swear word, and continued, "He is very sloppy and unprofessional. I was keeping tabs on him as much for his own protection as anything."

Cherise gasped. "Is he in trouble?"

Garneault laughed. "Of course he's in trouble, *cherie*."

"No, I mean has he been hurt? By the other bad guys? He seemed worried before I left."

"Men in his position have to be cautious."

"Yet you confide in me." Cherise tucked a strand of hair behind her ear. "How do you know I'm not going to tell him?"

"So your story has changed?" He gave her a sideways glance, a slight smile playing at his lips.

"No, of course not!" She pursed her lips with an indignant air and focused on the road ahead. The windshield wipers squawked a steady rhythm across the glass.

"I knew you weren't directly involved." A chuckle came from deep in his throat. "What kind of agent would I be if I didn't know such basic information?"

"Then why take me to the police station? Why all the questions?"

"If you were under police protection – even as a suspect – you would be out of harm's way. One less liability for me to think about while I try to catch the real criminals."

"Liability?"

"Yes, liability. Not only for yourself but for the entire operation. Unfortunately, the Italian police did not see things my way. Since your record is clean and there was no hard evidence linking you to the drug ring, there was no reason for them to keep you."

Cherise sat quietly for a moment, twirling a piece of her hair between her thumb and forefinger. "So, if I'm a liability, does that mean you're going to protect me?"

"Until I can get you to safety – *oui*."

"And where might that be?"

"Your embassy seems the best option." He glanced in the rear view mirror.

She nodded her approval. "My passport and all my other documents are gone." She scowled. "I knew Alistair was a creep right from the first time Dirk brought him home, but I had no idea he was this bad."

"This Alistair Montgomery. You know him well?"

"I thought I did." Cherise snorted. "Boy was I wrong!"

Garneault looked in the rearview mirror again. His mouth hardened and he accelerated. "We may need to postpone that trip to your embassy."

Cherise craned her neck to look out the back window. "Are we being followed?"

"It would appear so," he said through clenched teeth. "Hang on." He stepped on the gas, maneuvering dangerously past several other vehicles. Without signaling, he cranked the wheel to the left and they careened around a corner. Cherise let out a tiny squeal and clutched the arm rests.

They ran a red light, the sound of honking horns fading as they whizzed past at lightning speed. Garneault made a sharp right and then a block later another left. He checked the mirror and swore in French.

"I don't think the Virgin Mary would appreciate that," Cherise said lightly. Her knuckles were white on the interior padding.

He didn't respond but concentrated on the game of cat and mouse, accelerating again until he rounded a corner, slipping down a dim alley paved in rough cobblestones. He slowed the car and pulled into an alcove beside some garbage cans.

"Do you think we'll be safe here?" Cherise whispered. "What if he sees us?"

"We wait."

"Then what?"

"You'll just have to trust me."

Where had she heard those words before? She sighed. "Like you said, I guess I don't have much choice."

Time ticked by. Cherise opened her mouth once to say something but Garneault silenced her with a finger to his lips. A few minutes later, he maneuvered the car slowly out of the alley, leaving the headlights off. He pulled around the corner and coasted past a row of brick and stucco buildings, all four or five stories high and sandwiched together like tenement houses on the narrow street. The awnings and hanging signs in front of each one advertised the business within - bakery, restaurant, watch shop, shoe repair - while the tiny wrought iron balconies on the higher stories spoke of tenants. The neighborhood seemed vaguely familiar. When they passed a large warehouse with a steel door, Cherise's spine began to tingle.

"Is this... Oh no!" Her hand went automatically to her mouth. Almost instantly she grabbed for the door handle and tried to open it, but it was locked.

"What are you doing!" The car swerved slightly as Garneault reached across her body and stilled her hands with a steely grip.

"I'm not going back there," Cherise whimpered. "I knew I shouldn't trust you!" She squeezed her body up against the door as far away from him as possible.

"You would jump from a moving vehicle?" Garneault clucked his tongue. "*Mon dieu*! Relax. I am not taking you there."

"No? Then where are you taking me?"

"My place."

STELLA GAVE Dolly her full reins, letting the mare gallop freely for all she was worth. It might chase away the tension that seemed to press down at every moment. The home that used to be her safe haven had become a battleground, both outwardly and within the private recesses of her soul.

They reached the ridge in record time and slowed to a halt. Dolly was winded. With a few pats to the horse's neck, Stella slid off her back. She threw the reins over Dolly's neck and stepped closer to the edge of the ridge. The mare wouldn't go anywhere without permission.

This was Stella's favorite thinking spot. She sat down on a large rock that jutted from the edge and gazed down on the ranch. Nestled beneath the hills beyond, the ranch was a web of corrals, fences and buildings; a tangled interconnecting mass of circuits that mirrored her own jumbled thoughts. So much had happened in the short time she'd been home. Her father was sick, and yet, poor timing as it was, her own heart had been unexpectedly awakened. She just wasn't one hundred percent sure who was the real object of her affection.

When she'd told Gabriella that her heart was unreliable, she'd meant it. Blue was undeniably attractive. He was fun and funny and he made her feel like she had nothing to prove. She could be herself and she knew he would accept that. He'd made his intentions clear and the prospect wasn't totally unpleasant. She'd felt a base attraction when they'd kissed, and starting out as best friends wasn't the worst way to build a relationship. He made her feel soft. Sentimental.

With Zane it was different. There was fear mixed with excitement every time she saw him since they'd kissed. It was like that one act had opened this weird obsession. She wondered what it would be like to try it again, yet feared the prospect even more. They did nothing but bait one another, and sometimes she hated him for it - not just that he argued with her, but that he seemed to bring that contentious side out in her. People said passion was a two sided coin; that love and hate were closely related emotions. In their case it was true. He made her so angry at times with his stubbornness, but simultaneously she fantasized about him in ways that would make Cherise proud.

Stella shook her head. A relationship with either was out of the question. She couldn't do that to either of them and she wouldn't do it to herself.

With a sigh, she stood up, slapping the dust off her jeans with her palms. Some gravel beneath her feet gave way and she slid forward on her boots, flailing her arms in an attempt at righting herself. The movement landed her on her backside and she slid further over the ledge.

She came to a halt about ten feet past the lip of the ridge. It was steep, but not that steep and she knew she wasn't really hurt, except for some surface abrasions on her hands. How clumsy! "Way to go, Stella. It's what you get for letting yourself go soft over a man." She laughed out loud, as much to relieve her own tension as anything. "Make that two men."

She glanced over her shoulder. The climb wasn't very far and there were plenty of shrubs and weeds to grab hold of. She tried to turn onto her front so she could start crawling, but her foot was wedged in an awkward position between a boulder and a tree root. She scooted forward, bending her knees, and tried to push the boulder. It wouldn't budge. Next she tried twisting her foot so as to remove the boot. Nothing.

Stella relaxed for a minute, surveying her surroundings for something - anything - she could use as a lever. After a few more minutes of straining with the boot, she finally flopped back, panting. "Okay. Don't panic. Think, think!" She craned her neck around, looking up. Dolly was still standing where she'd left her. Would she go back to the ranch if she told her to? A dog might obey a command like that, but a horse?

"Go! Go, Dolly! Go home!" Stella waved her arms. The horse whinnied but stayed put. "Come on! Just this once be a disobedient horse and go get help." She picked up a good sized stone and flung it at Dolly's flank.

Dolly protested and jumped back a few feet. "Come on. Go!" Stella threw another stone and this time Dolly reared up on her hind legs. One more and the mare turned and trotted off.

Stella just hoped Dolly wouldn't take all day getting back to the ranch. It was really only a ten minute ride, but who knew what went through the mind of a geriatric horse? She lay back, closing her eyes from the afternoon sun and threw her arm over her face for further protection. Then she waited.

Perhaps she dozed off - she wasn't sure - but within what seemed a short time she heard the distinct sound of galloping hooves. She sat up, brushing the dust from her clothing and hair.

"Stella!" It was Zane. She heard the crunch of gravel as he jumped down from his mount.

"Down here," she called.

She saw his head appear over the ridge, obvious strain on his face. "Are you hurt?" He was already sliding down the slope toward her on his backside.

"I don't think so. Just stuck."

Zane surveyed the boulder then tried to push it off her foot with brute strength. It didn't budge. "And stuck good."

"Yeah." Stella tried to laugh, but she suddenly felt shaky. Like she might cry.

Zane's blue eyes bored into hers. "Hang tough. I've got an idea. Just stay put."

This time she did laugh. "Don't worry. I'm not going anywhere."

He scrambled up the steep incline and a few minutes later reappeared with a rope. After attaching the rope securely around the boulder, he made his way to the top again. Soon the rope went taut as he anchored it to the horn on the horse's saddle. "As soon as you feel that rock budge even a little bit, try to get your foot out of there. I don't want that boulder coming back down on it."

"Roger that." Stella braced herself as the rope tightened. Seconds later the boulder inched ever so slightly. Stella snatched her foot free just as it slid back into place. "I'm free," she shouted.

Immediately she started up the slope, grabbing onto every available branch on the way. Her foot throbbed, but she didn't stop to analyze the feeling. Zane's strong hands were there to help haul her body over the final few feet. Once over the top, she flopped down onto her backside, puffing.

Zane crouched beside her. "Let me take a look."

"It's fine." She waved him off.

"Don't be stubborn. Take off your boot."

The look in his eyes told her there was no use arguing. With a grunt she pulled on the cowboy boot, wincing as she slid it off. Next she removed the sock. "See? Fine."

Zane cradled her foot in his hand, gently turning it this way then that. "The ankle seems fine. The top looks a little bruised though." He ran his fingers over the area in question. "That hurt?"

"It tickles." She jerked her foot away from his grasp. The feel of his calloused hands on her foot had sent a tingling sensation up her spine, and it wasn't just ticklishness. She managed to get the sock back on, but when it came to the boot, she winced.

"Leave it off," he advised, standing. "Here. I'll help you up."

She took his proffered hand and hoisted herself up. She could put pressure on both feet, but having one boot off was making her feel slightly off balance. She let go of his hand anyway. "You got here fast. Where's Dolly?"

"Hopefully back at the ranch. I was halfway up the ridge when I saw her without a rider coming from this direction. I didn't bother taking her back first. I was more concerned about making sure you were okay."

"And you knew exactly where to find me?"

Zane nodded. "You're predictable."

Stella raised her brows. "Is that so?"

"Yes it is." Their eyes locked.

Stella sucked in a breath, her pulse beating wildly at her throat. "Then I guess you won't be surprised by this." With one fluid motion she grasped the front of his shirt, bringing him closer to her level while she strained up on tiptoe to meet him halfway.

Caught off guard, she thought he might pull away, but within seconds he was responding in kind. His hands bit into her shoulders as he pulled her even closer, until her own arms freed themselves to wind around his neck, her hands getting lost in his hair.

"Stella..." His voice was husky; the sound of her name like a prayer.

"Stop talking," she said, finding his mouth again. He did and for a few more moments all reasonable thought vanished.

Suddenly he stilled, jerking his mouth away from hers and cocking his head to one side.

"What is it?" Stella hardly recognized her own passion charged voice.

"Someone's coming."

Stella stepped back and turned in the direction of Zane's stare. Blue's familiar physique rode into view. He reined in his horse with a sideways jerk. His face was ashen. "What's going on? Dolly came into the yard rider-less and..." He jumped from his mount and strode toward Stella, placing his hands possessively on her shoulders. "Are you alright?"

"I fell down the slope and my foot got wedged beside a rock. I'm fine, now, though. Zane came along and got me out." She was surprised at how normal she sounded.

"Thank goodness." Blue pulled her into a rough embrace. "I was almost sick when I saw Dolly trotting into the yard without you."

Stella caught Zane's gaze over the top of Blue's shoulder. His eyes had hardened into an emotionless mask. "I'm fine," she lied, pushing Blue away. "It was just a freak accident. You'd think the world was coming to an end."

"Blue, why don't you take Stella back to the ranch while I get my rope?" Zane said, his voice sounding clipped.

"We can wait for you," Stella offered.

"It's okay. I'm heading in a different direction." He started over the ledge and soon disappeared from sight.

"Come on," Blue said, his voice barely above a whisper. "Let's leave grumpy goat behind." He mounted his horse and then offered Stella a hand so that she could slide up behind him.

Stella blinked back some tears, glad that Blue couldn't see her face. Maybe her world *was* coming to an end.

CHAPTER 27

"*Y*ou live here? In this neighborhood?" Cherise peered out the window and noticed the sign *"Granaio"* - the very bakery she had fled to earlier that afternoon. A lifetime ago.

"At present." Garneault turned down another alley which was barely large enough for the vehicle to fit through. To Cherise's surprise, he touched a remote garage door opener and a door rattled open in the back of one of the buildings, just large enough for him to pull into. Once the door had slid back into place, he cut the engine and unlocked the car. "Now you may exit the vehicle," he said with a slight smile.

Cherise climbed out of the sedan, trying to take in her surroundings. "And we'll be safe here? It seems awfully close to... you know."

"It will be the safest place for now. Like the eye of the storm. As soon as I can, I will take you to the American Embassy."

"So who was that chasing us back there?"

"In this business, there are many enemies," Garneault replied. He busied himself with another cigarette.

"An appropriately vague response, I suppose," Cherise said.

"The less you know the better." He squinted, those golden eyes surveying her through the curling smoke of his cigarette.

"Fine." Cherise flipped her hair back and straightened her spine in an effort to regain some dignity. "If I'm going to have to stay here, I'd like to freshen up a bit. I must look a fright. And I probably smell bad, too."

"Hm." Garneault had come around to her side of the vehicle. He scrutinized her from head to toe. "I'll see what I can do. This way." He butted the cigarette under his heel then turned.

Cherise followed him through a heavy door and up two flights of steps. At the end of a narrow hallway, he produced a key and unlocked a door, ushering her inside. The apartment was small; a one room bachelor suite with no balcony. The paint was yellowed and there was the faint smell of old cigarettes. It was sparsely furnished with a single bed in one corner, a minuscule kitchenette, a small table with two chairs, and two armchairs, one of which was pulled up by the window beside a telescope on a tripod.

Cherise walked toward the window and lifted one slat on the Venetian blinds. Below was a perfect view of the warehouse where she'd been held captive. "So you've been watching Alistair's comings and goings?"

"*Oui.*"

She let the blind clatter back into place and turned, giving him her most condescending stare. "And you didn't bother to rescue me sooner? Thanks a lot."

Garneault sauntered to the kitchen counter, ignoring the daggers coming from her eyes. He set his hat and glasses down. "I did not know he had you captive until you came running out. I had hoped instead that your disappearance at the airport meant you had gone home to America where you belong."

Cherise sniffed and tilted her nose up. "Sorry for being such a nuisance."

Garneault shrugged, apparently not at all put off by her haughtiness. "You do seem to be entangled with more than your share of disreputable men."

Cherise's shoulders sagged and she suddenly felt very tired. All aplomb whooshed from her body like air from a balloon. "I know. It's like I'm cursed when it comes to the male species."

His gaze seemed to soften. "I will find you some clothing and you will take a nice long bath, *oui*? Then I will find something for us to eat." He strode to the closet beside the entry and within seconds pulled out a men's shirt on a hanger. "This will do for now until I find something more suitable. The bathroom is the door to your right. You will find everything you need, although I must apologize in advance. I have not had a housekeeper visit and, well..."

Cherise smiled, taking the shirt. "I'm sure it will be fine. Thank you. For everything."

STELLA SAT HUNKERED over her laptop at the tiny desk in her bedroom. She stared at the screen, overwhelm threatening to engulf her as she tried to focus on various cancer treatment options. Anything to keep her mind off this afternoon's events and her own errant hormones. If Blue hadn't come along, who knows what might have happened? Now Zane would probably never speak to her again.

Her cellphone bleeped and she grabbed for it, eyes still glued to the screen. "Hello?"

"Stella! You answered!" Tempest's voice held relief.

"Of course. Why wouldn't I?" Stella propped the phone between her ear and shoulder as she clicked to a different site.

"This just might be the worst day of my life."

"Tell me about it. Mine's been a doozey. What's up?"

227

"Where to start? I got a message from Cherise." There was a pause. "A sort of bad message."

"Oh?" Stella squinted at the screen and opened another window. "Trust Cherise to be having a 'crisis' while on vacation."

"Well… I think it's a bit more than the usual. I know this is going to sound crazy, but she said she's been kidnapped."

"What?" Stella paused in mid click.

"But then she said she managed to escape," Tempest continued quickly. "But it gets worse. Apparently, Roberto is some kind of drug dealer and -"

"Hold it," Stella interrupted. "What did you just say? Repeat that. All of it." She swiveled away from the screen, giving Tempest her full attention.

"Cherise was kidnapped in Rome and Roberto is a drug dealer."

"That's what I thought you said."

"And that's not all," Tempest continued. "Zoe… Zoe…" Her voice began to wobble. "Somebody killed Zoe."

"What?"

"When I came home from apartment hunting today she was hung by a rope attached to the eavestrough. It was terrible!"

"I'm… I don't know what to say. Listen. Start at the beginning and tell me everything."

Tempest did, starting with Cherise's alarming phone call, Zoe's hanging, and ending with Dirk's appearance and continued chivalry.

"Let me get this straight." Stella pinched the bridge of her nose. "You've checked into a hotel that Dirk Hillyer is paying for?"

"Yes. Is that a problem?"

"I guess not. I'm just having trouble picturing it, that's all. The Dirk Hillyer I know wouldn't go out of his way to help others. Not unless he had ulterior motives."

"After everything I told you, that's the thing you focus on?"

"Sorry. You're right. I don't know what I was thinking." Stella stood up and paced to her dresser where she fingered the gilded edge of a trinket box sitting on top. "I guess I've just been under a bit of stress myself lately."

"Oh! I'm such a terrible friend. I didn't even ask you about that. What's happened?"

Stella shook her head. "Nothing to worry about right now. Sounds like you - and Cherise - have bigger problems. So you think Cherise might really be in trouble?"

"It sure sounded like it."

"And you think it might be related to Zoe being killed which is also related to that Ryan what's-his-face?"

"I don't know. Dirk doesn't seem to think the two are related, but I don't feel good about it."

"And what Dirk thinks matters."

"There you go again!"

"Sorry." Stella cleared her throat. "What did the police say?"

"They didn't seem all that concerned about Zoe. They just said they'd let me know if they find any leads. She's just a cat." Tempest's voice wobbled. "Of course, I didn't tell them everything. Not about me pretending to be Cherise. But I did tell them about the phone call and that her boyfriend might be dealing drugs."

"What did they say to that?"

"Not much. Just took notes and said they'd get back to me." Tempest sighed. "I'm not sure they took any of it seriously. Probably think I'm just paranoid."

Stella opened the lid of the box and withdrew a strand of woven embroidery floss. "Did they say you had to stick around?" She held the ankle bracelet up to the light, perusing the intricately woven colors.

There was a pause on the other end of the line. "No, I don't think so. They have my number."

"You should come here for awhile. We could work on this

together. If Cherise really is in trouble, we need to come up with a plan." Stella put the memento back in the box and shut the lid.

"Well..."

"Two heads are better than one. And friends stick together, right?"

"It's kind of far to Texas. And what about the dogs?"

"Are you kidding? This place is overrun with animals. A couple more won't matter."

"I'm not sure I can afford it," Tempest said hesitantly. "Unless..."

"Unless what?" Stella asked.

"Oh, I hate to do it. Not after everything else he's done."

"What are you talking about?" Stella crossed to her bed and sat down.

Tempest sighed. "Dirk. I know if I asked him, he wouldn't hesitate to pay my way. Me and the dogs. I just hate to do it after everything he's already done. I mean, the hotel room I'm in now is practically an apartment. I know he says he just wants to be friends, but I can't help feeling guilty."

"Then forget it. We'll think of something else."

"No, I'll do it," Tempest said with resolve. "Cherise needs our help. Besides, I can't wait to get out of L.A. Every time I'm here, someone I love dies."

"Oh Temp! Honey! You know none of this is your fault."

"How can you say that? I think God is punishing me for being such a bad person."

"You? A bad person? If that's the case, the rest of us are in deep trouble."

"No, I mean it. What kind of Christian tells so many lies she can't even keep them straight anymore? Or goes and takes money from a man even when she knows it's not right? Or has fantasies about some other guy who might be a killer?"

"What's that now? You lost me with that last part."

"Just forget it. I thought God was on my side, but my life just keeps getting worse and worse and I don't know how to fix it. My cat got killed and now one of my best friends might be in mortal danger. None of this would have happened if I'd stayed in Massachusetts."

"You're talking crazy. Just get out here as quickly as you can and we'll figure something out - together."

"Thanks, Stella. You're the best. I know I can count on you, at least."

They hung up and Stella sat for awhile pondering the conversation. It seemed each one of them was dealing with more than their share of trauma these days. Maybe the Almighty *was* trying to get their attention - all of them.

She'd never put much stock in the whole God thing before. Not since she'd left home and nobody was there to make her go to mass. But maybe it was time to start. She was definitely going to take Gabriella up on her offer and go to church with her this evening. Just in case.

THE STEAMING bubbles were nothing less than heaven. Cherise soaked in the tub long enough to reheat the water twice. She finally emerged and rubbed her skin vigorously with one of Garneault's towels, but before she let the water go, she scrubbed her undergarments clean and hung them over the towel bar. Too bad if he didn't like it. She had few other options. The shirt he had given her was long enough to cover whatever needed covering. She picked up the shirt and brought it to her nose, inhaling deeply. It smelled like laundry detergent and just the tiniest hint of male musk.

Garneault looked up from the newspaper he was reading as Cherise emerged from the steamy bathroom. Was that appreciation she saw in his eyes? If it was, it was quickly masked. "Feel better?" he asked.

"Much," Cherise breathed. She glanced around the tiny room, not quite sure what to do next.

Garneault folded the newspaper purposefully and set it down on the floor beside his chair. "Now for some food." He stood up and gestured for her to join him at the tiny kitchen table.

He held out her chair and Cherise nodded her thanks, all the while keeping a firm hold on the shirttails as she sat down. "This looks lovely." Spread out on the table was a baguette, cheese, grapes, and a bottle of wine.

"It's the best I could do at this hour," Garneault said apologetically.

"Alistair always brought fast food. This is very – European. Simple but classy. I like it."

Garneault tore off some bread and cut several slices of cheese. Next he deftly uncorked the wine with a pop and poured two glasses. He handed one to Cherise.

"Cheers," Cherise said, and took a sip.

They ate for awhile in silence. Finally, Cherise laughed. "This would make quite a scene. The abductor and the abductee sharing a glass of wine."

"I'm not your abductor," Garneault clarified.

"Oh right. It's kind of funny just the same."

"Not really."

"Now you're being a stick in the mud."

Garneault frowned. "A – stick in the mud?" he repeated.

"Just a saying. It means you're no fun."

"This is hardly fun. You are a very lucky woman. I don't think you realize exactly what kind of hornets' nest you've entered."

Cherise looked down at the glass in her hands. "Yes, I do know. Thank you." They sat quietly for a few more minutes until Cherise picked up the wine bottle and poured more liquid into her glass. "I should probably phone my friend. She'll be wondering what that message was all about. More wine?"

Garneault shook his head. "I'm on duty." He sat forward. "What did you say to her exactly?"

Cherise took a long swig of her wine before answering. "That I'd been kidnapped but that I escaped. And that Roberto was a drug dealer." She tilted her head to the side. "I think that's all. All I had time for, anyway, before you came barreling after me." She smiled at him over the rim of her glass, and took another sip.

"I hope I did not hurt you."

Cherise shrugged. "Nothing that won't heal. You're pretty fast on your feet for an old guy."

Garneault raised his brows but didn't respond.

Cherise giggled, and then downed the last of her wine. "Anyway, about phoning my friend?"

"I'm afraid that is not a good idea at the moment. Tomorrow when you get to the embassy would be safer, I think."

Cherise sighed dramatically. "Okay. Whatever you say, I guess." She reached for the bottle, but Garneault's hand shot forward and grasped it as well.

"Let's save it for another day, shall we?" He rose slightly as he leaned across the table and extracted the bottle from her hand. "It is very late and you need your sleep."

Her eyes flew to his and she sat up straighter, smoothing the edges of the shirt over her lap. "Um, about that. There's only one bed."

"Which you are more than welcome to." He focused those exotic golden eyes on her for a moment before stowing the wine in the refrigerator.

"But where will you sleep?"

"Don't worry about me. I am used to sitting up all night. If I get tired, I will simply find a spot on the floor."

"Alright. I just feel bad about taking your bed."

"It is no problem. I am going down to the garage to have a cigarette now while you get settled."

Cherise's eyes widened. "You're leaving me alone?"

His eyebrows arched over his magnetic eyes and his mouth turned up at one corner in a rueful smile. "Only for a few minutes, *cherie*, until you fall asleep."

It was a pity. She felt safe in his company.

CHAPTER 28

"*D*irk, I'm not sure coming to Texas with me is a good idea." Tempest focused on the ice cubes in her glass as she swirled it around. "I mean, I know it's a lot, asking you to finance the trip and all, but Stella asked me to come. Not you."

They sat in the hotel dining room at a table for two tucked in an out of the way corner. Instrumental music played in the background; the lighting was low and intimate; the tableware exquisite. Everything needed for the perfect date. Except this wasn't a date. They were talking about life and death - Cherise's.

"How can it not be a good idea?" Dirk countered, leaning forward across the table. "Cherise is my sister. Or did you forget that fact? If anyone needs to be in on a plan to rescue her, it's me."

Tempest sighed and looked up at Dirk's expectant face. He had a point. "I know. Stella isn't going to like it, though."

"Why? What have I ever done to her?"

Tempest shrugged. "I don't know. She just doesn't trust... your motives."

Dirk's frown deepened. "Surely she doesn't think I have anything to do with this?"

"More like your other motives. With me." She dared eye

contact before lowering her gaze again as a wave of embarrassment flushed her cheeks.

"Well, we just won't tell her I'm coming, then. Let it be a surprise."

"Have you managed to get ahold of Alistair yet?" Tempest changed the subject.

Dirk shook his head. "No. I'll keep trying, though." He sat back, stretched, and then slapped his linen napkin on the tabletop. "Well, I say we go online and check out the flight options to Fort Stockton. You never know. We might get lucky and be on our way first thing tomorrow."

Tempest nodded and tried to smile. Dirk was being such a good friend. She was so grateful for everything he had done so far. For everything he was willing to do. She was on the verge of trusting him completely - a scary prospect given her past experiences with men. Stella was being too hard on him. It was just too bad she couldn't seem to feel more for him in the way he wanted her to.

It was ironic, in a way. She was attracted to a possible cat-killer-con-artist, while the one man who seemed interested in her left her feeling nothing. It was the kind of twisted pheromones that always seemed to characterize her relationships, but it was nothing less than she deserved.

Had always deserved.

Back in college she had been goo-goo eyed over a guy named Jake. He was in one of her classes and she was sure he'd never even noticed her. Then one day he asked her out for coffee. Of course she'd said yes. It seemed like they had lots of interests in common and when he asked if he could come back to her dorm room, she'd said yes without hesitation.

Afterwards she'd cried in the shower, but she never, ever told anyone. Not even Stella and Cherise. They were both sexually active already and it was just too embarrassing. Besides, it wasn't rape - not really. The sex had been consensual, although rather disappointing. When he was done he made it very clear that she wasn't up to his standards and he wouldn't be seeing her again.

She probably should have known better when he'd kept asking about her roommate, Cherise. It was one of the reasons why she'd never shared the incident.

Then, when she accepted Jesus, He'd washed all that shame and guilt away and it didn't matter anymore. At least that's what she told herself. When she met Ron at church it looked like God was on her side after all. Ron was everything Jake was not. Honest, upright, and a man of deep integrity. Maybe a bit legalistic, but that didn't matter since he loved God and wanted to serve Him - just like she did.

Everything was going according to plan. Until Ron found out she wasn't a virgin.

Oh, he said it didn't matter to him, but she could see it in his eyes. The disappointment. Aversion, even. She was tainted and he made a clean exit to the mission field as soon as he could. End of story.

She'd dusted herself off and carried on, clinging to her faith like a life preserver. But lately, God seemed lost in the stormy seas. Her arms were weary from hanging on and soon, she just might sink altogether.

EVENING'S BLANKET settled over the ranch. Stella leaned against the veranda's railing and listened. A horse's whinny, a cow's moo, crickets, an owl... the comforting sounds of the night. She stood up straight and inhaled deeply. She'd promised Gabriella she'd meet her at the parish church and she'd meant it. Gabriella was a staunch Catholic and her church was in a small town about twenty miles away. It might take more than a few "Hail Marys" to cleanse her soul after today, though. Instead, she'd focus on praying for her father. And Cherise.

First, however, she had another item to take care of. Stella stepped off the veranda and headed to the most likely place. The stables.

The musky scent of horses and their accompanying snorts greeted her as she entered. A line of bare bulbs overhead cast deep shadows in the recesses of the building. As expected, she found Zane in one of the stalls, giving the animal within a rub down.

Stella cleared her throat as she approached. "Um... hey." She leaned over the stall and propped a foot on one of the rails. When he didn't answer or even look up, she added. "We need to talk."

Zane just kept on working. With a sigh, Stella tried once more. "Look. I just wanted to say, I'm sorry. For, you know... putting you in a bad position."

Zane stood up straight and patted the horse. Then he moved toward the stall's gate and swung it open, disregarding the fact that Stella had to jump out of the way or get knocked down.

"Hey! Wait a minute," Stella called after him. She scurried after his retreating figure. "Talk to me, Zane. Don't just walk away."

Zane stopped, visibly inhaling before turning around. "What do you want me to say, Stella?"

She stepped forward and he took a step back, keeping an arm's length between them. She blinked and stopped her advance. The space between them felt like a chasm. "I don't know what happened back there. It was my fault."

"It was as much my fault as yours." His voice was clipped and he sounded angry. She just wasn't sure if it was with her or himself.

Stella swallowed and let out a heavy sigh. "It's like something outside myself took over my body. I had no control. I'm just really confused right now, with my dad sick and everything..." She trailed off, hoping her poor explanation would be enough. When she looked up, she was met with angry blue eyes.

"What kind of game are you playing, Stella?"

"What... what do you mean?" she stammered.

"First you're throwing yourself at Blue, then me. It's like you're toying with us. Pitting us against each other for kicks."

"No, it's not like that."

Zane rubbed the back of his neck. "I can't take it. Maybe it means nothing to you, but I won't stand by and let you break Blue's heart." He turned to leave.

"What about your heart?" Stella held her breath. Zane had stopped in his tracks. "Zane?"

He slowly turned around again. What she saw in his eyes made her catch her breath. He looked sad. Beaten down. Hopeless. "What about it? I could tell you that I lay awake at night thinking about doing exactly what happened up there on the ridge. That I dream about it when I finally go to sleep. I could say that, but what's the point? Even if you did choose me over him, I would never do that to Blue. I *won't* do it to him."

Stella had no more words as she watched Zane stalk from the stables. He had just verbalized her own dilemma. And he had, for all intents and purposes, just told her he loved her.

~

CHERISE JUMPED when she heard the lock, bolting upright in the narrow bed as she clutched the sheet under her chin.

"It's you," she whispered when she recognized Garneault's silhouette.

"You were expecting room service?" A small grin pressed at the corners of his mouth. He set a paper sack down on the table, along with a cardboard tray with two paper cups in it. "I brought breakfast."

"I'm not sure I can eat anything, but the coffee smells divine." She slid out from under the sheet, scooting the dress shirt down over her buttocks as she did so.

Garneault held out another shopping bag, keeping his eyes averted. "I also brought you some clean clothes."

Cherise walked to where he stood and took the bag, peeking inside. Nestled with a pair of yoga pants and a T-shirt was a pair of delicate panties and a lace bra. "Thanks. I guess I'll go change."

Cherise shut the door to the tiny bathroom and pulled the clothing out of the bag. She slipped on the undergarments. They fit perfectly. The thought that Garneault had picked them for her made her tingle. Next she donned the yoga pants and contrasting T-shirt. Comfy, yet form fitting. Something she might have picked for herself for going to the gym. She smiled. She was filled with a new sense of peace and hope.

Cherise emerged from the bathroom and did a pirouette. "So? What do you think? They fit perfectly. How did you know my size?"

Garneault sat at the kitchen table, some fruit and Danish waiting on plates. "I'm trained to make those kinds of judgments. I have a good eye."

"Apparently." She smiled as she approached and sat down at the table. "This looks good. I'm hungry after all."

They ate for a few minutes before Cherise spoke again. "So? What time do we leave for the embassy?"

Garneault wiped his mouth, folded his napkin and carefully laid it on the table. "I'm afraid we may have to postpone that for a little longer."

Cherise's eyes widened. "Why? You said we'd go today. You said -"

Garneault raised his hand to silence her. "I said we would go when it was safe to do so. At present it is not."

Cherise summoned her best pout. "Why not?"

"Just trust me on this."

"No!" Cherise suddenly stood, shoving the table as hard as she could. The coffee cups toppled, their remains splashing onto the floor. "Trust me, trust me! How many times have I heard that?

And look where it's got me?" She paced away from the mess and kicked an armchair in passing. "Ow!"

"Calm down." Garneault stood, brushing some stray drops of coffee from his trousers.

"I don't want to calm down," she shouted, flailing her arms.

"You must. Your shouting may draw attention."

"So? Maybe someone will rescue me for real." She strode to the window and grabbed the tripod with the telescope on it.

"Stop!" With lightening speed Garneault was beside her. He caught her wrist before she could fling the mechanism to the floor, then extracted the object and set it aside, still holding onto her wrist. Cherise tried to twist away, but Garneault grabbed her other wrist and jerked her toward him, shaking her a few times until she stopped struggling.

"I just can't take much more," Cherise finally sobbed, suddenly melting into Garneault's chest.

He relaxed his grip, enfolding her in his arms instead. "There, there," he said, patting her back.

Cherise allowed herself the luxury of feeling his arms around her, even after her breathing had returned to a semi-regular state. She was a mess, emotionally and mentally, and right about now she would take whatever comfort she could get. After a few more minutes she gathered herself. "Thanks," she said, sniffing as she pulled back slightly. Her hands were still on Garneault's chest; his hands had moved to her upper arms, holding her a few inches away.

Blue eyes rose to meet golden ones. Cherise's lips parted and she sucked in a swift breath. His eyes were absolutely mesmerizing; golden orbs of fire waiting to ignite with passion. For a moment she thought he might kiss her, but his arms dropped to his sides and he turned away, picking up the telescope and placing it in its original position by the window.

Cherise took a step back, fidgeting with her hands. "I'm sorry.

I'll clean up the mess." She scurried to the kitchen area, grabbed a tea towel and started mopping up the coffee.

"Stop cleaning," Garneault ordered. Cherise's arm stopped in mid-stroke. "Come sit." He gestured to the armchair, standing with feet shoulder width apart and arms crossed until she did as she was bid. Once she was seated, he started pacing. "I've withheld some information which might make it easier for you to understand." Cherise simply waited. "I've been under cover. Your friend Alistair thinks I'm one of Roberto's rivals."

"Alistair is not my friend," Cherise clarified. A sharp look from Garneault made her clamp her mouth shut again.

"When I took you to the police station, I may have compromised myself. We were followed, as you know."

"Who was it?" Cherise followed his back with her eyes as he continued to walk back and forth.

"I can't be sure, but it is very dangerous for us to leave this place at present. Each time I leave I risk having my whereabouts discovered. Just this morning I was followed again."

"But... I can't stay here indefinitely." Cherise raised worried eyes to his.

"Of course not. If everything goes according to plan, it will all be over soon."

Cherise released a grunt. "Where have I heard that before? You sound like Roberto."

Garneault stopped pacing and squatted down in front of Cherise's chair. "I know this is hard. It is a very complicated... how do you call it in English? A sting? It has been in the making for months. There are those within the police department itself who do not know all the details. For the safety of everyone involved."

"And things are about to 'go down' as they say?" Cherise supplied.

He nodded. "*Oui*. That is it exactly." He stood and shoved his hands in his pants pockets. "As long as my cover hasn't been blown."

Cherise sighed. "Well, can I at least phone my friend Tempest? She's going to be worried sick."

"I'm afraid not."

"Why not?" Cherise demanded.

"This is where it gets even more complicated. We have intelligence that your friend - this Tempest - has been involved in some suspicious activity."

Cherise laughed outright. "That's ridiculous! Tempest is the sweetest, most trusting person on the face of the planet. She wouldn't hurt a flea if she could help it."

Garneault shrugged. "Maybe, maybe not. Apparently, she is involved in something with your own brother. What do you have to say about that?"

Cherise blinked. Her heart suddenly fell into her stomach. Dirk she could believe. Hadn't she wondered about his involvement herself?

"I see now that I have your attention. Whether they are involved or not, it is too risky. As for you, this is the safest place for now."

"So says you. I still don't understand why I can't just walk out that door and go home. This whole thing has nothing to do with me. I mean, Roberto was all paranoid about my being out alone, presumably because he thought someone might try to get at him through me. But now, other than Alistair, I'm not under threat anymore. I could probably just take a taxi to the U.S. Embassy and be done with it. No one would even know."

Garneault scrutinized her features and shook his head. "You still don't understand, do you?"

She looked up at him, wide-eyed. "What?"

"How deeply embroiled you are. There are those besides Alistair that would use you at the drop of a hat, just to make a point."

"In other words, I've become a pawn in their game."

"Unfortunately, you have been that from the moment you stepped off the airplane."

Cherise took a moment to digest that information. The fear that suddenly gripped her chest could almost not be contained. With mock cheerfulness she stood up. "Well, since I'm stuck here anyway, I say we get drunk. Where's that bottle of wine from yesterday?" She strode to the refrigerator and yanked it open.

"I'm sorry if I've frightened you, *cherie*. I am just trying to be honest." His penetrating gaze was full of compassion.

She leaned against the counter and took a swig straight from the wine bottle.

"It is early for drinking, *non?*"

"So? And don't think you're going to take it away this time, either." She pointed at him, the bottle still in her hand. "I need something to calm my nerves." She walked back to the armchair and flopped into its depths, taking another drink once she'd landed.

"Go easy. I don't need you drunk when it's time to evacuate."

"Want some?" She held the bottle aloft. "I'll share. We can pretend this whole thing isn't real."

"No thank you." He glanced at his watch and then sat down on a kitchen chair.

"Oh right. You're on duty and all that." Cherise took another sip and then scrutinized Garneault through narrowed lids as she swished the remaining liquid around in the bottle. "You ever sleep with someone you're protecting?"

His eyebrows rose. "That is personal."

"I'll take that as a 'yes'." She took another gulp - a big one this time - and giggled once it finally went down. "You're kinda cute, you know that?"

"Perhaps the wine is not a good idea."

"Maybe I'm suffering from that condition. You know – where the victim falls for her captor?"

"The Stockholm Syndrome," he supplied. "And I'm not your captor."

"Rescuer then. Either way." Cherise leaned forward and gave him her most seductive smile. "So you wanna? I mean, it would sure pass the time."

"I am going down for a cigarette." He stood up.

"No wait! Don't run away." She waved the near empty bottle. "Okay, that was way too forward, I realize. It's my stress behavior. I didn't even think to ask if you were married or 'involved' or something. Are you? Married or involved?"

He shook his head. "No."

"Really?" She squinted. "A man like you must have lots of women who are interested."

"And now that is definitely enough." He walked the few steps to where she sat and took the bottle from her hands. "I must go out now, but you will stay here. Out of sight. Do not answer the door. Do not look out the window. Do you understand?"

She nodded mutely. All the excitement had definitely been sucked out of the situation.

CHAPTER 29

Tempest squinted, shielding her eyes from the assaulting flashes of sunlight as they drove down the tree lined driveway that led to the Crayton ranch. She glanced over at Dirk, who appeared quite relaxed as he maneuvered the rented Escalade down the long lane. He drove with his right hand, his left arm propped out the open window and his blonde hair ruffling in the breeze. Carefree and confident. Why couldn't she be like that?

I'm sorry that I've been such a bad Christian lately, God. If You could just find Zoe's killer... and make sure Cherise is okay... and maybe sort out this weird relationship with Dirk... I promise I'll try to get back to doing what's right. Tempest sighed. It felt like her prayers were bumping against a glass ceiling. Was God even listening?

As they rounded the last corner, Tempest caught sight of the buildings – enough to comprise a small town. Barns, garages, corrals – all entangled in a maze of fences. After all their years as friends she had never actually visited Stella at her own home. Too bad it was under such trying circumstances.

Tempest spotted Stella as she emerged from the front door of the rambling ranch style house and crossed the veranda. Relief at seeing her friend's familiar face sent a wave of emotion through Tempest's stomach. Do not cry! Blubbering now seemed weak indeed.

The vehicle came to a rolling stop and Dirk put it in park. He turned in his seat. "Ready?"

Tempest nodded and wiped some stray moisture out from beneath her glasses. Paddy barked in response from the back seat while Jupiter yawned widely, his gigantic tongue rolling out of his mouth.

"Looks like they're ready, too." Tempest laughed. She opened the door and jumped down onto the gravel.

"Tempest!" Stella rushed forward and the two friends hugged each other for several long minutes. Finally Stella stepped back, holding Tempest at arm's length. "How was your trip?"

Tempest let out a sigh. "Long. I feel like a rag doll. But I can't tell you how relieved I am to be here, finally."

Dirk emerged from the driver's side of the dark blue vehicle. He was still wearing his designer sunglasses and looked the picture of the debonair playboy despite the two connecting flights and the long drive from the airport in Fort Stockton.

"Hello, Dirk," Stella greeted coolly. "I didn't know you were coming."

"Did you think I was the chauffeur?" He patted the hood of the Escalade as he rounded the vehicle to join the women.

"Obviously I knew it was you once you drove up. And of course you're welcome," she added.

"Tempest warned me you might not be on side, but Cherise is my sister. I had to come."

"Of course," Stella said.

"We should probably let the dogs out," Tempest said, pointing to the vehicle. "It's been a long trip for them, as well."

"I'll help," Dirk offered, moving toward the cargo door.

"Wait. They need to be on leash." Tempest retrieved the leashes from under the passenger seat.

"Once they're used to their surroundings you could probably just let them run," Stella said.

"You think so?" Tempest let Jupiter out first, holding him by the collar as he jumped down from the back. She clipped the leash onto the collar's ring.

"We're out in the middle of the country, remember?" Stella laughed. "Besides, look around. No shortage of animals."

Dirk had already scooped Paddy into his arms and set him on the ground as Tempest attached his leash. "I'd hate for them to get into anything," Tempest said.

The crunching of gravel underfoot told them someone else was approaching. "Hi, there. You must be Stella's friend Tempest."

"Hi." Tempest smiled tentatively at the man as he tipped his cowboy hat in greeting. He had longish sandy hair and insanely blue eyes.

"Tempest, this is my friend, Blue Shepherd. Blue, this is Tempest Ross," Stella introduced. "Oh. And Dirk Hillyer, my friend Cherise's brother," she added, almost as an after thought.

"Pleased to meet you," Blue said, offering his hand to first Tempest and then Dirk.

"Likewise," Dirk responded, taking Blue's outstretched hand and shaking it.

"And who do we have here?" Blue asked, patting Jupiter's head. The large dog leaned into the welcome ministrations. Paddy barked and Blue reached down to scratch his head also.

Tempest smiled. "Looks like you've just made a couple of friends. They've been cooped up for so long they'll lap up what-ever you can dish out."

Blue straightened. "You want me to make a place in the barn for your horse?" He gestured at Jupiter.

Tempest blinked. "Um..." She swung to Stella with questioning eyes.

Stella laughed. "He's just kidding. They can both stay in the house with you."

Tempest expelled a breath and smiled. "Of course. I knew that." She reached to scratch Jupiter's head. "You're too much of a momma's boy for that, aren't you?"

"I could take them for a walk," Blue offered. "Give y'all a chance to catch up."

Tempest's eyes widened. "Would you? That would be great. As long as it's no trouble."

"No trouble at all." He smiled disarmingly. "Anything for a friend of a friend." He winked in Stella's direction. Stella just laughed, but Tempest noticed she avoided his gaze. "Come on, then." Blue started off in the direction of the barn, dragging his feet slightly to slow Jupiter down. Paddy's little legs were going a mile a minute.

"He seems nice," Tempest said.

"What? Oh, yes." Stella smiled brightly. "Well, I suppose we should get your stuff to the house."

"I'll get the suitcases," Dirk offered. "You two go on ahead. You've probably got lots of catching up to do."

Stella blinked in surprise. "Okay." She took Tempest's arm and led her toward the veranda. "I never thought I'd see the day when Dirk Hillyer would offer to carry someone else's suitcases," she whispered.

"It seems chivalry is catching." Tempest nodded in the direction that Blue had taken the dogs. "Speaking of... Blue seems nice. And very good looking, too." She glanced at Stella, an inquisitive smile on her lips.

"Now you're sounding like Cherise. Come on. I need to let Gabriella know we have an extra houseguest."

Tempest got into step with Stella's purposeful strides. Just being in the presence of her friend was making her feel stronger already.

THE WOMEN WAITED for Dirk in the foyer after alerting Gabriella to the extra houseguest. He was an unlikely bellman, but Stella had to admit he was acting quite sincere.

"Just put Tempest's in here." Stella gestured to her open bedroom doorway. "You might as well sleep in here with me," she directed at Tempest. "We have lots of catching up to do."

"Sounds good." Tempest stifled a yawn.

"In fact, why don't you get settled while I show Dirk to his room?" She waited while Dirk rolled Tempest's medium sized suitcase to a halt just inside the door. Then she continued down the hall, turning left. She stopped and gestured to his designated bedroom. "Here you go. Gabriella always keeps this one made up, just in case. You should find everything you need in the adjoining bathroom."

Dirk nodded. "Thanks." He entered the room and rolled his large designer suitcase to a stop.

Stella followed him into the room and shut the door. She smiled when a look of alarm crossed his perfect features.

"Anything else?" he asked.

"Yeah. What's up with you and Tempest?" She crossed her arms.

Dirk's eyebrows rose. "Not one to beat around the bush, I see."

"You got that right. So?"

"We're friends," he said, shrugging his shoulders.

Stella laughed, not convinced. "You forget I know you, Dirk. At least I know about you. And you're not one to just up and make friends with somebody like Tempest."

"I'm not sure I understand what you mean," Dirk replied. "If you mean someone engaging and beautiful, then you're wrong. She's exactly my type."

Stella narrowed her eyes. "You're not going to make this easy, are you?"

Dirk looked directly into Stella's gaze. The sincerity she saw there surprised her. "You might think you know me, but you really don't. Sure, maybe I've used women in the past, and maybe I even had fun doing it. But every one of those girls knew exactly what they were getting. I wouldn't do that to Tempest. I like her. For real."

"You're sure?"

Dirk nodded. "Absolutely."

"As long as you're sure," Stella repeated. "Cause I won't put up with any crap from you. Tempest isn't like the rest of us. She's fragile."

"You might be surprised," Dirk said. "I think she's got more strength than you give her credit for."

Stella left him, his words echoing in her mind as she made her way back down the hall to her own room.

Tempest had her faith, she knew that. It was the one thing that Stella envied at times.

Somewhere along the line, she had lost her own belief in a higher power. The closest she'd come to retrieving it was last night when she'd gone with Gabriella to the church.

The air had been musty like the smell of an old book, layered with burning wax and mouldy plaster. But the familiar scent brought back memories of a time when she did believe.

As a little girl she had gone faithfully to mass with Gabriella every week. Her own mother had been a devout Catholic and it was something that her father allowed - encouraged even - in her mother's memory.

In those days, her heart reached out to God each time she entered the building; the mechanics of the service an anchor for her little soul. Despite the loss of her mother, she knew that God loved her. She could hear it in the swell of voices as they recited the holy words in unison; see it in the shaft of light that streaked from the narrow windows across the face of the suffering Savior, hanging in perpetuity on the cross at the front of the sanctuary.

Even the echo of shoes on the cool tile floor, or the rustle of clothing as the congregation knelt in unified prayer, felt like a message from above.

Last night, as she'd entered the dim interior and followed Gabriella in solemn procession to the altar where the candles burned, it had all come rushing back. Just when had she stopped believing? Trusting? Crying out to God, her maker?

Even as she knelt beside Gabriella in prayer, a thought flashed across her mind. How could a loving God allow such pain in the world? Allow her own dear father to die from a horrible disease? She'd opened her eyes, then, waiting for lightning to strike.

When it didn't, she rose from her prostrate position and retreated to a seat at the back. She was a hypocrite. At least Tempest's faith was real.

When she got back to the room, Tempest was sitting on the bed, hunched over a book.

"What you reading?" Stella asked.

"Oh, just this little devotional book. I haven't been the best about keeping up with it, but I thought maybe it was time I started."

Stella forced a laugh. "We can use all the help we can get, I guess. I want to show you something," she said, changing the subject. She walked to her dresser and retrieved the little trinket box and came back to sit on the edge of the bed. "See?" She pulled out her old friendship bracelet. "I told you I never threw mine away."

Tempest took the twisted yarn and examined it. "It's in a lot better shape than mine was."

Stella smiled. "No kidding. I still can't believe you never took yours off."

Tempest shrugged. "I guess you and Cherise are like my true family. I want to always feel like you're a part of my life, even if we're apart."

Stella nodded. "All for one." She placed the bracelet back in the keepsake box. "Which is why we need to figure out a way to find Cherise."

"Agreed. And thanks for being so good about Dirk showing up unannounced. I could hardly say no when he was paying for the trip."

Stella scrutinized her friend, cocking her head to one side. "So exactly what's between you two, anyway?"

"Nothing," Tempest denied. "That's the honest truth." She pushed her glasses up on her nose, avoiding Stella's penetrating gaze.

"Hm. Maybe true now, but not what he has in mind, believe me."

"I feel grateful for all he's done for me – and for his friendship. And I guess it's kind of flattering to have someone like him take an interest in me. But honestly, I'm not feeling any sparks. I feel bad, but I can't help it." She screwed up her face.

"You never did tell me what you meant the last time we talked. Fantasizing over some other guy?"

Tempest waved a dismissive hand. "Please forget whatever I said! I was in a tizzy over Zoe. Not thinking straight."

"I'm so sorry about that, by the way. It must have been terrible for you."

"I'm trying not to think about it," Tempest said. She took a deep breath. "Changing the subject, what about you and your friend Blue? I noticed a look between you two."

"Oh you did, did you?" Stella laughed, but the sound was not quite as confident as usual, even to her own ears. She took a few minutes to replace the keepsake box on the dresser. "Actually, I'm not really sure how I feel at the moment. Confused would best sum it up."

"Oh? How so?"

Stella sighed. "Blue and I used to be like brother and sister. But something's changed. He's definitely interested in becoming more than just friends."

"And what about you?"

"Well…" Stella looked up at the ceiling and laughed. "This is embarrassing."

"What is it?"

"There's also this other guy. Zane, his brother."

Tempest's eyes blinked behind her glasses. "Wow."

"I know. I sound like Cherise."

"So what are you going to do?"

Stella shook her head. "Nothing. I won't be the one to break up a family. I just wish I could turn back the clock to before things got awkward." Suddenly her mouth turned down at the corners and she looked down.

"It's not the worst scenario," Tempest said. "And sometimes these things have a way of working themselves out."

"It's not just that." Stella blinked rapidly.

"Stella? What is it?" Tempest crossed to where Stella stood and took her hands in her own.

Stella dragged in an unsteady breath. "Oh, boy. I told myself I wouldn't even go there. We've got enough to think about with Cherise, and you've already had your share of problems."

"All for one. Remember?" Tempest reminded gently.

Stella took another deep breath and then let the air out slowly. "My dad is really sick. Probably dying." Tears welled up in her eyes.

"Oh, Stella!" Tempest fully embraced her friend and they rocked for several minutes. "Why didn't you tell me sooner?"

"I'm still having trouble believing it myself," Stella admitted. "I found out by accident. I was so mad when I found out. Like my dad had betrayed me or something. Of course, I know that's not true, but…"

"I'm so sorry. Maybe you should just focus on your family. Dirk and I can figure something out."

"Not a chance," Stella said. "Cherise is my family, too, remember?"

"Hm. Maybe we should pray about it. Do you mind if I pray?" Tempest asked.

Stella blinked. "No. Go ahead."

Tempest led Stella to the bed and they both sat down on its edge.

"Lord, I haven't been a very good Christian lately. I know that, but You haven't changed and I'm beginning to see that, so could You just forgive me - forgive us - and help us to work out all these issues we're having? Could You heal Stella's Dad? Could You touch his body right now with Your healing hands and make him well? And could You show us how to help Cherise and keep her safe while we figure something out? There's a lot more I need to say, but for right now, I just want to lift up my friend Stella to You, Lord. She needs Your peace. Flood her with Your peace that passes all understanding. In Jesus name. Amen."

Stella kept her eyes shut for a few seconds, for she was sure an angel was in their midst. Why else would she feel such a sense of calm rushing through her body?

CHERISE MUMBLED and tried to squeeze her eyes more tightly shut. Someone or something was shaking her in her dream, but she wasn't ready to wake up yet.

"Wake up, *cherie*. It is time to go."

Cherise cracked one eye. It was Garneault's voice and the man himself was standing over her as she lay in his bed. "What time is it?" she asked, squinting as she opened both eyes.

"Early or late, depending on your point of view," he replied. "Time to go."

She blinked and tried to focus on his still hazy form. She propped herself up on one elbow. "We're going to the U.S. Embassy? At this hour?"

Garneault stood with arms crossed. "*Oui*. Now get up and get dressed."

Cherise sat up and realized his shirt that she wore as sleeping attire was gaping open in front. Embarrassment at her behavior that morning came back to taunt her and she pulled the shirt front more discreetly over her chest. "Right. It'll just take me a minute to get changed." She gathered her clothes and scurried to the bathroom to get ready.

Garneault sat at the kitchen table when she emerged, his holster strapped over the shoulder of his dress shirt. Cherise cleared her throat. "Ready, I guess. I didn't come with much to begin with."

He nodded and stood, avoiding her gaze as he donned his suit jacket. Next he placed his dark glasses over his beautiful, exotic eyes. Would she ever see those eyes again, she wondered? Finally, his fedora completed the ensemble.

"I... I just wanted to thank you again," Cherise stammered. "For putting yourself at risk and putting up with me these past couple of days."

Garneault simply gestured at the door. Cherise swallowed the lump in her throat and marched toward it with her head held high. She was finally going home. Then why did she feel so sad?

Garneault led the way down the stairs and into the dim interior of the garage. Even this change in scenery was welcome. When she finally got home she would never complain about boredom again. Garneault held the passenger side door of the vehicle open and she slid into the front seat. She watched as he walked around the front of the sedan and got into the driver's side. He started the engine then opened the secret entrance to the garage.

"I'm sorry about - you know." Cherise glanced at his profile as he backed the car out of the enclosure. "Like I said, it's my stress behavior. That and maybe I had too much wine."

"It is no matter. We are on our way now."

Cherise blinked back the tears that suddenly threatened to spill over. "I know it's silly, since we hardly even know each other, but I'll miss you."

Garneault maneuvered the vehicle down the narrow alley and came to a stop at the intersection to the main street. The car only had time to roll forward a few feet when the distinct click of a handgun being cocked sounded from behind them.

"Turn left."

Cherise gasped and turned her head to get a glimpse at the stowaway. She already knew who it was by the familiar tone. "Alistair."

CHAPTER 30

*W*aves of shimmering sunlight danced across the water, reflecting onto the poolside patio. The pool was not overly large, but its aquamarine depths, surrounded by the tiled deck, greenery, and shrubs made the Crayton backyard seem like an oasis in the desert. Tempest stretched lazily before she lowered herself into one of the lounge chairs. She'd changed from her traveling clothes into shorts and a tank top. "I definitely needed that nap," she said to Stella, shielding her face with her arm. "Although you should have woken me earlier. The day's half gone!"

Stella was already positioned in her own chair, wearing a two piece coral bathing suit and dark glasses. "You needed it. Besides, the dogs and I were getting to know each other better."

As if on cue, Paddy lifted his head and "gruffed" before laying it down again on his paws. He was comfortably out of the sun underneath Stella's chair. Jupiter was further away on the grass under the shade of a tree.

"Thanks for looking after them," Tempest said. She looked down at her own attire and back up at Stella. "I didn't think to bring a bathing suit. I could be working on my tan, but I burn so easily. Not like you. Look at you!"

Stella surveyed her own skin and shrugged. "Definitely darker since I've been home, but not that even. I usually don't bother with suntanning."

Gabriella emerged through the French doors carrying a tray laden with three glasses of iced tea. "Thought you might enjoy a cool drink about now."

"Thank you Gabriella." Stella sat up a bit as Gabriella set two of the tumblers down on a small table between the lounge chairs. Beads of moisture had formed on the outside of each one.

Tempest noted the third glass. "Are you joining us?"

"It's for your other friend. He was in the house asking after you and I told him you were out here by the pool. I expect he'll be here any minute."

Dirk appeared just as Gabriella made her exit. He was wearing Bermuda shorts, flip flops, and no shirt. His tan was salon even. His designer sunglasses effectively hid his eyes, but she wondered if he was staring at Stella's perfect body, and then wondered why she would even care. "Gabriella brought us iced tea." She pointed to his glass which was waiting on a larger table under an umbrella. "What did you do with yourself all afternoon?"

Dirk sauntered to the table and sat down on one of the chairs. His blonde hair lifted off his forehead with the slight breeze as he took a sip of the tea. "Research," he finally said, setting his glass down. He held up an electronic tablet. "And I found something very interesting that I think you ladies will want to see."

Both women left their lounge chairs and joined Dirk at the table. He opened a well-known social networking site and went to Cherise's profile page. "I don't know why I didn't think of it sooner," he said, clicking through several photos she'd posted about a month ago. "Ah. Here it is. This is from a party she went to."

Tempest peered at the picture. It showed Cherise and some other friends posing with their drinks aloft. "Okay... so? She's at a party."

"Not just any party," Dirk replied. "This is the party where she met Roberto. I know, because I was also there. It was out at the yacht club."

"Of course it was," Stella commented dryly.

"As you can see, there's Alistair and there's Roberto." He clicked onto another picture, showing the two men with their arms slung around each other's shoulders.

"So that's the infamous Roberto." Stella scrutinized the picture. "Not sure he's worth crossing the Atlantic for." She sat back in her chair. "So if Alistair and Roberto are friends and Roberto is a drug dealer, how do we know Alistair isn't into drugs, too?"

Dirk just laughed. "Alistair is one of my oldest friends. He is many things, but drug smuggling and kidnapping aren't his style. Far too messy and it would take work, which he isn't fond of."

"And how is this relevant?" Stella asked.

"I'll show you." Dirk spoke directly to Tempest this time. "Who do you see in the background?" He pointed to a spot on the screen.

Tempest leaned forward then adjusted her glasses and squinted. The image was small and the person was in shadow. "I'm not sure. It could be anyone."

"Okay. How about this?" He clicked back to the first picture of Cherise and her drinking buddies. He zoomed in as much as possible to a person in the background; the same person from the previous photo. This time his face was in full view.

Tempest gasped. "It's Ryan!" She looked over at Dirk for confirmation.

He nodded. "That's what I thought, too."

"Let me see." Stella moved the screen so that she could take a better look. "Are you sure about this?"

Tempest nodded her head. "That's him."

"Which means, either his being at that party was a really big coincidence, or he's in on this whole drug thing," Dirk stated.

"Which also means he knew all along I wasn't Cherise." Tempest felt the cold fingers of fear crawling up her spine.

"Good thing you decided to come here when you did," Stella said. "Although, I'm not sure how this helps. It might just prove that this is bigger than we can handle. We'll need to go to the police."

"Not so fast," Dirk interrupted. "We tried that route already without much success. I think I might have another idea."

"Okay. What is it?" Stella asked.

"I finally got ahold of Alistair earlier this afternoon. I figured since he and Roberto were friends, he might have some knowledge about where to start looking for Cherise."

"And?" Tempest prompted.

"He was just as surprised as we were that Roberto was involved in drugs. Anyway, it just so happens he's in Europe on vacation, so he offered to go to Rome and scope things out for us. See what he can find."

"That's convenient," Tempest said.

"Can we trust him?" Stella glanced across at Tempest for support. "I wish there was something more we could do."

"Of course we can trust him." Dirk lifted his sunglasses so that he could look directly at one woman and then the other. "And that's just the beginning. I'm taking the next available flight to Rome, myself. If you're coming along, you better get your tickets booked."

"You're what?" Tempest felt her pulse kick into high gear. Things were moving way too fast.

"You heard me. I'm meeting Alistair in Rome the day after tomorrow. I've already booked my flight."

"Hold on." Stella held up her hand. "I thought we were going to come up with a plan together. You're pretty much calling all the shots, as far as I can tell."

Dirk shrugged and placed his sunglasses back on the bridge of his nose. "Take it or leave it. You got a better plan?"

"Oh dear!" Tempest glanced from Dirk to Stella. Both had that determined look about the jaw that meant no arguments.

"When does your plane leave?" Stella asked.

"Tomorrow. With the connecting trans-Atlantic flight and a seven hour time difference, I'll be in Rome by noon the day after tomorrow."

Stella turned to Tempest. "How's your passport?"

Tempest's eyes widened. She knew where this was going. "Aunt Rose always insists I keep it valid. You just never know when you'll need it, she says. But what about the dogs?"

"They'll be fine here," Stella said. "Blue will look after them, no problem."

"You seem awfully sure about that."

"Hey, who was the one who prayed earlier and asked that things work out? Where's your faith?"

Where indeed.

Oh God! If this is an answer to prayer then help me trust You!

CHERISE HELD her breath and tried not to whimper as Alistair held the gun to the side of Garneault's fedora. "Just keep driving, copper. And don't do anything stupid or I blow your brains out."

He glanced at Cherise and smiled wickedly. "Good to see you again, Cherise. Looks like our friend the copper has been treating you well. Now, just up the street a ways. That's it. And then right back into my little hiding spot."

The familiar warehouse loomed in front of them and Cherise felt her mouth wobbling as she tried to control herself. "I won't go back in there," she said, her voice barely above a whisper.

"No? I think you'll do whatever I tell you to do, or it'll be your new flame that gets it right in the brains." Alistair chuckled as he pressed the gun into Garneault's hat. "What do you think, frog? You willing to take a bullet for her? I'd think twice if I were you. She tends to change men like most people change their socks."

Garneault pulled up in front of the warehouse doors and Alistair pressed the remote opener that was in his other hand. Soon they were inside the cavernous interior and the door was clanking into place behind them.

"You should let her go," Garneault said. His voice sounded amazingly calm despite the circumstances. "You have me for collateral."

Alistair laughed outright. "Oh right. You think I'm that stupid? Just let her fly back to Boston and tell the world about all of this? Not a chance."

"What are you going to do?" Cherise asked.

Alistair cocked his head to one side, an amused expression on his face. "Eventually you'll have to meet with an untimely end, and Roberto will get blamed, of course. I'll make sure of that."

"I can't believe you'd do such a thing," Cherise said between clenched teeth.

"You should have listened to your parents in the first place, and stayed away from such an unsavory boyfriend." Alistair's eyes hardened. "Although, your taste in men has always been questionable. Now, get out of the car."

Alistair opened his own door and backed out of the vehicle, all the while keeping the gun trained at Garneault's head. Once they were all out of the car, Alistair waved for Cherise to come his way. "Come here. Now. And you, get your hands up," he added, pointing at the Frenchman.

"Stay where you are, *cherie*." Garneault's voice was low, his hands chest high in surrender.

"Don't play martyr, frogman," Alistair chirped. Cherise slid her feet forward one at a time until she was close enough to Alistair for him to grab her and wrench her against him. He yanked her around to face front and transferred the gun to her head. "Now, I want all your weapons. Everything. Don't try to play me or I'll shoot her."

"I thought you just said you wanted to make it look like Roberto did it?" Garneault asked calmly, his hands still raised. "You can't do that if you shoot her now."

Alistair raised his brows and opened his mouth in surprise. "Very clever, froggie. You willing to try me? One, two, three..."

"Okay, okay." Garneault slowly put his hand inside his jacket and withdrew his gun. He crouched slightly, keeping his other hand raised as he let the gun clatter to the floor.

"Lift up your pant leg," Alistair ordered.

Garneault did so and withdrew a smaller weapon, which he threw to the floor with the other. "That's it."

"You better not be lying."

"I swear."

"Okay, turn around and head up those stairs. And don't try anything funny or she gets it."

Garneault turned and slowly mounted each step. Alistair forced Cherise up after him, tripping over her own feet as he half pushed, half dragged her along.

"You know, I find it rather amusing the way you cops are so incompetent," Alistair continued to banter. "I mean, you're supposed to be the professionals, and here I am with a gun to your head. Well, technically her head, but you know what I mean."

"You're a sick man, Alistair," Cherise whispered.

He laughed. "Honey, you haven't seen just how sick I can be."

STELLA TIPTOED into the hall and pulled her bedroom door closed with extreme care. Insomnia had become her companion of late, and she knew she would just wake Tempest if she tried to lie there in the dark beside her.

They had talked for awhile, mostly about the upcoming trip to Rome, but they also did some reminiscing. The thought that Cherise might no longer be part of their threesome was never voiced, and they approached the topic of Italy as if they would find her and bring her home without any difficulty. Still, doubt remained. What in the world were they going to do once they got there? In an ancient city full of millions of people, Cherise could be anywhere.

Stella wanted to ask about Tempest's faith, but somehow the topic never came up. When Tempest had first gotten 'religion' a year or so ago, Stella had been worried that it would change their relationship. But Tempest never pushed her beliefs on her friends. It just became part of what was, not what should be.

But now Stella wanted to know more. How was it different from the faith she'd had as a child? The faith that Gabriella professed, or even the Shepherd clan, whom she knew had some kind of belief in God. Duke liked to quote scripture on occasion and the boys had both gone to Sunday school, if she remembered correctly.

She shook her head and let it go. There would be time for introspection later once Cherise was safe and sound and back in the States.

Stella headed down the hall, intent on the kitchen. She noticed in passing that a light shone from under the door of her father's study. She stopped for a moment, considering her options, and then rapped lightly on the solid wood of the door before slowly pushing it open.

Rod Crayton was sitting in a comfortable armchair, flipping through some paperwork. He glanced up when she entered. "Hello, my girl."

"Awfully late to be up working, don't you think?" Stella noted the darkness under his eyes and the sallowness of his cheeks.

"I suppose I could say the same." He flipped the top page of the stapled document back into place and set it on the end table beside him. "I couldn't sleep. What's your excuse?" He removed his glasses and looked at Stella.

"Same." She perched on the arm of his chair and slung her arm across its back.

He focused on the bookshelves across the room as he spoke. "You'll be glad to know I'm going to start treatments. I said I didn't want to be sicker from the cure than from the disease, but Helen and I talked about it and she's convinced me otherwise."

"Good. I'm glad to hear it." Stella gave his hand a squeeze.

"I was going to tell you earlier, but you seemed busy with your friends and I didn't want to worry you."

"Not knowing worries me more."

"Well, now you know. We're heading into the city tomorrow for a couple days. I guess it's worth a shot, and a person has to at least try, right?"

Stella nodded her agreement.

"Either way, I'm ready to meet my maker."

"Are you, Dad? Are you really?"

He turned his gaze toward her. "You sound surprised. I know I'm not perfect and I've never really been religious, but I believe in God, Stella. Always have. Now your mother, she was the saint. There's no doubt in my mind where she went. I'm looking forward to seeing her again someday."

"All this talk of death! Let's talk about life - your life and the fact that you still have lots of good years left."

"You don't know that for sure, my girl. No one does. But I've had a good run. I just thought you should know that I'm not afraid to die."

"That's good, I guess." They sat quietly for a moment before Stella spoke again. "I used to believe in God when I was a kid. Maybe I still do. I don't know for sure. I just find it a bit confusing, to be honest. Tempest believes, but the way she talks about it is different from what I'm used to - the way Gabriella raised me. And you... I don't know if I've ever seen you step into a church."

"It's not about the shingle over the door. It's about what's in your heart." He tapped his chest.

Stella leaned back so she could look at her father more closely. "Wow. Pretty sage words from an old keester like you."

Rod laughed. "Duke said that once. I'd like to say I came up with it myself, but I'd be lying."

"You and Duke are both pretty wise, I'd say."

They sat for a few more minutes. Stella wasn't sure about her own beliefs, but it was a relief to know her father took comfort in believing in something. She surveyed his craggy features. "I have a question."

"Shoot."

"What would you do if you had a friend who was in trouble, and you knew you needed to help, but it could be kind of risky?"

"Depends on the trouble and depends on the risk." Rod narrowed his eyes as he looked at her. "Why? This have something to do with those friends you have stayin' here?"

"Just another mutual friend. We were talking about it earlier, that's all." She tried to smile brightly.

"Don't you go doin' anything foolish, now, hear?"

"I won't." It was a lie. She'd already committed to something foolish. At least her folks would be gone for a few days so there would be fewer questions. Once her father found out, a certain barnyard element would literally hit the fan. "Well, I guess I better get back to bed. And you, too, Mister. You need to be fresh for your trip tomorrow."

She kissed him on the forehead and then exited the room.

Well, God. I know I haven't tried this praying thing much, but now seems as good a time as any. If you could send some angels out to help us I'd appreciate it. And maybe a couple to watch over Dad and Duke, too. That would be cool. And Zane and Blue. Amen.

CHAPTER 31

"*A*re you awake?" Cherise whispered into the darkness. The windowless room was pitch black except for a sliver of light peeking through from under the door.

Garneault coughed before answering. "*Oui.*"

"Are you okay?"

He let out a small snort. "I am alive. And that is enough for now."

"I can't feel my hands. How long do you think it's been?" Cherise's extremities had long since tingled into deadened numbness.

"Eight, maybe ten hours. I may have passed out briefly."

Alistair had made Cherise duct tape Garneault to a chair while he kept the gun trained squarely on the other man's chest. Then he'd proceeded to tape her hands behind her back, ordered her to sit, and taped her feet to the legs of a second chair, back to back against Garneault. Lastly, he'd pummelled Garneault with several blows to the face and head before shutting out the light.

"I'm not sure I can hold it much longer," Cherise whimpered. "I really have to pee." The thought itself brought a rush of warm relief. With it came accompanying shame, and tears started streaming down her face. "I'm so embarrassed."

"It is only natural," Garneault soothed.

She took a shuddering breath. Every last vestige of pride was gone.

Garneault's voice reached out to her in the dark. "I am deeply sorry, *cherie*. It is my fault that we are in this predicament."

"I'm the one who's sorry - for coming to Rome in the first place. If it wasn't for me, none of this would have happened."

"Still, I should have known better. There is no excuse."

"Do... do you think he'll kill us?"

"It is probable, though not certain. His movements have been erratic from the beginning. He seems to be operating under the false assumption that he is invincible. That there are no consequences to his actions."

"That's Alistair."

"You know him well, I take it."

"I thought I did. He was my brother's friend, not mine." She hesitated. "What you said earlier... about my brother and my friend Tempest. You seriously don't think they're involved, do you?"

"Sometimes those we trust the most also deceive us the most. It may be that they are innocent, but they are definitely involved in some suspicious activity."

"I can't believe it." Cherise shook her head in the dark. "Tempest is a saint - even before she got religious. She wouldn't knowingly be involved in anything bad. Certainly not drugs."

"Perhaps she got involved by mistake. Sometimes that happens, as you well know."

"Do I ever."

"And your brother?"

"I'd like to think he's clean, but then again, I can't really say for sure. We haven't always seen eye to eye."

"Hm. Hopefully my contacts will notice my absence before it's too late."

"You have a plan, then?"

"Only the barest of one. It hinges on freeing ourselves from these bonds."

Cherise grunted as she struggled against the tape that held both her hands and feet fast. "It's no use. We're going to die. I know it."

"Do not give up hope quite so quickly, *cherie*. I've found patience to be a more successful tool than strength."

Patience? That had long since fled along with hope. Cherise squeezed her eyes tight against another onslaught of tears. Right now she wished for a little bit of Tempest's faith, but it just seemed too far away.

STELLA HEAVED her suitcase into the back of the Escalade and then lowered the cargo door with a clunk.

"I coulda done that for you." Blue stood nearby, hands in his jeans pockets.

"Oh!" Stella glanced in his direction. "I didn't hear you come up, but I got it."

"I sure hope you know what you're doing." Skepticism laced his voice.

"We don't have a lot of options." Stella rounded the vehicle to join Blue.

"How about the police?"

"Don't make me sorry we let you in on it." Stella pointed an accusing finger at him. "You promised you could keep a secret and so help me..."

"You'll what? Somebody has to take care of your friend's dogs."

"True. But the last thing I need is a lecture, okay? Cherise needs our help. That's what friends do."

Blue kicked at the dirt with the toe of his boot. "Fine. But I'm not entirely happy about you flying off to Rome with pretty boy. I could get jealous." He glanced up and scrutinized her with his intense blue eyes.

"Of Dirk?" Stella waved dismissively. "That would be the day."

"Well, be careful. I want you back in one piece."

"Not now, okay?" His eyes were like magnets and she had to look away.

"I meant as a friend."

Angry footsteps crunched toward them and Stella's gaze drifted toward the source of the sound. She stiffened. Zane.

"What's this about some hair-brained scheme to fly off to Rome and save your friend?" Zane crossed his arms and stood with his feet apart, military style.

Stella turned to Blue with accusatory eyes. "I thought I told you to keep quiet."

Blue shrugged. "I might have mentioned something to Dad, just in passing. I figured you'd be gone before it leaked."

"Stop and think for a minute," Zane interrupted. "You have no idea what you're getting into. You should be going to the police."

"That's what I said," Blue agreed.

"You can't stop me." Stella looked from one to the other. "Neither one of you."

Zane threw his hands in the air. "You're in way over your head." He turned on his brother. "And you! You're in on it? You're lucky I don't drop you right where you stand."

"I didn't do anything wrong." Blue's voice rose in volume. "They're grown women. What was I supposed to do?"

Zane let out a frustrated breath. "You'd go along with anything, even if it puts her in danger. That's your idea of the ideal man?"

"Now you're getting personal. It's no secret that I like Stella. Am I supposed to feel bad about that?"

"If you like her so much, how can you put her in danger like this?" Zane poked his index finger into Blue's chest.

"Excuse me! You're talking about me as if I'm not even here," Stella stated.

"Touch me again and you'll be sorry," Blue said, his tone menacing.

"Oh really?" Zane growled. "Put your money where your mouth is."

Blue's comeback was a left hook to the jaw. Zane staggered back but quickly regained his footing. He lurched forward and the two men locked bodies in an all out wrestling match that landed them on the dusty ground.

"Stop it!" Stella yelled.

Barking added to the chaos - one deep, the other sharp and frantic. Stella looked over to see Tempest holding the dogs at bay, their leashes taut. Dirk was behind her with their suitcases.

"What in blazes is going on here?" another person hollered above the din. Duke Shepherd grabbed Zane by the shoulders and hauled him off of Blue.

"Just settling our differences," Blue panted as he scrambled to his feet.

"I haven't seen you boys fight like that since you were teens. Zane? You're not one to get in a scrap over nothing. What's going on?"

"This is between me and Blue." Zane rolled his shoulders to straighten his back.

Duke rubbed his stubbly chin, then turned to Stella. "Well?"

"It's about my plan to go to Rome." She looked down at her feet. That wasn't the whole truth, but it would do for now - especially in front of an audience.

"Can't say I approve, but you're determined, I take it?"

Stella just nodded.

"Then I can't stop you."

Zane was still breathing hard through his nostrils. His mouth hardened into a line as he shook his head. "Thanks, Dad." He stooped to pick up his cowboy hat from the dusty ground and stalked away.

Stella watched his retreating figure then looked back at Duke. "I suppose you're going to tell my dad?"

"I'll wait till he gets home. If I were you, I'd say a little prayer in the meantime, though." Duke winked. "If you survive the trip, he might want to kill you himself."

Dirk pointed to his watch. "I hate to break up the fun, but we really should get going."

"I'll take the dogs now," Blue said to Tempest.

"Oh. Thank you. I'm glad to know they'll be in good hands while I'm away." The dogs were milling around her legs in an arc the radius of their leashes. She handed them over, giving each dog a final pat. "Be good, now. Hear?"

Stella gave both Duke and Blue a quick hug before heading to the Escalade. She wanted to run after Zane, too, but knew it was foolish.

All the praying in the world wouldn't repair their damaged relationship.

THE LOCK'S rattle woke Cherise from a fitful doze. She jerked her head upright as Alistair entered the windowless room and switched on the light. "Ah!" She squinted in reaction to the glaring onslaught.

Alistair reached into his jacket pocket and drew out a switchblade.

"Don't kill me!" Cherise whimpered.

"Quiet!" He began sawing at the duct tape around her ankles.

"Do not hurt her," Garneault said. "Kill me instead."

"Shut up, frog. You'll get yours soon enough. Now, if you don't want me to slice her throat right here and now, keep your mouth shut."

He jerked her to a standing position, wrenching her shoulders as her bound hands were forced up and over the back of the chair.

Cherise yelped in pain as the blood rushed to her numb extremities. Her legs were useless and with a shove from Alistair she collapsed onto the couch.

Alistair clicked the switchblade back into place and pocketed it with a leer. "Now we'll have some fun, eh Cherise?" Suddenly he scrunched up his nose and looked down at the wetness on the knee of his trousers. He'd knelt in the puddle of urine. "Ew! Disgusting!" He pointed to the obvious wet stain on her yoga pants. "I was going to screw you in front of the frog, here. But consider this your lucky day. I'm not touching *that*." He strode to the door.

"Wait!" Cherise cried. "Where are you going?"

"To change my clothes. You just ruined my favorite suit. You'll pay but good when I get back."

"Let's talk about this. You don't want to add rape to what you've already done," Garneault called out.

"Who said anything about rape? Get ready to meet your maker."

"You're a monster!" Cherise cried.

"You won't get away with it. You'll spend the rest of your days behind bars," Garneault continued reasonably.

"Please! Anything is possible when your pockets are deep." He smiled wickedly. "I haven't quite figured out how I'm going to do it yet. But I'm starting to see why serial killers get into it so much. Just the anticipation alone is a bigger rush than the best drugs money can buy."

He shut the door behind him and locked it from the outside,

the slide of the deadbolt adding finality to his words. They were once again cloaked in darkness.

"He has given us a gift," Garneault said.

"What's that? Death?"

"In his squeamishness he left your feet unbound. Turn on the light and we will see about the rest. I was making progress with my own wrists, but not quickly enough."

Cherise stood up slowly and tested her balance on her still tingling feet. She shuffled in the darkness to the door and using her shoulder, managed to flip the switch.

"Your face!" Cherise cried out. "It's purple and swollen." She rushed to Garneault's side, but with her bound wrists she couldn't sooth his pain the way she wanted to.

He cracked a slight smile, despite the lopsided nature of his bruised lips. "A sight for sore eyes, I am sure. But never mind that. Let's get your hands free."

"How are we going to do that?"

"Teeth can be quite efficient. Stand with your back to me and I'll see what I can do."

Garneault began gnawing on the tape, pulling and tugging with his teeth until a large flap was released and he was able to unravel it from Cherise's wrists. She wiggled her fingers to get the circulation going.

"And now if you will reach around behind my belt, you will find a pocket knife that should be quite useful for the rest."

Cherise's eyes widened. "You kept a knife on you? What if Alistair had found it?"

"He didn't did he? Now hurry."

Cherise found the small knife, a miniature Swiss Army variety, and used it to free Garneault's hands. He rubbed his wrists while she sawed the tape from his ankles.

When she finished she flung herself at his body, not carrying if she smelled bad or not. "We're free!"

He cleared his throat. "Not quite yet. *Excusez-moi,* but I must use the facilities."

"Oh! Of course!"

He shuffled to the bathroom on stiff legs. He emerged several minutes later and gestured toward the tiny room. "Now it is your turn. If you rinse out your clothing in the sink it will be dry in no time, hm?"

She looked down at the floor. "I'm just so embarrassed about that."

"Don't be. It is what saved us. Now hurry so we can make a plan."

"Um, what am I supposed to wear in the meantime?"

Garneault began unbuttoning his shirt. "This seemed to work last time." He stripped off the shirt, revealing a sleeveless white undershirt beneath. It showed off his sinewy but well muscled torso. Their eyes met briefly and he handed Cherise the shirt.

"Thanks," she murmured, and pushed past him into the bathroom.

She cleaned herself up as best she could and then rinsed out her slacks and panties before hanging them over the towel bar. She secured Garneault's shirt into a wrap around skirt of sorts, took a deep breath, and then opened the bathroom door. Garneault sat on the sofa, his hands clasped between his legs as his elbows rested on his knees. He looked up as she sat down beside him, but then turned his attention back to the wall on the opposite side of the room.

"Surprise is our best option," he said.

Cherise closed her eyes and leaned back in exhaustion. "I don't know how you can be so optimistic."

"I am not one to give up."

"But what if... what if this is it? Our last night on earth?" She cracked one eye open and surveyed Garneault's form. The soft fabric of the undershirt stretched over his back like a second skin. She had the sudden urge to touch him and she slowly lifted her hand. Tentatively she allowed her fingers to rest on the smoothness of his back just below his shoulder blade.

He twisted and grabbed her hand off of him, holding it in a steely grip for a few seconds before releasing it. "Do not go there, *cherie*. My stress behavior may not be as pleasant as yours."

"Sorry." She blinked, her chin beginning to wobble.

"We must remain focused," he said more gently.

"I know. I'm just… Oh! What's wrong with me?"

With a murmured oath he turned to face her, still keeping his distance, but there was softness in his eyes. "You asked me if I had ever become involved with someone I was protecting. The answer is 'yes'. It was a difficult lesson and one I have not forgotten."

Cherise swiped at an errant tear. "What happened?"

"She died," he said simply.

She blinked. "What?"

"I let my emotions get involved and I got careless. She took a bullet for me. I swore to never let it happen again."

"I see."

"I hope you do. And now we will formulate a plan."

CHAPTER 32

*S*tella rotated her neck to try and get the kinks out as she passed through the security area leading to the main terminal. It was good to be back on solid ground after such a long flight.

Rome's International Airport was a rush of humanity of all shapes, sizes and fashion sense. "Stick close," Dirk said over his shoulder as they walked briskly through the throng. "Alistair's meeting us beside the luggage claim area."

They spotted Alistair, who waved in their general direction, and Dirk trotted to where his friend stood. "It's good to see you, man." He slapped Alistair on the back as they embraced briefly. "Thanks for meeting us."

"Of course." Alistair turned to Stella and Tempest. "I'm surprised to see you lovely ladies here in Rome, too. I had no idea you were coming with Dirk."

"When we found out Cherise was in trouble it was a no-brainer," Stella said. She glanced at the conveyor belt for any sign of their bags.

Alistair shook his head. "I couldn't believe it about Roberto. I just hope Cherise is okay." He turned to the women. "How was your flight?"

"Long," Tempest admitted.

"I hear you. Jet lag is such a bummer."

"So what should we do first?" Stella asked. "You know what they say about 72 hours... and it's been more than that already."

Alistair smiled. "As soon as we get your luggage we'll check you into my hotel and try to figure out what to do next."

"There's mine," Tempest said, pointing at a small black bag.

"Let me get that for you." Alistair reached out and retrieved the suitcase with one hand.

"Dude! What happened?" Dirk pointed at the swollen knuckles on Alistair's right hand.

The other man looked down and chuckled. "I shut it in the cab when I first got to Rome. Clumsy or what?"

"I see the rest of our luggage," Stella said. "The sooner we start looking for Cherise the better."

"THIS SEEMS like an awfully expensive place if you ask me." Tempest looked around the posh hotel lobby. An opulent chandelier the size of her car hung from the ceiling. Shimmering brass accents, and lots and lots of crystals, made the interior look like a wedding cake gone mad.

Stella shrugged. "Dirk insisted on paying for everything, so why should you care?"

Why indeed? Dirk continued to be generous, but that didn't mean she had to like it. Soon she'd be in so deep she'd have to hock her firstborn. If she ever had one, that is. Tempest shifted in her seat - a stiff damask chair with ornately carved wood trim. Dirk and Alistair were at the front desk checking in. "Do you trust him?" Tempest kept her voice low.

"Which one?" Stella replied cryptically.

"Alistair, of course." Tempest scrutinized the two men at the registration desk. They were so similar on the surface. Blonde, tanned, fashionable, rich... But Dirk had become so much more. He had proved his sincerity and integrity. Alistair, on the other hand, was still untried.

Stella grunted, swinging her crossed leg impatiently. "There's definitely something about him that rubs me the wrong way."

Tempest couldn't agree more.

With a final nod to the receptionist, Dirk turned from the counter and sauntered toward the women. He held out a key card. "Hope you don't mind sharing. There weren't enough rooms for you to get your own, but it's a double room, so you'll each have your own bed."

"It'll be perfect," Tempest said, standing.

"The bellman's already taking care of your bags, but I thought you might like to freshen up and then we can meet to discuss our next move." Dirk turned toward Alistair as his friend approached. "I was just saying we could start searching as soon as we freshen up a bit."

Alistair rocked back and forth on his heels, his hands in his pants pockets. "You're probably exhausted from the flight. Why don't you relax a bit first. Get acclimatized."

"I'm not sure we have that luxury," Stella said. "Every moment could mean the difference for Cherise."

"Of course, of course." Alistair rubbed the back of his neck. "It's just that I actually have something rather important that I need to take care of this afternoon. Something... unexpected."

"I don't know about you, but I didn't come here to sit at the hotel." Stella's unrelenting gaze swept from Dirk to Alistair.

Alistair straightened. "Absolutely. Why don't you three go on ahead? Just keep me informed and I'll join you as soon as I can."

Dirk shrugged and looked from Stella to Tempest. "Sounds fair, I guess. What do you two think?"

"Sounds reasonable to me," Tempest said.

"Alright then. You've got my number, so let me know where and when we can meet up later." Alistair nodded farewell and took his leave.

Tempest watched Alistair's figure as he pushed out of the glass and brass doors and onto the sidewalk. Something was off, but she just couldn't put her finger on it. She closed her eyes and said a little prayer. *Lord, I don't know what it is, but please keep Cherise safe, wherever she is. And guide our steps, today. Help us find her. In Jesus name.*

"I don't trust your friend," Stella was saying. "What other business could be more important than finding Cherise?"

"That's not fair. It could be anything," Dirk said in Alistair's defense. "So? What should we do first?"

"Go to the police?" Stella suggested. "That seems like the most logical place to start."

Tempest furrowed her brow, a sudden thought popping into her head. "We could do that. Or..." She looked from Stella to Dirk. "We could track Alistair on our way to the police station."

"Wow. That's unexpected, coming from you," Stella said.

"Seems a bit drastic," Dirk added.

"If he's innocent, then there's no harm done." Tempest looked at Dirk. "You've got his cell number. I saw on TV once how they tracked the person with an app that uses the cellphone's GPS."

Dirk frowned. "Really? Seems like an invasion of privacy."

"Just give me the number," Stella demanded. "I'm installing the app right now."

"Okay, okay!" Dirk recited the number and Stella typed it into her phone.

Tempest sent up a quick prayer of thanks as they scurried out of the hotel onto the street. They found several cabs waiting right outside the doors. They piled into one and Stella read the coordinates to the cab driver.

The middle aged man raised his hands in a sign that he didn't understand.

"Let me," Dirk said. He took the phone out of Stella's hands and repeated the directions in Italian.

Tempest looked at Dirk with wide eyes. "I didn't know you spoke Italian."

"There are lots of things you don't know," Dirk said under his breath.

Now what did that mean, Tempest wondered?

~

"ARE YOU READY? I think I hear the garage doors."

Somewhere between consciousness and delirium, Cherise heard Garneault's voice. She nodded and sat up. She'd been dozing on the soiled couch. She was totally exhausted, both mentally and physically.

"Get behind the door. When you hear the deadbolt, get ready. He will need to reach in and turn on the light. You will slam the door back on him before he has a chance, either on his arm or in his face – just enough to knock him off balance so I can get the gun."

Cherise nodded again. She was fully awake now. "Be careful," she whispered. She tiptoed forward in the dark and flattened herself into the corner perpendicular to the door. Garneault took up his position against the wall beside it. The lock clicked open followed by the deadbolt sliding from its chamber.

The door swung open and Cherise held her breath. Just as the light flicked on, she slammed her body into the door with all her strength. As planned, Alistair's arm was caught between the door and the jam, and he bellowed – in pain or surprise, she wasn't sure. Garneault grasped the flailing hand with both of his and motioned for Cherise to release the door.

Alistair tumbled into the room, his own momentum combined with Garneault's pull making him stumble forward.

Garneault tackled the intruder, but not before Alistair made a quick recovery and met him head on.

There was no way for Cherise to get past and she stood frozen, watching as the two men grappled for superiority right in the doorway. Suddenly there was a flash of light, accompanied by a resounding bang and the hot smell of gun residue. Cherise watched Garneault go down, jerked backward by the force of the blast, and she screamed.

"Shut up!" Alistair yelled. His chest was heaving as he staggered to straighten himself. "That was really stupid. Do you hear? Stupid!" The last word came out like a full blown war cry.

Cherise whimpered, her eyes like saucers as she watched the dark puddle forming under Garneault's body. "You killed him." Her voice was barely above a whisper.

"You'll be joining him in the afterlife soon enough," Alistair ground out. "Now get moving." He grabbed her roughly by the arm and pushed her forward through the door, the gun cocked and ready at her back.

Cherise stumbled forward, almost falling down the flight of stairs as Alistair pushed her from behind. She couldn't see for the tears that were streaming down her face. Garneault was dead.

"You know, we could have had this over and done with a lot sooner, except your brother went and showed up."

Cherise turned her head. "Dirk is here?"

Alistair jerked her back into a forward position. "Yes, Dirk is here. Now, shut up. Nobody said you could talk."

Cherise ingested this new information. Why was Dirk here? Was he here to rescue her? Or was he part of the drug world with Alistair? And even if that were the case, surely he wouldn't stoop to killing his own sister?

"You know, I won't say that I'm not going to enjoy this. Seeing your poor family's faces when they get the news that the beast Roberto had you murdered. Your father's reaction will be stoic, of course. Maybe he'll take up drinking full time, so your mother won't have to do it alone."

They reached the main floor and Alistair shoved her toward the car. "You're probably wondering how I'm going to pin this on Roberto. True, the frog upstairs makes it a little more complicated, but I've got it all worked out. Roberto was always a trusting fool and I've managed to gather some forensics that should implicate him quite nicely. That, combined with the testimony of your friends, should be enough. By the way. Thanks for that phone call. It worked out quite nicely in my favor."

The sound of tires rolling to a stop outside the garage brought Alistair to a halt. "If you so much as make a peep, I'll blow your brains out right here and now."

He maneuvered them both to the grimy window that was high up in the door and stood on tiptoe to peek out. Alistair hit the automatic door opener and with slow motion precision, the door rose inch by painful inch.

Cherise's eyes widened in shock. There on the other side stood Dirk, Stella and Tempest.

"Hello," Alistair said. "Here for the final act? I can't say I'm surprised. " He laughed and pressed the revolver into Cherise's temple, the distinct click as he cocked it in readiness resounding in her ears.

CHAPTER 33

*C*herise started shaking, sweat beading on her skin, running down her forehead. All three newcomers were frozen in time. The waiting taxi cab took off like a bullet.

"Don't do it, man." Dirk's voice was calm. Steady.

"Shut up!" Alistair barked, tightening his grip. "Why couldn't you leave well enough alone? Unfortunately, I like you, Dirk. We've always been good pals. I wasn't planning on hurting you. But you've gone and made things complicated. Now I'm going to have to make it look like Roberto killed all four of you rather than just one."

"Not today."

Roberto. Cherise recognized that voice anywhere. A whimper escaped her lips.

Roberto approached from the outside, his gun trained on Alistair. He stepped forward steadily, both hands holding his revolver at the ready. "Get back," he instructed. Dirk, Tempest and Stella obeyed, sliding slowly out of her line of vision.

"Well," Alistair said conversationally. "Isn't this an interesting reunion? So nice of you to join our little party, Roberto."

"Let her go," Roberto said, his voice calm and full of steel.

"Stop right there or I blast her," Alistair warned. He tightened the wrestling hold he had around her neck.

Roberto came to a halt just outside the garage doors. "Shut up and let her go," he repeated.

"Why?" Alistair asked. "You were done with her, weren't you? Although you might like to know that it didn't take her long to find another gigolo. Isn't that right, Cherise? A French cop. Rather old, in my view, but beggars can't be choosers."

"You will stop talking now and you will let her go. Or I shoot."

"The moment your gun goes off I'll squeeze my trigger. You might kill me, but Cherise will be dead, too. We could strike a deal, I suppose. You help me eliminate all of them and I won't try to pin it on you. How does that sound?"

"You are a sick man," Roberto replied.

"Really? So maybe you'd like to die instead?" Alistair whipped his gun arm forward and aimed at Roberto, still holding Cherise around the neck.

What happened next took place so quickly, Cherise wasn't sure of the sequence. Suddenly, Alistair was stumbling forward, his arm slackening around her neck. Simultaneously, she saw Dirk diving sideways, knocking Roberto off balance as gun shots sounded.

She spun around to see Garneault kneeling on the floor over Alistair's body, the small Swiss Army knife sticking out of the younger man's neck. "Garneault! I thought you were dead!" She scrambled to his side.

"I am sorry, *cherie*," he whispered. "But you are safe now." He slumped forward onto Alistair's prone body, their blood mingling in a grisly puddle on the cement floor.

"No! Wake up!" Cherise shook Garneault by the shoulder. She looked around wildly. "Somebody help!" Then she saw him. Another man down in a pool of his own blood.

"Dirk!" With a strangled cry she stumbled across the floor toward Dirk's fallen form. How could she have doubted him?

Tempest and Stella were already bending over him. "Hang in there partner," Cherise heard Stella say as she applied pressure to his stomach. Blood was seeping through her fingers.

Tempest's hand rested on Dirk's forehead, her other tightly in his grasp. She was saying something soft and gentle - perhaps a prayer - and he was gazing up at her with glazed eyes, his gaze fixed on her face.

"Oh, God, no! Dirk, you can't die!" Cherise threw herself at his body.

"Give him space," someone said behind her and she felt strong arms pulling her away from her brother. Her mind struggled to decipher the voice.

Roberto.

"Get away from me!" she screamed. She flailed her arms, trying to beat him with her fists. "It's all your fault. You're a monster! A drug dealer and killer!"

Roberto grabbed her wrists and held them in a steely grip, even as she flung her body from side to side to try and get away. "Settle down! I'm a cop. One of the good guys."

Sirens sounded in the distance and every last bit of fight drained from her body. "A cop?" Her chest heaved. "You're a cop?"

Roberto nodded. "Yes."

"Why didn't you tell me?" she whispered. Her whole body slumped and she slid to a sitting position on the cold floor.

"I couldn't." Roberto knelt down by her side. His eyes held apology but not contrition. "I'm sorry."

"But all that time... in Boston... here in Rome -" She choked on the last words. "You used me."

"When you're under cover you're expected to do things that would seem... authentic."

"Authentic? Is that what you call it?"

"I'm sorry," he said again. "Not all of it was an act."

Sirens blazed to a stop as police vehicles and an ambulance

screeched into place outside the doors. Roberto stood up and strode to meet them.

With the surreal quality of a dream, stretchers were wheeled into the garage as ambulance attendants and police bustled about. A woman came to her side with a blanket and helped her stand. She glanced at Dirk, covered with blood, an oxygen mask over his mouth and nose. Nearby, Garneault was already on a stretcher, as was Alistair, only a sheet was pulled right over his face.

Tempest and Stella threw their arms around her and although she hugged them in return, her wounded mind could hardly register what was happening. It was too much to take in. So she closed her eyes and let sleep take over.

CHAPTER 34

"*A*re you feeling any better?"

Cherise blinked back to reality and tried to focus on Stella's face. Both friends sat on either side, holding a hand each. She shifted on the vinyl waiting room seat. Somewhere in the background a voice over the intercom called for a doctor. "Um, yeah. Fainting is nothing compared to…" Her voice wobbled. "Well, you know."

"Are you kidding? You've been through hell and back," Stella said.

"Psychological wounds can take longer to heal," Tempest offered. "I'm just so grateful that God showed us how to find you."

"God showed us?" Stella asked. She sounded skeptical. "It was an app, if I remember correctly."

"Yes, but I prayed right before that and asked Him to help us. Then I thought of that app and…" Tempest smiled.

Stella shrugged. "He works in mysterious ways, or so I'm told."

Someone approached, but Cherise refused to look up and

acknowledge his arrival. She had nothing to say to Roberto Percelli - if that was even his real name.

"Any word on Dirk or the other officer?" Stella asked.

"Garneault. His name is Jean Yvres Garneault," Cherise informed, keeping her gaze on the specks in the tiled floor.

"Not yet," Roberto said. "They are both still in surgery, but the prospects for both look good, I'm told. If it wasn't for your brother, I'd be the one in surgery right now. Or worse."

Cherise swallowed hard.

"He was very brave," Tempest offered.

"We've recovered all your personal effects," he directed at Cherise. "You can pick them up at the police station when you're ready."

Cherise nodded. "Good."

He cleared his throat. "I would like to talk to you privately, if I may?"

"I have nothing to say to you."

"That may be, but I have a few things I'd like to say to you, if you would allow me the privilege?"

"Come on, Hon. It couldn't hurt," Stella said.

"And we won't be far," Tempest added. "If you want to, that is."

Cherise just shrugged. She refused to meet his gaze.

"Why don't we go get you a coffee?" Stella suggested. "And a muffin or something. You're probably starving."

"I suppose." Cherise gave Tempest's hand a squeeze before releasing it. "But don't be too long."

"Promise." Tempest kissed her on the cheek and both friends stood up. Cherise watched Tempest and Stella walk toward the elevator then turned her gaze back to the floor. She felt, rather than saw, Roberto sit down in the chair that Stella had vacated.

"I never meant to hurt you," Roberto began.

Cherise expelled a pseudo snort. "Of course not."

"I know that sounds cliche, but it's the truth."

"Then why get involved in the first place?"

Roberto sighed. "I admit, at first it was a way to get close to the drug ring running out of Boston. We knew Alistair was involved, but weren't sure how deep, or who else might be involved."

"So you *did* use me."

"You didn't put up much of a fight," he said.

Cherise couldn't deny it. She'd practically thrown herself at him. It must have felt like a gift. "You're a good actor."

"I'm not going to lie to you," Roberto said candidly. "I *was* playing a part, but when I left Boston, I thought you'd forget all about me. Move on."

"And then I showed up in Rome."

"Yes. Then you showed up in Rome." He sighed. "I should have sent you packing the moment you landed, but something in me didn't want to do that. It was selfish and I'm sorry."

She dared look at him for the first time. What she saw was a tenderness she had not expected and she flicked her gaze away. "But why didn't you tell me you were a cop? All the secrecy just made me suspicious. I would have gone home before anything happened if you'd just been honest."

"Would you?" he asked.

"Well... maybe."

"In any case, I couldn't risk blowing my cover. Especially not with your connections. For all I knew, you could be part of it. That was one explanation for your sudden appearance in Italy. Plus, your brother and your friend were acting suspiciously. What was I supposed to think?"

"That was all my fault. It had nothing to do with drugs."

"So I've since found out."

Cherise furrowed her brow. "Whatever happened to Dominic? I hope he survived."

Roberto nodded and smiled. "He most definitely survived. His ego was wounded more than his head. To be taken out by an amateur American... It was difficult for him to take."

"I'm glad." Cherise smiled for the first time since the conversation began. "I just wish that some of what we shared was real. It was for me, you know."

"It was not all a ruse. It's what made it difficult, in the end. It's why I chose to send you away, even though it almost compromised the operation."

"So…" She searched his handsome face. "Is there any chance that…?"

He shook his head. "I can't make any promises. You deserve better."

"I see."

The clack of approaching shoes on the tiled floor made them both look up. The newcomer wore dark pants and a polo shirt; his hair crisp and black. Reflective glasses shielded his eyes.

"You made it." Roberto stood up and the two shook hands.

"Just arrived." The mystery man turned to Cherise. "Cherise Hillyer?"

"Yes." Cherise glanced from the reflective glasses to Roberto and back again.

The man lifted the glasses and rested them on his head. "It's good to finally meet the real you."

Cherise looked at his proffered hand. "And you are?"

"Ryan O'Toole - F.B.I. I've been chasing you all over the world."

THE ELEVATOR DOORS swished open and Tempest stepped onto the gleaming tiles of the waiting room floor. Stella followed, carrying a cardboard tray containing three disposable cups of coffee.

"Muffins were a good idea." Tempest held up a paper sack. She took a tentative sip from her own steaming cup.

Stella gestured with the tray. "Who's that talking to Cherise?"

Tempest's coffee splashed to the floor and she danced back with a shriek to avoid the hot liquid. "Goodness!" She brushed at a few droplets that had landed on her peasant skirt. When she glanced up her gaze collided with a familiar blue one. There was no doubt.

Ryan crossed the short distance between them. "We meet again." He turned to Stella and took the tray. "Let me help with that. And you must be Stella?"

"What are you doing here?" Tempest managed. Her voice cracked.

"Let me introduce myself, first. Ryan O'Toole. F.B.I." He smiled in that same disarming way that Tempest remembered.

Understanding dawned on Stella's features. "The infamous Ryan, I take it?"

"Infamous?" He laughed. "Probably."

"Nice to finally meet you face to face. Well, I'll go get some paper towels to clean up this mess," Stella said.

"You led me on quite a merry chase," Ryan said once Stella left them. His tone was rather chipper under the circumstances.

Tempest frowned. "If you knew I wasn't Cherise all along, why did you keep following me?"

"Why did you keep lying? The charade is what kept you on my radar."

Tempest screwed up her forehead. Her mind was in a muddle. "I was… I was afraid." She narrowed her eyes. "Speaking of lies, why did you kill my cat?"

"Your cat? I don't know what you're talking about."

"You don't?" Tempest blinked. "Someone killed my cat. On purpose. I thought it was you - well, the drug dealer you - trying to warn me."

"First I heard of it."

Stella returned with some paper towels. "What did I miss?" Tempest scowled and Ryan chuckled. "Coffee's probably getting cold," she said, pointing at the tray in Ryan's hand. "You deliver the goods while I clean this up."

"Right," Ryan said. He and Tempest walked toward Cherise and Ryan held out the tray of coffee. "Any particular order?"

"They're all black," Tempest said.

Stella joined them and took her cup. She frowned and looked around. "Where's Roberto? We brought one for him."

Cherise cradled her cup in both hands. "He left." Her tone held defeat.

"Perfect. Since you spilled yours, you might as well have this one." Ryan handed a cup to Tempest.

She shook her head. "You go ahead. I take cream and sugar."

"Okay, thanks." He lifted the cup and took a sip.

"Ryan tells me he followed you all the way out to L.A." Cherise said to Tempest.

"When you showed up at the restaurant with your boyfriend that first time pretending to be Cherise, it made you a 'person of interest'."

"My boyfriend?" Tempest frowned.

"Dirk Hillyer." He smiled over the rim of the cup, as if they were having an ordinary conversation.

"Really?" Cherise's eyes widened. "You and Dirk?"

"He's not my boyfriend," Tempest clarified.

"You sure about that?" Stella asked.

"He's *not* my boyfriend," Tempest repeated more forcefully.

"It took some unraveling to figure out you weren't involved," Ryan continued.

"I had no idea my little ruse would cause such a fuss," Cherise said.

"One little lie can have far reaching consequences." Ryan's tone was pleasant enough, although the words seemed like a reprimand.

"I'm sorry." Cherise looked down at her hands. "I caused a lot of trouble."

"All's well that ends well," Ryan said.

"Really? Two men are fighting for their lives and another is dead. I hardly call that a happy ending," Stella said.

"Alistair put himself in that position. It's just too bad we didn't get more intel before he passed."

"You mean he wasn't working alone?" Cherise asked.

"It's doubtful. He was definitely the wildcard in the whole equation, though. Totally unpredictable."

Tempest felt a wash of sadness come over her on behalf of Alistair. She hadn't liked him, that much was true, but he was a human being - one of God's creations.

A doctor came through the swinging emergency room doors and headed their way.

"What's the news?" Cherise asked as soon as the doctor arrived.

"Your brother is out of danger. The bullet entered through the lower right side of his abdomen and made a fairly clean exit. No vital organs were damaged. You may visit once He's transferred to a regular ward."

Cherise heaved a sigh of relief. "Thank heavens! What about Detective Garneault?"

"He'll survive. I'm afraid I can't tell you much more since you are not a relative."

Ryan held up his badge. "We were working the case together. You can tell me."

The doctor scrutinized Ryan down the length of his nose. "His wound went through the shoulder. I'm afraid it damaged the joint quite severely, but with reconstructive surgery, he will recover. He may need to take an office job after this." The doctor nodded before taking his leave.

Stella shook her head. "They were both so lucky."

"I'm not sure luck had anything to do with it," Ryan said. "I'd say the Almighty has had His hand on both of them. On all of you, for that matter."

Tempest's gaze jerked to meet Ryan's. "You believe in God?"

"Of course." He smiled. "Don't you?"

Tempest looked away, unable to speak let alone look him in the eye.

Ryan was a Christian. The thought went round and round in her brain. Not that is should matter. She would never see him again after today.

But it did matter. It mattered a great deal.

CHAPTER 35

The rhythmic swish and beep of the medical equipment attached to Dirk's still form was the only noise in the room. Cherise sat by his side, holding his hand while Tempest and Stella stood near the foot of the bed. Tempest fidgeted with her fingers. He'd been in the regular ward for an hour but he hadn't wakened fully yet.

Lord, please help him to recover. Not just from this injury but from the injury to his heart when I tell him we can never be more than friends.

Dirk's eyes fluttered open. "Water," he croaked.

"How about an ice chip?" Cherise asked. He managed a nod. Stella retrieved the container full of ice chips and Cherise slid one into his mouth.

"You're a hero." Tempest touched his foot lightly with her fingers.

He cracked an eye open and squinted at her. "Yeah? I feel like crap."

Cherise squeezed his hand. "I'm just glad you're alive."

Dirk's face contorted as he tried to shift his weight. "Some hero. I don't think I can even go to the bathroom by myself."

"Until you're ready to fly, you'll stay put and do as you're told," Cherise scolded.

Dirk grimaced. "Thanks for stating the obvious, sister. So... you're going to leave me in this god-forsaken country?"

"Absolutely." Cherise smiled. "The sooner I get back on American soil the better."

Dirk's eyes roamed to where Tempest and Stella stood. "What about you two? A little 'vaca' in beautiful Rome? I could use the company."

A twang of guilt tightened in Tempest's stomach, but she shook her head. "I don't think so. I still have to sort out whether I'm staying in California or moving back to Massachusetts."

"The house is still free, isn't it?" Stella asked.

"Yes, but I'm not sure how comfortable I am living there. I mean, there doesn't seem to be a connection between what happened here and... and Zoe." She paused and swallowed the lump that had formed in her throat. "I'm not sure I can live in a place where hanging someone's pet is just a prank."

There was silence in the room for a moment.

"Um, Temp? Can I talk to you a minute? Alone?" Dirk's gaze caught Tempest's and then he turned to look at Cherise, as if to ask for permission.

"We won't be far," Cherise said as she got up from her station beside the bed. She kissed Dirk's cheek and eased her hand away from his.

Tempest watched Cherise and Stella leave the room. She felt an uneasy knot growing in her stomach. Somehow she needed to muster the strength to tell him the truth. He had turned out to be a good friend. A loyal friend. She hated to hurt him, but she needed to set the record straight before it went any further. *Lord, give me the right words.*

"Come sit," Dirk said.

"Okay." Tempest moved to the side of the bed and perched on

the edge of the chair Cherise had vacated. "Um, there are a couple things I think we need to talk about."

"Before you say anything, I have a confession." His voice was very quiet.

She stiffened. Here it was. He was about to confess his undying love. "Yes?"

"Obviously, it's no secret that I've been vying for your attention this last little while." His voice sounded strained and he reached for her hand.

"Dirk." She said his name in protest, but allowed him to cradle her hand in his as it rested on top of the sheets.

"I'm just sorry I let myself get so carried away." He searched her face.

"I'm flattered, really - and I do want to be friends. But -"

"I doubt that. Not once I finish what I have to say." He looked away.

She frowned. The anguish was deep, far beyond the physical pain. "You don't have to say anything, Dirk. Not right now. Wait until you've recovered a bit and then we'll talk it through."

"No. It's eating me up inside. You're going to hate me, and I deserve it. All I can say is, I'm sorry – a thousand times sorry."

"What... what are you talking about?" An uneasiness settled over her. This didn't sound like the confession of a man in love.

"I thought it would drive you to me. I'd be the guy you'd lean on."

"What?" she whispered.

Dirk's face contorted and he closed his eyes. "I hired someone to kill the cat."

A small cry burst out of Tempest's mouth. She catapulted to a standing position, toppling the chair backwards.

"What's going on?" Stella bolted into the room.

Tempest stood with her hand over her mouth. No words would come.

"Dirk? Tempest? Is everything alright?"

Dirk expelled a long drawn out sigh. "I killed her cat." At Stella's gasp he clarified. "Well, I had someone else do it." He winced. "I just told the guy to get rid of her. I never expected… *that*."

Tempest's fists clenched at her sides. "Cat killer!" she spat.

Stella squeezed Tempest to her side. "Sh. Just calm down."

"Where's Cherise?" Dirk asked.

"Went to visit the police officer," Stella said. "What were you thinking?" she asked, keeping a firm grip on Tempest.

"I thought if Zoe went missing, Tempest would need a shoulder to cry on. My shoulder."

"You're pathetic," Tempest seethed. "And to think I thought you were a true friend." She shook Stella's arm off her shoulder, her fists still clenched.

"Now, don't do anything rash," Stella warned. She took a stance between Tempest and the bed. "He's not worth it."

"You can be sure of one thing, mister. I will never, ever forgive you."

Tempest whirled and fled from the room.

"THANK YOU FOR ESCORTING ME." Cherise smiled at Ryan as they paused just outside the door to Garneault's room.

"It was the only way they'd let you in to see him and it seemed important to you." His eyes were kind. "I'll be right here guarding the door. You go ahead and have a few minutes to yourself."

Cherise peered around the half closed door into the hospital room. Garneault lay very still, tubes and cords strung around him like a game of cat's cradle. She stepped softly into the room and approached the bed. Just one more glance before she never saw him again.

"I see you found me," he said, his voice a barely audible croak.

Cherise let out a tiny squeak, her hand flying to her mouth. "I'm sorry. I thought you were asleep."

"Plenty of time for that." His eyes opened and she found herself drawn into their golden depths.

"Are you in much pain?" Cherise stepped quickly to his bedside and grasped the hand that lay on top of the pristine white sheet.

"I can't feel a thing." He smiled weakly. "Too much medication for that."

"Thank you, again. For everything you did." Cherise felt her eyes fill up with tears. "I'm just so sorry you got hurt."

"It is part of the job."

"I know you think what I feel for you isn't sincere. That it's just an emotional reaction. But..."

"Sh. No more words. You are young. You will love again, I think."

Cherise sighed and swiped at her cheeks. "So this is goodbye?"

"It is best."

Cherise nodded mutely and released his hand. She noticed his fedora sitting on the nightstand and she picked it up, gently rubbing her fingers along the rim. She met his gaze, then positioned the hat on top of her own head. "To remember you by?"

Garneault's eyebrows rose but he gave a slight nod of assent. "If you think it necessary."

Cherise leaned over and placed a kiss on each of his cheeks. "Goodbye Jean Yvres Garneault. I hope you let yourself love again, too. You're too good a man to waste away single."

She backed out of the room and blew one more kiss in his direction.

CHAPTER 36

*C*herise recovered her carry on items from the security tray and waited for her friends to make it through the line-up. A slight, involuntary shudder ran down her spine. The last time she'd been at this airport she'd been abducted by Alistair. Now he was dead.

She shook her head to banish the memory. It would be a long time before she felt normal again, but it was important that she put on a brave front. It's what her people did. No matter what lay under the surface, always smile, her mother said. "Let's go find a seat," she said brightly once Tempest and Stella had gathered their things. "I have something for you."

Both friends followed her to some vacant seats in the airport lounge and all three flopped onto the black leatherette. Flight numbers and boarding instructions blared on the speakers over their heads.

"Nice hat." Stella nodded at the fedora.

Cherise touched its brim and sighed. "Thanks. I didn't want to crush it in my suitcase."

"There's a story there, I'll wager," Stella persisted.

Cherise smiled coyly. "Maybe."

"When we get home and everything is back to normal, you two should come out to California for a visit," Tempest said. "I'll have my own place by then, I hope."

"You're staying, then?" Stella asked.

Tempest nodded. "I decided I'm not going to let some cat-killer ruin my life." She glanced at Cherise apologetically. "No offense."

"None taken," Cherise said. "I just can't believe we're related."

"We can spend time on the beach and forget this ever happened," Tempest continued. "No men allowed."

Cherise furrowed her brow. "Hm. Not even cute cabana boys?"

"She's back!" Stella sang. They all laughed.

"Oh, whatever! Right now I've got presents and I want you to open them before we get on the plane." Cherise reached into her carry-on and withdrew a velvet jewelry bag. Inside were three identical items: long, slim boxes. She handed one to each friend and smiled widely.

"You had time to go shopping?" Stella asked, turning the box over in her hands.

"I bought them before. I thought they were lost, but they recovered everything. So... open them." She clapped her hands like a child as she waited for her friends to obey.

Stella and Tempest exchanged glances then simultaneously opened the lids. They both gasped. Inside were the bracelets she'd bought at the market that day with Dominic, each made of three finely twisted chains - one gold, one silver and one copper.

Cherise opened the third box and lifted an identical bracelet from its nest. "See? I bought us new friendship bracelets. These ones shouldn't wear out."

"They're beautiful!" Tempest exclaimed. "But so expensive. You shouldn't have!"

"Of course I should have. You two are the best friends anyone could have. When I needed you, you came halfway around the world to find me. I'll never be able to repay you."

Stella hugged Cherise. "Friends don't need repayment. It's just what friends do."

Cherise shook her head. "Sometimes I just don't know what I did to deserve friends like you. I love you, you know that?"

They embraced again, a group hug that lasted until they heard their flight number over the loudspeakers. They broke apart with emotional laughter.

"All for one," Cherise said, raising her fist.

"All for one," all three repeated.

She didn't know what she had done to deserve such loyalty and love, but she thanked God for letting her be a part of it.

TEMPEST SETTLED INTO HER SEAT, ready for the long flight home. Stella and Cherise were sitting across from her a couple of rows back. She glanced down at the in-flight magazine, but couldn't focus. It was mostly in Italian anyway.

Instead, she closed her eyes. She was exhausted, both physically and emotionally. That Dirk Hillyer could do such a thing was still beyond her comprehension. She'd trusted him. Thought he was her friend. She would never forgive him. Never!

A small voice penetrated through the fog. *I FORGAVE YOU.*

She felt tears rush to the surface and swiped under her glasses. *I know, Lord, but he killed my cat!*

THEY HUNG ME ON A CROSS.

She dropped her head in shame. *God, forgive me. I know that - but it's so hard! Help me to be the person that You want me to be, no matter what. Help me to forgive Dirk - even though I don't feel like it right now. Somehow show him you love him. Show all of them you love them, Jesus.*

She opened one eye just a crack. It was uncanny how the body could sense that someone was near, even when one couldn't see the person. Ryan O'Toole was perusing the numbers above the seats. His eyebrows rose in surprise and he smiled before proceeding to stow his small carry-on in the storage unit above their heads. Then he swung down into the seat next to hers.

"Looks like we're seat mates for the long haul," Ryan said, glancing her way with a ready smile. He was not wearing the dark glasses for a change, and his eyes danced with amusement.

"Looks like it." Tempest adjusted her body so as to avoid touching his arm.

"Don't you find that even a bit ironic?" he asked.

"I suppose. Maybe it's karma. I deserve the humiliation of sitting beside you all the way home."

"I prefer destiny. Maybe once this is over we can get together for coffee, sometime. Only we can use our own names and be ourselves. What do you think?" His smile was mesmerizing.

Tempest felt her cheeks suffusing with heat. "I'd like that."

"And by the way, I actually live in L.A. I wasn't just visiting."

Tempest let this information settle into her brain. "Really? Me too."

Noise from the engines readying for take-off temporarily drowned out any more prospective conversation.

Tempest smiled. *Thank you God. You really do have a sense of humor, don't You?*

CHAPTER 37

They parted ways in New York - Cherise to Boston, Tempest to Los Angeles, and Stella back to Texas. Blue promised to help send the dogs once Tempest arrived home.

It was silent in the big ranch house as Stella opened the front door as silently as possible and then shut it again just as carefully. She'd worry about her luggage tomorrow. She looked around the familiar foyer and felt strangely empty inside – like the let down after Christmas once all the hype was over.

She'd been through a lot these past few days - and her friends had, too. It could have broken them all, but it hadn't. Instead, the bond that had been forged between them was even stronger than it had been before.

She'd also seen a glimpse of what faith could do. Tempest had apologized for her outburst at the hospital and said she was writing to Dirk as soon as she got home to tell him she forgave him for what he'd done. That took courage - and strength beyond what was humanly possible. Stella knew she had some tough decisions to make in the next few days herself, and wanted that same sense of purpose and peace.

God, I want that kind of faith, but I don't know exactly where to go to get it. Show me how it's done.

That same strange feeling of peace stole over her and she smiled. Tempest would be happy.

Thoughts of her father crept into her mind. She tiptoed toward her parents' bedroom, led by a faint wedge of light. She paused at the bedroom door. It was open a crack. She could see Helen sitting up in bed reading, her father apparently sleeping beside her.

Helen glanced up and held a finger to her lips for silence. She slipped from the bed, donned a housecoat that was slung over a chair, and joined Stella out in the hall.

"Thank God you're safe," Helen whispered, pulling the bedroom door shut behind her. "It was quite a worry when we got home and found out where you'd gone."

"Sorry." Why did Helen always make her feel like she needed to apologize?

"Let's go to the kitchen for a cup of tea, shall we?" Helen suggested.

Stella shrugged. "Okay."

They walked down the hall and Helen switched on the light when they got to the kitchen.

"How did Dad's treatments go?" Stella asked.

"Quite well, I think. He's sick of course, but only time will tell if it'll help or not."

"Let's hope."

Helen readied the kettle then sat down opposite Stella at the counter. "I know you and I haven't always seen eye to eye, but I know one thing we agree on. We both love your father."

Stella shifted uncomfortably and waited for Helen to continue.

Helen cleared her throat. "I know you blame me for a lot of things, but not telling you about your father's sickness sooner isn't one of them. I told him he should tell you right away. It wasn't fair for you not to know. But he's a stubborn man, as you know, and he didn't want any undue sympathy. The only reason I found out was because I was with him the day he went to the doctor and asked the doctor outright what was going on."

Stella felt a lump beginning to form in her throat.

"It's been hard this past while, keeping up appearances while keeping it to myself. He wants to split the estate up, too. Divide it three ways. Part for me, part for you, and the other part for Duke. Of course, you know that Duke is sick as well, so his part would eventually go to his boys."

"None of that will matter if the insurance is no good."

"I think he's coming around on that front, too," Helen said. "I told him he's being a stubborn old goat not to at least look into it. After all, honesty is always the best policy, and even if it means less money in the long run, it's probably safer to have everything above board."

Stella nodded. "I agree. Totally."

Helen smiled. "See? We have more in common than you think."

Stella let her gaze drop. "I should probably apologize to you, too. I haven't been a very good step-daughter."

Helen patted Stella's hand. "I wasn't a very good step-mother. I'm sorry. I should have been a better mother to you." Helen's eyes were full of sadness and regret.

"It's okay," Stella whispered, lowering her eyes.

"No, it's not." Helen's gaze fixed on something the distance. "You were such a beautiful child when I first married your father. So like your natural mother, and I think that made me jealous. I didn't realize that you were also hurting and just needed someone to love you." She straightened and looked at Stella. "I've often thought what a fool I was. I always wanted a child of my own, but by the time I accepted that I couldn't conceive, it was too late to repair the damage to our relationship."

Stella blinked rapidly. She could feel the sting of tears forming around her eyes. This was not the conversation she'd expected.

Stella's heart ached for the lonely and bereaved little girl she had been – that she still was sometimes, on the inside. But she also felt for Helen. The other woman was hurting, too.

She pictured the suffering Savior at the front of the church and thought of all that He had been through. Her woes were nothing compared to His. She took a deep breath and sat up straighter on the stool. "You'll never be my mother, Helen, but you could be my friend."

This time she could see the tears shining in Helen's eyes. "I'd like that."

STELLA LEANED on the railing and surveyed the familiar scenery from her vantage point on the front veranda. Someday this would be partly hers.

But for today, she'd said her prayers and it was time to bite the bullet. "These last few days have really put some things into perspective." She turned to Blue, who was standing next to her, one foot resting on a rail. "Life is too short to mess around. You're like my best friend, but that's all it'll ever be."

"That's what you called me about?" he asked. She saw the hurt flash across his face.

"Yes. I'm sorry."

He put on a brave smile. "Can't blame a guy for trying."

Stella gave him a playful shove with her shoulder. "I'm too bossy and stubborn for you anyway. You need a girl who'll dote on you and think you can do no wrong. I know better."

"Thanks," he said sarcastically.

They both sobered. "Blue." Stella's lashes fluttered downward. "There's more and you mean too much for me to lie to you."

Blue's eyes narrowed. "There's someone else, isn't there?" Her silence was the answer. A dark cloud descended on his features. "It's Zane, isn't it?"

Stella took a deep breath. "It doesn't matter. It will never work out."

He stood up straight. "Well, I better get back to work." He tromped down the veranda steps and stalked away.

"Blue!" Stella called after his retreating figure. He ignored her and she watched him go, embarrassment at making himself vulnerable showing in his gait. He would get over it, she hoped, but it stung that she'd hurt him.

With a heavy sigh she swung down from the veranda herself and headed for the barn. Taking Dolly for a ride was always her first line of defense whenever things went badly.

She walked into the dark interior and went straight for Dolly's stall. "Now what am I going to do, girl?" she directed at Dolly as she pulled the bridle down from its hook.

"That depends on the problem."

She spun around. It was Zane. Her heart pounded in her chest at the sight of him and she caught her breath. "Zane."

"I'm glad to see you got home safe."

"Of course I'm safe."

"I was - that is, we were, worried."

"There was some danger, I won't lie. But everything turned out, I think."

"That's good."

Awkward silence followed.

"So what's the problem?" he asked. He hadn't moved from his position about six feet away.

"The problem?" She frowned.

"Yeah. You said, 'What am I going to do?' and I said, 'That depends on the problem.'"

Stella considered the question for a moment until a smile began to slowly spread across her features. "You," she stated. "You are my problem, Zane."

"Me?" His eyebrows rose in surprise.

"Yes, you." She took one step toward him. "I just broke your brother's heart a few minutes ago when I told him we could never be more than friends."

"I told you I didn't want to hurt him."

"The damage is already done. But I think he'll get over it." She took another step.

"And what does that have to do with me?" He folded his arms over his chest. A small grin was turning the corners of his mouth up ever so slightly.

"You're going to make me say it, aren't you?"

Zane nodded. "Mmhm."

Stella took another step, leaving only two feet between them. "You see, there is this other man who has somehow managed to steal my heart. Despite my better judgment."

Their eyes locked for a moment before Zane took the final step toward her and dragged her to him. He didn't wait for an invitation, but caught her mouth against his own in a passionate kiss.

This was her answer. This was where she belonged. This was home.

MORE IN THE SERIES

There's more in this series!

Can siblings Cherise and Dirk Hillyer redeem themselves after losing at love? Will Blue Shepherd be able to accept his brother's choice? Find out in **Blood Ties**, book two in the
Three Strand Cord Series.
https://www.tracykrauss.com/books/blood-ties/

And things aren't over for Tempest, either. Follow her continuing trials of love and faith in **Tempest Tossed,** book three in the series — a story full of danger, intrigue and redemption.
https://www.tracykrauss.com/books/tempest-tossed/

OFFER

Join Tracy's mailing list and get up to date info on all new releases, promos and giveaways when they happen. You'll also get a free book!

https://tracykrauss.com
- fiction on the edge without crossing the line -

If you enjoyed this novel, or any of Tracy's books, please consider writing a review online. Reviews help readers find books they'll love and are tremendously helpful for today's authors. Thank you in advance!

ABOUT THE AUTHOR

Tracy Krauss writes contemporary Christian romance with a twist of suspense and a touch of humour. Her books strike a chord with those looking for a hard hitting yet thought provoking read. Her work has won multiple awards and has been on Amazon's bestsellers' lists. She also writes stage plays tailored to a high school audience, and has contributed to several anthologies, devotional books, and one illustrated children's book. Tracy has a Bachelor's degree from the University of Saskatchewan and taught secondary school Art, Drama and English—all things she is passionate about. She is a member of ACFW, The Word Guild, and Inscribe Christian Writers' Fellowship, a Canada wide organization for writers of Christian faith. She and her husband have lived in five provinces and territories including many remote and unique places in Canada's far north. They have four grown children and now reside in beautiful Tumbler Ridge, BC where she continues to pursue all of her creative interests. Visit her website for more: https://tracykrauss.com

ALSO BY TRACY KRAUSS

Novels

Wind Over Marshdale

Lone Wolf

Play It Again

Conspiracy of Bones (And the Beat Goes On)

My Mother the Man-Eater

Neighbours Series I

Keeping Up with the Neighbours Series II

Three Strand Cord

Blood Ties

Tempest Tossed

Aliens Among Us

Out of This World

Stage Plays

Dorothy's Road Trip

Ebenezer's Christmas Carol

Hook's Nemesis

Ali and the Magic Lamp

Mutiny On Mount Olympus

A Midterm Eve's Phantasm

The Western Tale

Little Red In the Hood

King William Travels The World

Non-Fiction

Life is a Highway: Advice and Reflections On Navigating the Road of Life

Thirty Days of Targeted Prayer

Divine Appointments: Daily Devotionals Based On God's Calendar

Children's book

The Sleepytown Express